The coven's under investig
troubled young psychic, the
freedom—and brir

MW00330924

...gerous desire . . .

Exploited as a child medium, Emily Adams escaped to grow up on the streets—and hit rock-bottom. She took shelter with the prestigious Northern Circle, intent on staying only long enough to get back on her feet. But the Circle is still reeling from a devastating supernatural attack and betrayal. And vengeful High Council of Witches investigator Gar Remillard is determined to make Em surrender the truth—and disband the Circle forever.

When Em's psychic ability allows her to see Gar is haunted by a formidable ghost, her attempts to free him challenge Gar's rugged French Canadian heart and rancorous loup-garou instincts. But even as their new alliance and past connection kindles into raging desire, a malevolent force rises up to destroy them—the Circle and even the High Council.

With all she's grown to love on the line, Em must draw on her darkest nightmares and alliances with the dead to outwit and out-magic a force who can imprison souls with a flick of the fingers and command legions of wraiths with one word. . .

ALSO BY PAT ESDEN

The Northern Circle Coven series
His Dark Magic
Things She's Seen

The Dark Heart series
A Hold on Me
Beyond Your Touch
Reach for You

Things She's Seen

A Northern Circle Coven Novel

Pat Esden

LYRICAL PRESS
Kensington Publishing Corp.
www.kensingtonbooks.com

LYRICAL PRESS BOOKS are published by

Kensington Publishing Corp.
119 West 40th Street
New York, NY 10018

First Electronic Edition: October 2019
eISBN-13: 978-1-5161-0632-5
eISBN-10: 1-5161-0632-6

First Print Edition: October 2019
ISBN-13: 978-1-5161-0633-2
ISBN-10: 1-5161-0633-4

Printed in the United States of America

For those brave enough to change paths and start again.

Acknowledgments

I'd like to thank everyone at the New Orleans writers' retreat, especially Melissa and Kelly for inviting me. Spending time on the bayou with an amazing group of authors was exactly what I needed to bring *Things She's Seen* together. I truly felt blessed to be a part of the group.

As always, a million tons of gratitude goes to Jaye Robin Brown for your sharp eyes and brilliant suggestions. Enough said, you're the best.

Special thanks to K. Bird Lincoln for coming to my rescue at the last minute. And to Casey Griffin for reading quickly and all your support. Thanks to Vikki Ciaffone and Suzanne Warr. So much gratitude for you all.

Extra special thanks to my editor, Selena James. You'll never know how much your patience, wisdom, and especially your faith in my books means to me. A special nod to James Akinaka. And a huge round of cheers for the rest of the Kensington gang. I'm privileged to have such a wonderful team behind my books.

I'd like to give a nod to my sister Ruby Rice for listening and brainstorming. And to Meghan W. for a couple of amazing real-world suggestions that were beyond perfect.

Finally, a huge thank you to readers, booksellers, librarians, reviewers, and bloggers everywhere for supporting books so authors like me can continue to write and share our stories.

Prologue

I walked in the mist between worlds,
a ghost among the dead,
a child more lost than those I freed.
—Journal of Emily Adams
New Dawn House. Albany, New York.

Before

Slush splattered the police cruiser's windows. Em focused on the *schwup-shuwupp* of the windshield wipers and tried not to think about the stench of vomit coming from the seat beside her.

Her stomach cramped. She folded forward. The floor. She needed to hit the floor this time. But the target was a narrow space, and the wooziness in her head and the handcuffs biting into her wrists made it impossible for her to lean far enough forward.

Relax. Breathe deep, she told herself. *Sit still. Stay quiet.*

She swallowed the taste of bile and turned slowly toward the side window, swiveling only her shoulders so the seat wouldn't squeak and the handcuffs wouldn't rattle. Beyond the slush-coated glass, motels flickered into view, darkness returning as they passed. An inn materialized. A life-size statue of a horse. Old-fashioned streetlights glimmered in the haze. Wet snow. Empty streets...

Her head bobbed, eyes closing. Her thoughts wavered toward oblivion. How much had she drunk, anyway? A bottle. Two. Wine. Vodka. Gin. She remembered them all. She remembered. A concert. They were going to one. Or everyone else had. No money. No ticket. Tired. Cold. A stretch limousine. Unlocked. She needed to lie down. Sleep for a minute. She'd be gone before the owners returned. The limousine's overhead light flashed on. Someone screamed. Security. Police. She didn't remember having drugs on her. No needles. Never needles. The cop had asked her about that.

Her forehead thumped the window, snapping her back to her senses. Slush and haze. Slush and haze. The rhythm of the windshield wipers. The world dipping and reeling—

A voice touched her ear. *You stand at a crossroads, my child.*

She jolted fully awake, her sixth sense screaming for her to look out the window.

In the haze, a ghost stood on the sidewalk at the entrance to a city park. Congress Park, the sign said. An older woman. Modern. Not someone from the distant past. Statuesque. Stylish coat. Boots. A cashmere scarf flowing out from around her neck. Her gray hair piled on top of her head, defiantly exposed to the elements.

The ghost of a witch.

Em knew that's what the woman was with profound clarity, a lucidness that defied her drunken state. A lucidness that was as strong as Em's gift for seeing and speaking with the dead.

The witch's gaze locked onto Em's—and across the distance she offered Em a choice to either be accepted or refused. In that frozen moment there were no second chances. This was it. She could stay on the road she was traveling or take a new one. No promise the new road would be easy—it wouldn't be. But what Em chose to do would make all the difference.

Not just for her, but for the ghost on the sidewalk and for others as well, the living and the dead.

Chapter 1

A ghost followed me home from the school bus stop.
We had a home back then, not an endless string of hotel rooms.
I can't recall the ghost's name. Mine was Kate,
back before I became Violet Grace.
Before the beginning. The middle. And the end.
—Journal of Emily Adams, age 22
Memory from second grade. Massachusetts.

190 days later

Em lengthened her strides, hurrying to get ahead of the crowd leaving the A.A. meeting. The last thing she wanted was for someone to offer her a ride home. Not that she didn't like the group. Since she'd left the halfway house in Upstate New York less than a month ago and moved to Vermont, they'd made her feel more than welcome.

She picked up her pace, jogging through the slush, across a narrow street, and down the sidewalk. She totally got why the group didn't like the idea of a woman walking home alone at night, especially someone as small and skinny as her. But she'd lived on the streets in much larger cities. She knew how to handle herself. She had a phone—and a knife, if worse came to worst. Besides, walking in the dark and slush was a good reminder of the night she'd bottomed out, of what life had been like before she chose to live sober, a choice that had led her to join the Northern Circle coven and live at their complex here in Burlington. On top of that, there was an even more vital reason for her to walk alone: During the A.A. meeting a spirit had reached out to her, begging for help. She needed to locate it and find out what was going on.

Em stopped on a curb, shifting her weight from one foot to the other while she waited for the crossing signal to change. Damp leaves shone in the gutter, their bright autumn colors darkened to brown and black. Some people might have thought this time of year gloomy, but she found comfort in everything about it: the lengthening nights and leafless trees, the pumpkins and cornstalks on the front stoops of homes and shops, all the witch decorations. She smiled. If only those people knew that all the powers they imagined around Halloween were real, that witches and psychic mediums with powerful inborn gifts were right here in their midst.

A lifted pickup truck with four doors and oversize tires rumbled up to the intersection. Country music thudded out from the open driver's window. The driver glanced her way, camo cap pulled low over black curly hair. She couldn't see his eyes, but she could feel the intensity of his stare, studying her as if she were someone he knew. But her gaze only stayed on him for a second before it flicked to the occupant of the passenger seat, an apparition so misty it was almost imperceptible, even to her.

A haunting, her sixth sense murmured.

Sadness gathered in Em's chest. It was impossible to know in such a brief encounter why the ghost was haunting the guy, but she had no doubt the ghost was in turmoil over something it couldn't resolve. That was the heart of all hauntings. In turn, the ghost's unrest would reflect in every aspect of the man's disposition—spikes of frustration, seething anger, restlessness…. It was a horrible situation, and the fact that hauntings weren't common didn't make that any less true.

As the truck moved on, the ghostly outline swiveled to watch her out the back window. Em sighed heavily. If only she were in a position to help them. But the truck was already disappearing around a corner and she needed to focus on the troubled spirit who'd reached out to her at the meeting. She was certain they weren't one and the same. The spirit at the meeting had felt small, young—and frantic.

Traffic slowed to a stop and the crossing signal changed. Em dashed across to the other side, past a bookstore and a jewelry shop. She let her sixth sense draw her down Church Street, with its restaurants and boutiques. The tug grew more insistent, the small spirit's pull becoming even more desperate with each passing moment.

She headed into blocks of apartment houses, bars, vacant lots. The distance between streetlights lengthened. Her focus narrowed, her vision of the world constricting into a tunnel. As late as it was, she was grateful the tug was taking her closer to the coven's complex, closer to home rather than farther away. But what if—

She shuddered as she remembered last week, when she'd been at an A.A. meeting and felt a similar tug, only to discover the other coven members had been trapped in a fire at a nightclub. She should have left that meeting—and this one—sooner.

Something low to the ground slapped her ankle, claws digging in.

She wheeled around, backing up and glancing down.

A kitten. A ghost kitten. The small spirit that had reached out to her, she was certain of it.

It vanished into the roadside darkness, a vacant lot of rain-soaked weeds and tall grass. She followed, the tangle of plants taller than she'd expected, the darkness more encompassing. Muck sucked at her feet. Her teeth chattered from a sudden drop in temperature. Her breath became white vapor. Something was wrong here. Very wrong. One small spirit couldn't affect the temperature like that.

The kitten circled back, its ethereal glow urging her on. Another glow joined in. Then a third. A fourth. All ghostly kittens, their mews wailing in the darkness. Their tails swished like eerie torches, leading her farther from the street, past a shack, and up a coarse gravel bank to a line of railroad tracks.

Something black lay on the tracks. The size of—

A trash bag.

Kittens.

"Fuck!" Em shouted, running to the bag. No need to look for trains. The only light came from the kittens' glow. There had to be a live kitten in the bag. Why else would the ghosts have reached out to her?

She dropped to her knees, and the railroad bed's sharp stones stabbed through her jeans. She clawed at the bag's drawstring, struggling to rip it open. It didn't give. She tore at the plastic with her fingernails, panicking until she remembered her knife.

She pulled it from her peacoat and flipped it open. Carefully she cut the drawstring, then worked her way down, slicing the bag from top to bottom like a coroner opening a corpse. Garbage and stench spewed out. Milk cartons. Banana peels. Balled up paper towels. Rags. Meat wrappers—

A dead kitten. Its body covered with coffee grinds, stiff and gray.

Another kitten. Dead. Cold.

Her stomach lurched. Hot tears rolled down her cheeks as she rifled through the rubbish.

The ghost kittens' yowls circled her, panicked sirens, bringing on more tears. She winced as one of the ghosts batted her hand, claws slicing. Above their cries another sound caught her ear. The whistle of a distant train. Approaching. Quickly.

She grabbed hold of the bag to drag it to safety. But she'd sliced the bag in half and the contents tumbled out onto the rails. She dove her hands into the pile, feeling her way through the garbage. It was too dark to see well, just dim outlines—and stench.

Her fingers found damp, cold fur. Another stiff body. What if there wasn't a living kitten? What if the ghosts just wanted their murder discovered?

The clang of lowering railroad-crossing arms echoed nearby. Another whistle sounded. Louder this time.

A soft mew reached her ear, barely discernible. Not ghostly.

Her fingernails caught on wet things, hard things.

The train's rattling vibrated through the tracks on either side of her. The brightness of its headlights reached her, widening and surrounding her, moving closer.

Please, please, she prayed. *Please. Let me find it.*

Light brightened the wasteland all around her, the tracks, the garbage bag. Brightness growing stronger by the second. Rattling echoed in her ears.

She touched something tiny and warm. Her fingers found a second one. Lukewarm, gritty fur. Unmoving.

The train's whistle shrieked. The ghost kittens scattered into the weeds. She scooped up the warmer body, then the cooler one. Not wriggling, but maybe alive.

Another mew came from the rubbish.

With one hand, Em claimed the third kitten, then she slid down the gravel bank and away from the tracks just as the train's engine screamed past.

The ground shook, the train clattering and clanking behind her as she wiggled out of her coat and bundled the kittens up in it. She was sure they were alive. But how close to death they were, she wasn't certain. They were far too still and quiet. And small.

She got out her phone and called the Northern Circle's complex.

Chloe—another recent initiate—answered. "Hello."

"I need a ride," Em blurted. "It's an emergency."

"What's wrong?"

"I'm okay. Sort of. I found some kittens. They're in bad shape."

"Is that a train I hear?"

"Yeah. Hurry. I'll be on Pine Street. The north end." Now that she thought about it, she wasn't certain where she was. Sometimes when she was with ghosts it was like that, time and space evaporating as she reached into the ethereal. "If I'm not there, look down by the ferry docks."

"I'll be right there."

As Chloe hung up the last of the train cars rattled past, dragging their noise and vibrations with them as they moved on. The air stilled. Darkness settled around her, except for the glow from her phone. She realized then that she could have used its light to help her find the kittens in the garbage. But she couldn't change that now. The important thing was that the ghost kittens had vanished, a sign that she'd found all the living ones—living for now, at least. Truthfully, she might have been a skilled medium, but she was no kind of adept witch or healer. She'd never even had a pet. All she could do was keep them warm and hurry.

Em gathered up the coat, snugging it against her chest as she started back through the weeds. When she reached the street, half of her wanted to keep walking toward the complex. A wiser part pulled her under the safety of a streetlight to wait for her ride.

Minutes passed. She paced to the edge of the streetlight's brightness, then paced back. She adjusted the coat to give the kittens more air. But she didn't want to risk looking at them. Not here in the cold. Not until they were safe.

Finally, a familiar orange BMW coupe pulled up to the curb. Em climbed in with her bundle. The car belonged to the coven's high priest, Devlin Marsh, but Chloe was driving. Em was glad about that. She really liked Chloe. She was not only pretty, in a long-legged and fashionable-blonde sort of way, but she was also kind and headed-for-med-school smart. Best of all, it wasn't just people Chloe cared about. She loved animals, especially cats and Devlin's excitable golden retriever. She'd know what to do for the kittens.

"How many are there?" Chloe asked, pulling the car away from the curb.

"Three. But one is barely moving." Em dared to open the bundle and take a closer look under the brightness of the car's interior light. Two sets of shiny eyes stared up at her. The third set were closed. The kittens didn't look quite as tiny as she'd thought. Still, they were really young.

"I messaged my friend Juliet. She used to volunteer at a cat rescue. I'm sure she'll have all kinds of advice."

Em cradled the kittens closer. "I just hope they all make it."

"I do too." Chloe fell silent, then stepped heavily on the gas.

Em glanced Chloe's way. She'd expected her to ask how she'd found the kittens or to give her advice about what they should do. But Chloe's attention was trained on the road ahead, her jaw working as if she were lost in thought.

"Is something wrong?" Em asked.

Chloe skimmed her hand along the steering wheel, leaving behind a slight sheen of sweat. "Yeah. Something happened at the complex while you were gone."

Em swallowed hard. There was only one thing that could have upset Chloe this much—and the coven had been worried about it. Despite the upturn Em's life had taken since she'd joined the Circle, the coven itself had gone through a terrifying upheaval that had culminated on the night of the club fire. Actually, "upheaval" was far too mild a word for what had happened, and for the depth of the threat it represented to the coven.

Rhianna Davies—a witch with a longstanding grudge against the Northern Circle—had murdered Athena Marsh, the coven's high priestess and Devlin's sister. She'd then used necromancy and strips of Athena's skin to create a necklace that allowed her to transform into a likeness of Athena. In that disguise, Rhianna had manipulated the coven members into awakening the wizard Merlin's demonic Shade. The coven had later managed to banish it. But Rhianna had escaped, leaving the Circle holding the bag for bringing the Shade into this world, an incident the Eastern Coast High Council of Witches and their legal system would never overlook.

Worry sent a chill up Em's arms, and she shivered. To make matters worse, awakening the Shade wasn't the only violation the High Council could accuse the coven of committing. Their battle to banish Merlin's Shade had caused citywide chaos and briefly exposed the existence of true witches and magic to the mundane world. No matter how good a cover story the coven created, it was still impossible for an entire city to overlook flying monkeys made from scrap iron rampaging through the streets, not to mention glowing swords, energy balls, and the strange lightning that had caused the club fire.

Em steadied her voice. "I'm guessing you heard from the High Council?"

"Worse. They've sent a special investigator."

"What? The investigator is here already? That was quick." Em rubbed a hand over the bundle in her lap, feeling the stir of the kittens' tiny bodies. An investigator. At the complex. That wasn't good. They could recommend the coven be disbanded for their violations. If they saw fit, they could even abolish individual coven members' ability to work magic and seize their assets, including sacred objects and the complex itself.

Though Em hated how selfish it made her feel, an investigation like this could also put an end to her personal plans. She'd joined the coven mainly so she could live in the sanctuary of their complex while she got her act together. Once she reached a year of sobriety, she intended to leave and never be dependent on anyone or anything again. But right now, she wasn't prepared to leave. She had no money, no job, no other place to live—other than the hellish halfway house or the streets.

"The investigator is interrogating Devlin right now." Chloe's voice strained upward, her anguish for her boyfriend undisguised.

"Shit." Em's chest tightened. Devlin was usually cool and collected, a poster boy for Ivy League success. But right now, he was suffering deeply, full of remorse and guilt, shaken by the loss of Athena, a sister he loved with all his heart.

The car tires skidded as Chloe winged into the complex's driveway a little too fast. Anger tinged her voice. "I knew the Council would send someone soon. But this soon? It's ridiculous. It's barely been a week. Devlin—all of us—are grieving. It's not fair."

"It'll be okay. Devlin can handle himself," Em said. A lump knotted in her throat. She looked down at the bundle of kittens. This certainly wasn't the best night for bringing home orphans.

Ahead, the outline of the complex's main building came into view, an old three-story brick factory that the Circle had transformed into an artsy group living quarters. Devlin and Athena technically owned it and the adjoining smaller buildings, all surrounded by a chain-link fence broken only by an elaborate and funky arched gateway—but Devlin owned the entire complex now that Athena was gone.

Em's gaze went back to Chloe. "So what's the investigator like? A man or a woman? Suit-and-tie, by-the-book asshole?"

"You got the asshole part right. He walked in the front door, then just hauled Devlin into the office and started firing questions at him. He barely took time to introduce himself." As Chloe drove under the gateway, she glanced through the windshield toward the peak of the gate where the remaining flying monkey sculptures stood sentinel, their non-animated wings glistening in the darkness. "I bet the inspector will have a field day quizzing Devlin about them."

Em cringed. "I feel so bad for Devlin. What's wrong with the investigator? Is he just old and crotchety?"

"No, not at all. He's only a little older than Devlin, maybe thirty. He's more of a backwoods enforcer, all alpha and bad attitude. Not at all like the elderly examiner that investigated my dad's business. His name is Gar Remillard..."

Chloe kept talking, but her voice faded into the background as Em's entire focus went to a vehicle parked by the front door of the complex's main building. Most likely the special investigator's ride. A vehicle that should have been unfamiliar to her. But she knew the big, lifted truck instantly, its oversize tires made for mudding. The truck she'd seen right after she'd left the A.A. meeting. The guy with the camo cap, the black curly hair, and intense stare.

The haunted man.

Chapter 2

Invisible friends. Vivid imagination, other parents would have said.
My aunt knew the truth. She sold my mother
on the possibilities, as shiny as a new car or a diamond ring,
their ticket away from sugar daddies and welfare fraud.
—Journal of Emily Adams, age 22
Memory from second grade. Amherst, Massachusetts.

It was almost eleven. Em sat on her bed with a nurser bottle, feeding the littlest kitten an emergency formula she'd made from a recipe on the Internet. The other kittens slept curled up in a box, kept warm with a heating pad and towel.

The kitten stopped sucking and closed its eyes, a purr vibrating from its scrawny body. The other two were brown tigers with the incandescent blue eyes of super young kittens. This one was white, and its eyes were changing to golden-amber. Em had originally thought it the weakest kitten, but it had drunk greedily and kneaded its claws into her as it sucked.

She glanced away from the kitten to where her phone and a six-month A.A. medallion sat on the nightstand. It was late, and she didn't feel like calling, but she needed to touch base with her therapist or she'd catch hell tomorrow. Her therapist wasn't just the person at the halfway house in Albany who had hooked her up with the coven, she'd also agreed to be her temporary A.A. sponsor: someone she was supposed to check in with daily.

She put the kitten in the box with the others and retrieved her phone. She could leave a message if no one answered—better to do that than nothing.

The phone rang once. Twice.

Her therapist picked up. "Hey, Emily. I was just thinking about you."

"Sorry it's so late. I found some abandoned kittens in a trash bag on my way home from a meeting."

"That's horrible. Are they going to be okay?"

"I think so. We're going to take them to the vet tomorrow. They're really little."

Her therapist's voice went from concerned to firm. "While you were at the meeting, did you talk to anyone about being your sponsor? You're welcome to call me anytime, day or night. But it's important for you to have a local support system."

"Ah—I was planning on asking someone at the women's meeting later this week." She glanced at her six-month medallion. One of the tenets of A.A. was rigorous honesty. But what she'd said wasn't a total lie, any more than not mentioning the trouble the coven was in was a lie. She intended to go to that meeting, eventually.

"That sounds like a good plan." Her therapist's tone lightened. "You're still writing in your journal?"

"Yeah, every day." That was the full truth. Along with everything else, she owed her therapist for turning her on to working through her feelings and past by freewriting—especially poetry. She really enjoyed that. "One of the coven members gave me a cool book. *Return of the Great Goddess*. It's really inspiring."

"I'll have to look it up." The therapist's tone became more casual. "I read a wonderful poem about the Goddess this morning. Maiden. Mother. Crone..."

Em's attention shifted away from the phone as a rumble of raised voices came from somewhere beyond her closed bedroom door. Half-listening to her therapist, Em tiptoed to the door and stepped out into the hallway so she could hear the argument. It was coming from somewhere on the floor below, reverberating up the stairwell.

"It's the truth," Devlin's voice growled.

"So you say," a man's voice answered, dangerously low and cool. Gar Remillard. She was sure of it. His voice didn't have anything distinctive about it, just the rock-hard tone of a man not about to give an inch.

Devlin huffed. "Wherever you got your information, it's wrong."

"I'll see you in the morning, Devlin." Gar's voice paused for a second, then he went on. "I recommend between now and then, you find yourself some proof."

The tap of footsteps sprinted up the stairwell toward her floor. Em started to retreat, but she wasn't fast enough; Gar reached the top before she could get out of sight.

Devlin was well-built, the kind of put-together handsome that was hard to overlook. Gar in his faded jeans and taut T-shirt was even harder not to notice, but for entirely different reasons. He stood broader and taller than Devlin, a good few inches over six feet. Slashes of dark ink marked his biceps and forearms. A five o'clock shadow stippled his rugged chin. Unruly black hair. Steel-blue eyes darkened by the hallway's dim light. Behind him the ghost whirled, an all but invisible tempest tagging his every move.

He nodded a brusque greeting to her, his surly expression unwavering.

She feigned a smile and retreated into her room. He went into the one next to hers and thumped the door shut. The guest room. She should have guessed that's where he was staying.

"Em? Did you hear me?" her therapist said.

"Oh, yeah—sorry." Em eased the door to her room closed and bolted the lock. "I lost the connection for a second. It's this cheap phone."

"That's okay. I should get to bed. Don't forget about the sponsor."

"I won't."

Relieved to have the call over with, Em stashed her phone on the nightstand, her thoughts already returning to the room next door and its surly occupant. When she'd arrived at the complex a couple of weeks ago, Devlin had let her pick out her own room. She'd chosen this tiny one up on the top floor with the empty guest rooms. He'd encouraged her to change her mind and suggested she take a larger room with a private bath down on the second floor, the one that Brooklyn had ended up moving into recently. But this little room set all by itself had felt right to her, tucked out of the way like a bird's nest in the canopy of a tall pine. She'd never dreamed that she'd end up sharing her retreat so soon, and with someone as troubled and dangerous to the coven as Gar—and his ghost. She felt so bad for both of them.

Em crawled into bed and shut off the light on her bedside stand. She curled up and murmured her usual prayer of gratitude for a safe place to sleep and a refrigerator full of food. For not throwing up every morning like she used to and for the money she made doing cleaning chores around the complex. "Dear Goddess, protect the coven, protect the kittens too."

The whoosh of a shower whispered out from the other side of her bedroom wall. The guest bath. It was interesting how she and Gar had noticed each other even before he arrived at the complex. She'd been mistaken to assume it was nothing more than a fleeting connection, brought on by his haunting and her psychic ability. In truth, Gar and the ghost were smack-dab in the middle of her business. If she could figure out who was haunting him, and why, then she might be able to free the ghost from whatever was keeping it earthbound. Without question, breaking that attachment would make Gar less volatile and easier to reason with. She should have mentioned the haunting to Chloe, but she'd been so worried about the kittens that it had slipped her mind. First thing in the morning, she'd tell everyone. Some of them might have sensed something was off about him, but more likely they hadn't. She was the coven's only psychic medium, after all.

As she curled up tighter, a memory slipped into her mind. Another haunting. Years ago. She was fifteen, sitting on the loading dock at a conference center in Atlanta. The hot sun. The stench of garbage. The clank of pans in the kitchen behind her. Next to her, Alice. Sixteen years old. Haunted blue eyes, so much like Gar's. Full, beautiful lips. The two of them holding hands as they plotted Em's escape from her aunt and mother.

Em squeezed her eyes shut, trying to hold back the inevitable flood of harder memories: Alice, her kisses. Her trembling hands. Her craziness brought on from being haunted by the baby she'd lost, a spirit too young and fiercely attached to listen to Em's pleas for it to move on and let its mother live in peace. Another memory. The Royal Palm Playhouse in Tampa. Alice lying dead on the bathroom floor. A syringe on the tiles beside her.

Em's throat tightened until she couldn't swallow. She wriggled across the bed and grabbed the bottle of water from beside her phone. But the bottle's thin plastic felt wrong in her grip, not at all like the hard surface of the travel mug her fingers had reflexively expected to feel. The mug she'd kept filled with vodka and Coke. The burn and forgetting.

She shoved the bottle back on the stand. She'd gotten over the cravings. She'd gotten through detox months and months ago. When was the reptilian part of her brain going to forget and let go? Water was good. Liquor wasn't an option. Not today. Not tomorrow.

Taking a deep breath, she picked the bottle back up and took a long sip, the tepid water moistening her mouth, soothing her throat. She took another breath and sent the thoughts out into the darkness. *Alice, I miss you. Watch over us all, especially the haunted man.*

She didn't expect to physically hear an answer. She never had, at least when it came to Alice. But she often sensed Alice watching over her like a guardian angel.

A muffled squeak reverberated through the wall as the guest room shower shut off.

Em held motionless, hands clamped around the bottle as she listened. She couldn't hear Gar's movements or anything else. But she could imagine him and what he was doing, unfolding the towels she'd set out when she'd

cleaned the guest room a few days ago. Wiping moisture from his legs...
Gar Remillard. A haunted man. Curly black hair. Camo cap pulled low.
Looking at her.

Careful to not make a sound, she put the bottle back on the nightstand
and scrunched down under her blankets.

A thump came from directly behind her headboard—his headboard,
bumping into the wall as he got into his bed. When she'd left the clean
towels in his bathroom, she also put fresh sheets on the bed and scented
them with a spray made from lavender and sage. Hopefully the herbs would
ease the ghost's anguish and bring Gar gentle dreams.

An ache tugged in her chest as thoughts of Gar and his burden twisted
with memories of Alice, her half-crazed eyes and the soul-deep connection
they'd shared. Haunted.

Em tucked her knees to her chest. She filled her mind with a peaceful
image of tall evergreens and a river washed gold by the sunset. The cool
smell of a breeze wafting off of the water. The warm aroma of pine.
Peaceful. Tranquil. Comforting. She counted slowly, lulling herself. One.
Two. Three...

Her mind drifted to that slushy April night in Saratoga Springs, New
York. The witch ghost standing at the entry to the park. Their eyes had
met, so much warmth and strength conveyed in that one frozen moment,
and then the choice had been laid before her. Freedom. Death. Love.

It was funny how connections worked. She and the ghost in the park.
Alice and her. Her and Gar. She had the strange feeling she might like
Gar, if she could talk the ghost into moving on. In a way, it felt like maybe
she already did.

Chapter 3

TAMPA—Teen tarot reader found dead in theater bathroom. The body of nineteen-year-old Alice Brown was discovered in a backstage bathroom after an anonymous 911 call reported an overdose at the Royal Palm Playhouse. According to Tampa Police Sgt. Phillip Ball, the tarot reader was a well-known transient in the Tampa area. How she gained entry to the theater remains unknown.
—From *Florida Daily Herald*, March 23

Em woke up to the hungry mews of kittens. She slid out of bed, made a fast trip to the bathroom in the hall, then returned only long enough to collect the box full of kittens before heading downstairs.

Traces of pre-dawn light glimmered in the building's tall windows, casting shadows on the artsy graffiti-covered hallway walls and worn floorboards. Normally, she didn't get up before anyone else, but it wasn't fair to let the kittens go hungry any longer—nor wise to let their cries wake up the investigator in the room next door. Besides, the solitude and quiet felt good.

She padded in stocking feet past the office where Gar had interrogated Devlin last night, then down the wide main staircase to the first floor and the living room that overlooked the gardens. The room was enormous, its vaulted ceiling stretching up two stories. The sleek, modern furniture interspersed with potted palms reminded Em uncomfortably of the hotel lobby in Atlanta where her aunt had booked events every year. She could still see the moniker her aunt and mother had given her on the sign out front: *This Weekend Only. Violet Grace. The World's Youngest Psychic Medium.* She had to admit, seeing signs like that had been a thrill at first.

But facing rooms full of people had always frightened her. That was, until her aunt started plying her with "special" sodas and Creamsicle-flavored drinks, not to mention the whipahol and Jell-O shots.

The box of kittens tilted in her hands as the white one scrambled to the edge, crying as if begging to be let out.

She took a fresh grip. "Hold on. I'm going to make you breakfast, then I'll clean that smelly box of yours."

Em hurried around the room divider and into the lounge. As she headed for the hallway to the dining room, she made a point of keeping her steps quick and her eyes averted from the bar that spanned one wall of the lounge.

A rustle came from near the bar.

She stopped midstride. She'd been certain no one was up. Maybe it was Devlin's dog.

She pivoted. A towheaded boy slept on the sofa, dressed in Spider-Man pajamas. There was another rustle and a snuffle of breath as he shifted in his sleep to face her. It was Peregrine, Chandler's son. Chandler was one of the witches who lived at the complex, but her apartment and artist workshop were in a concrete building near the main gate. There was no reason for Peregrine to be here, especially since he was in the third grade and this was a school day. But that wasn't the only thing that was off.

Em sniffed the air. Coffee. Freshly brewed.

She tiptoed out of the lounge and went into the dining room. That room was empty, but a murmur of voices echoed out from the kitchen. What was going on?

She nudged the kitchen's swinging door open with the kittens' box. As she stepped inside, the ever-present aroma of homemade bread and drying herbs mingled with the coffee scent. Everyone who lived at the complex was gathered around the kitchen island: Devlin, Chandler, and Brooklyn. Chloe was there too. Technically she had an apartment by the University of Vermont campus, but she spent most nights with Devlin. The only missing full-time coven member was Midas. Like Chloe, he had an apartment elsewhere and attended the university, which most likely explained his absence.

"Good morning, sleepy head," Chandler said, smiling at Em. She was close to thirty years old with broad shoulders, short-cropped hair, and sleeves of dragon and monkey tattoos. Her tattoos resembled the sculptures she created out of scrap metal and car parts, including the flying monkeys decorating the complex's gateway, and the other ones that had been animated by Merlin's Shade and wreaked havoc around the city.

"I was about to come up and get you," Chloe said. "Didn't you get my text?"

"Ah—I didn't check my phone. What's going on?"

Devlin cleared his throat. "Gar went for a run. While he's not around, I thought we should all talk." There were pieces of toilet paper stuck to Devlin's chin and jawline as if he'd nicked himself shaving. He had on the same cable-knit sweater and shirt as yesterday—not normal at all for him. Not that he was overly prissy about clothes, but he usually looked as neat as a cover model.

He took a sip of his coffee, then shoved it aside. "Things aren't looking good."

A wave of dread rolled over Em. She rested the kittens' box tentatively on the empty stool next to Brooklyn's. They needed to be fed, but they'd have to wait. This sounded even worse than she'd feared.

Brooklyn glanced at the box. She was younger than Chandler by at least five years. She had thick dark hair that brushed her shoulders and soul-deep eyes that hinted at her Haitian heritage. "Chloe told me you rescued some kittens. They're so tiny and sweet." She wrinkled her nose. "They stink. You want me to feed them while you change their box?"

"Um." Em glanced at Devlin. His jaw was set, impatience written on his ordinarily relaxed face. She turned back to Brooklyn. "Maybe after we talk?"

Devlin's expression softened. "This won't take long. But we need to get to it. Gar could come back at any moment." He scrubbed a hand over his head and took a breath. "The issue is, Gar doesn't believe Athena is—" His voice choked.

Chloe rested her hand on his arm. "I can tell them if you want."

"No. I'm fine." He lifted his chin and continued in a measured voice. "Gar and the High Council don't believe my sister's dead. They're convinced she deserted the coven, like our mother did."

"What?" Em couldn't believe her ears. Even if Athena wasn't dead, she'd never have deserted the Northern Circle. She'd spent years rebuilding the coven after their mother's irresponsibility had nearly bankrupt it.

"Are they crazy?" Brooklyn said.

"In Gar's case, that might be true." Devlin offered Brooklyn a smile, but it instantly faded. "The Council claims Rhianna has an airtight alibi that proves she was elsewhere during the time when we claim she was here impersonating Athena. Supposedly she has witnesses who are beyond reproach."

Chandler thumped her coffee mug down on the island. "That's ridiculous. What does the Council think we have to gain by lying?" Her voice dropped. "I smell something stinky, and it isn't just those kittens."

Heat seeped up Em's neck. She sidestepped away from the island, carried the kittens' box to the other side of the kitchen, and set it on the floor by the fridge. They didn't smell that bad, though she agreed that there probably was something going on with the Eastern Coast High Council.

She opened the fridge and took out the jug of kitten formula, listening to Devlin explain that Gar had refused to say who Rhianna's witnesses were or where she claimed to have been during that time.

"There has to be a way to convince Gar we're telling the truth," Chloe said.

Brooklyn's voice turned sly. "I could whip up some special brownies. Bend him to our will."

"No potions or spells," Devlin said firmly. "That would be one way to get in even deeper. Make no mistake, Gar is a smart and powerful witch."

Chandler blew out a frustrated breath. "He reminds me of my birth mother. She always ran hot and cold. But after my father died, trying to communicate with her was like talking to a brick wall."

Em listened closely, intense sadness gripping her as Alice's unstable moods and torment flashed through her mind. She felt bad for Chandler's mother, and stranger still, she felt worse for Gar. He was in anguish. But he was a good person, her instincts told her that—and they screamed for her to defend him. Devlin, Brooklyn... none of them got what his problem was, not at all.

"What do you expect?" Chloe said. "Gar's father is a loup-garou."

Em's eyes widened. *A loup-garou?* Her aunt had claimed she'd met one once, a human who could shift into wolf form at will. It made sense that genes like that could make a man aggressive and instinctual—doubly so if he were haunted. It also explained why Gar had gone running before daylight, a time when normal humans would have a hard time seeing. But it didn't make him a horrible person.

"He's a loose cannon," Devlin added. "Even if he most likely can't shift, given his mother's a full-blooded heritage witch."

Chandler nodded. "Definitely trouble with a capital T."

"It's not Gar's fault!" The words flew from Em louder than she'd intended, and they landed in a lull in the conversation.

Everyone swiveled to look at her.

Devlin frowned. "What are you talking about?"

She thumped the jug of kitten formula down on the counter by the fridge. "Gar can't help the way he is. He's haunted—in turmoil."

"How do you know that?" Chloe asked. "You haven't met him yet, have you?"

"Before you picked me up last night, I saw him driving through the city. We met in the upstairs hallway for a second too. Both times I saw the ghost. I'm a hundred percent sure it's a haunting." She bit her bottom lip. "I should have said something sooner. It was stupid not to. I was going to tell you first thing this morning. I guess… I was so worried about the kittens, and tired."

Chloe raised her hand to quiet Em. "It's fine. Do you know who's haunting him?"

"Not yet. But once I meet him face-to-face I will, especially if I touch him."

Devlin jumped up from his stool, his gaze hard on Em. "Stay away from him. He may not be planning on interrogating you. I'd like to keep it that way."

"We should banish the ghost," Brooklyn suggested. "Wouldn't that solve the whole issue?"

Em folded her arms across her chest. "No. We need to figure out why it's not at rest and help it find peace." Her body went hot as she resisted the urge to state the obvious. After Athena had been killed and Rhianna had used her skin to make the necklace, Athena's spirit had come to them in the form of an orb. None of them had realized who the orb was at the time, and Rhianna had shouted a spell to banish it from the house. If the orb hadn't been evicted so quickly, they most likely would have figured out it was Athena and put a stop to Rhianna before things went as far as they did.

Chandler raised her voice. "I think we need to determine who the ghost is before we decide anything. Definitely before we confront Gar about it."

"I agree," Devlin said. His gaze remained on her. "Do you have something in mind?"

Chandler rubbed her arm, her sleeves of dragon and monkey tattoos radiating energy. "I'm not a medium like Em, but my psychic powers are probably second to hers. If the two of us went somewhere private—like my apartment—we could work together to draw the ghost away from Gar. It would have a hard time resisting the pull of our conjoined energy. We could find out who it is that way."

Eagerness coursed through Em, and her pulse picked up. "That's a great idea. While we're at it, we could also try again to reach Athena.

With Rhianna gone, the banishment spell has probably weakened. If we could find out where Athena's body is and prove to the High Council how Rhianna used her skin…"

She let her voice trail off, embarrassment prickling the nape of her neck as everyone fell silent and the conversation died. Why had she said such an inconsiderate thing? Her aunt would have given her a backhander for being so cavalier in front of a murder victim's family.

"If you want"—Brooklyn came to her rescue—"I'll make sure Peregrine gets to school on time, then you and Chandler could start right away." Her gaze went to the kittens' box. "I don't mind taking the fleabags to the vet either. Personally, I think the coven should adopt them. I saw a mouse in the greenhouse this morning."

Em's emotions shifted, a mix of gratitude and determination washing away her self-reproach. She smiled at Brooklyn. "Do you mind telling the vet about the garbage bag and the railroad tracks? The police might be more likely to do something if the vet's the one who reports—"

She stopped talking as the door to the kitchen swung open and Gar swaggered into the room as if it were a coffee shop he visited every day. The sheen of sweat from a hard run shone on his face and soaked the front of his T-shirt. Mud splattered his shoes. His camo cap was turned around backward. Everything about his stance said, "Don't mess with me." Not to mention the hazy tempest of the ghost slicing the air behind him.

His gaze cut a path across the room to her, steel-blue eyes zeroing in like a bullet from a sniper rifle. "I haven't talked to you yet."

The unyielding timbre of his voice shot straight into the center of Em's being, making her pulse jump from fear and reminding her that Gar saw her as a member of a disreputable coven he was investigating, not as someone determined to help him.

Devlin stepped between them, his back to her as he blocked Gar's line of sight. His shoulders squared. "She is a new initiate—brand new to the Craft. She has no responsibility for what happened."

"Of course she doesn't." Gar's tone was so level that Em couldn't tell if he was being sarcastic or sincere. He sidestepped Devlin and advanced on her, bringing with him the frenzied energy of the ghost.

She swallowed drily and lifted her head to meet his steady gaze.

"You're the famous Violet Grace. The world's youngest medium. I believe that's your moniker."

"That was my moniker," she said, matching his even tone. "But I'm not that person anymore. She's gone. Dead."

A pleased smile flicked across his lips, one that touched his eyes. She caught a glimpse of something else in his eyes as well, a question burning in their depths so fiercely it made her heart skip a beat. His eyebrows raised.

"Yeah?" she said, confused.

He swiveled away from her and toward Devlin, as if he'd changed his mind about asking the question, or perhaps he'd never intended to. The ghost's hazy outline flared upward into the air behind him, and his voice sharpened. "Well, Devlin, it looks like I'm late for breakfast."

The cords in Devlin's neck tensed. "We weren't having breakfast. We were talking about you. You didn't think we wouldn't, did you?"

"I suppose not." Gar took his cap off and ran a hand over it. "What I'm contemplating is who I should question first this morning."

Em raised her voice, hoping to draw his attention back to her so she could look in his eyes again. "I know Rhianna is lying about Athena. I saw her spirit. It came to us in the form of an orb."

Ignoring her, Gar glanced at Chandler. "I'll speak with you first. Eight o'clock in the office."

Chandler? Em could only stare as Gar snagged an orange from the fruit bowl by the fridge, then marched back out the kitchen door and vanished as it swung shut behind him.

What had he avoided asking her?

And, Dear Goddess, what was she going to do? Without the addition of Chandler's energy, it would be a lot easier for Gar's ghost to refuse her summons.

Chapter 4

Etched goblets tiny enough for fairy hands,
Cinderella champagne flutes sparkling with candy-flavored liquor.
Drink this. The Queen of Hearts smiled.
—Journal of Emily Adams
Memory from third grade. First Drink. Aunt Lynda.

Once Chandler went into the office for her interrogation, Em slipped upstairs with a bundle of clean towels. She waited by the window in her room until she saw Chloe take off for the university and Brooklyn leave to bring the kittens to the vet. They all assumed she'd head to Chandler's apartment and attempt to lure Gar's ghost by herself, since Chandler's interrogation could go on for hours, or even all day. But Em had come up with a new idea.

Carrying the bundle of towels in her arms, she tiptoed back out into the hallway and paused, listening for sounds. No voices or footsteps filtered up the staircase from below. No sounds at all. She crept to the guest room door. Nerves fluttered in her stomach as she eyed the doorknob. As a High Council investigator, Gar had to be experienced with staying where he wasn't welcome. It wouldn't be out of the question for him to have cast a spell against intruders. Unless, of course, he was so messed up or egotistical that he believed no one would dare intrude on his privacy.

She prodded the knob with a fingernail. No electric prickle or vibration shot up her finger, nothing to indicate the presence of a spell. She grasped the knob and turned it. So far, so good.

Slowly she pushed the door open and stepped inside, leaving it ajar so she'd hear if anyone came up the stairs. She might not have enough time to escape, but she had the perfect alibi for her intrusion. After all, there was nothing suspicious about a housekeeper dropping off towels and straightening up a guest room.

She inched forward, her steps silent against the floorboards. The sultry aroma of soap and shampoo from a recent shower hung in the air. She set the towels on the dresser and switched on a small lamp. Turning on the overhead light made more sense for her housekeeping lie, but ghosts as a rule preferred to materialize in twilight conditions. And ghosts were why she was here—or at least, one specific ghost. Without the addition of Chandler's energy, her chance of drawing the ghost away from its attachment to Gar was remote. However, the closer she was to Gar physically, the greater her odds were. They'd increase even more if she held something personal to him.

She scanned the room, letting her instincts guide her. Gar's canvas duffel bag sat on the luggage rack, still zipped closed and bulging as if unpacked. She wiped her hands down the legs of her jeans. If worse came to worst, she could use a piece of his clean clothing to help with the summoning. But that was far from ideal.

She moved on to the bathroom. The clothes he'd worn running were hand washed and thrown haphazardly over the shower curtain rod. His toiletry bag, razor, and toothbrush sat beside the sink. Next to them was a metal box the size of a large wallet—and an elastic arm brace with what looked like a poison dart gun from Assassin's Creed attached to it. The gun's barrel was decorated with a golden arrow.

Unable to believe her eyes, Em took a closer look at the arm brace gizmo. *Holy shit.* It was an actual dart gun, the kind that was meant to be worn on a person's arm. And definitely *not* a toy one.

She picked up the metal box and opened it. Sure enough, it held a selection of darts and labeled vials: *Panaeolus cinctulus, Vinca major, Artemisia absinthium…* She closed the box and put it back exactly where she'd found it. An unstable man with chemical weapons. Not a good combination—though she wasn't surprised, nor did she blame him for bringing a weapon. She'd stayed in strange places and slept with her knife close by many times over the last few years. She wouldn't have minded having something more intimidating than her knife. Not that Gar had to be afraid here at the complex, nor was a dart gun ideal for stashing under a pillow.

Her gaze landed on his hairbrush, bringing her thoughts back to the job at hand. She needed something personal for the summoning, and you couldn't get more personal than that.

She snatched the brush and carried it to the bed. The quilt and sheets were pulled up, but the pillows still wore indents from where his head had been. As she sat down, the aroma of lavender and sage surrounded her. A second, fainter scent reached her nose: an earthy mix of moss and evergreen forest. The scent of Gar's magic and spirit.

Em took a deeper sniff of the aroma and a sense of serenity stole over her as her subconscious drew a connection between the fragrance and her past. A river in the pines, a fifteen-year-old her, and hazy memories of a guy she'd known. Johnny Brighton. Skinny. Long, dark hair. Scruffy beard. Early twenties, maybe. She'd only known him for two days, maybe a little less. But since then, the smell of evergreens always made her think of him. His kindnesses. How he'd made her feel safe.

Warmth radiated through Em's chest. She smiled and shook her head. This was definitely not the time or place to go on a sentimental journey. Besides, no matter what her subconscious thought, comparing Johnny to Gar was weird.

She turned the hairbrush over in her hands, feeling the soft scrape of the bristles against her palm. Now that she thought about it, maybe her subconscious had a point. Johnny and Gar really were similar in a lot of ways. Both had eyes full of secrets and raven-dark hair—and Johnny had also worked for the Council. In fact, Johnny was the first and only other person she'd met who did. Back then, that had soothed her fears. Her aunt and mother had only mentioned the Council a few times in passing, but always with great venom. To her, that automatically made Johnny someone she could trust. He'd proved to be more than that. He'd been her skinny rebel knight, the guy who helped her kill Violet Grace and get to Alice. Also—and she'd even admitted it to Alice—she'd crushed on Johnny something awful. He'd even regularly starred in her erotic fantasies.

A tingle of lust began to coil low in her body. She laughed at herself. Sure, she hadn't hooked up with anyone since she'd gotten sober, but this was a ridiculous time to get horny.

With a sigh, she surrendered to her libido. *I'll make you a deal. Let me get my work done. Later, we'll think about Johnny some more. In bed or the shower. But not now.*

She took a deep breath, cradled the hairbrush lightly between her hands, and switched her mental image of Johnny for one of Gar with his broad-shoulders and the ghost's hazy tempest swirling behind him.

Tension rose from her chest as she drew up her magic. It skimmed her neck, filling her sinuses with a coppery smell as she sent the command out toward Gar's ghost. "I beseech you, spirit," she murmured. "Show yourself."

One minute passed. Two. Three.

She sent out her magic again. "Show yourself. I beseech you."

Her skin prickled, anticipating the stroke of a presence. She tilted her head, listening for the slightest sound. Nothing.

She set the hairbrush on her lap, her voice firmer this time. "Appear to me. I summon you, come now."

When she'd been Violet Grace—all those years on the road with those tight patent leather shoes on her feet and pink girly ribbons in her hair—she'd rarely had a problem contacting spirits. She'd sit across the table from some rich person or walk through an audience in a conference hall and ghosts would reach out from this world and beyond, scrambling for a chance to speak with their loved ones. The few times she'd encountered hauntings—four that she could remember, including Alice—the contact had been different. Those ghosts were aggressively stubborn, refusing to communicate and even less agreeable when it came to putting distance between them and the person they were attached to. Getting them to move on was even worse, sometimes impossible.

"Show yourself!" She drew up all her energy and visualized a wall of waves surging toward her, wind in her face. She thrust her power outward against the tide, a widening mesh of magic, a fisherman's net casting for spirits. She drew the net back in, swift and hard, feeling the familiar pull of a spirit's resistance.

The resistance vanished.

She tried again. Sweat soaked her back. Her hair hung heavy against her shoulders. The room around her came into sharp focus, her eyes now a force in the low light as she concentrated all her energy. She glanced around, looking for indications of a spirit's presence. The white pillar candle on the table beside the bed sat undisturbed and unlit. No shadows in the corners. The air temperature hadn't changed. No new smells.

Em focused her energy again and cast out her net. Gar was one story below with Chandler, almost directly beneath her. Not far at all for her to draw an ethereal being. She could clearly sense it again, firmly anchored to him.

Please. She tried a more persuasive tactic. *You have nothing to fear. I won't banish you. I want to help you.*

The sensation of the ghost loosened its grip on Gar and moved toward her—

Abruptly it stopped and then spun away, every hint of it vanishing from her detection like a fish sucked down a whirlpool.

Em pressed her lips together. This was seriously strange. The ghost was gone, not just from her net. It was gone from the building. Gone from Gar. From her. From everywhere.

Something's coming! Her sixth sense shrieked.

Every hair on Em's body stood on edge as the air around her suddenly crackled with electricity. The floor began to shimmer, the knots in its wood darkening and spinning like the eyes of a hundred hurricanes. Energy ruptured through the boards, a geyser of exploding sparks: Gar's ghost, agitated, terrified.

"Welcome," Em greeted it, her voice shaking.

The vaporous form twisted, fighting to materialize. But as it fought, the air pressure in the room soared, cycling higher and higher.

Em clamped her hands over her ears, unable to stand the forceful sensation.

Pop! The pressure vanished. And with it, the ghost.

Em froze. The room was silent; no lingering energy, nothing out of place, not a single indication that something out of the ordinary had just happened. Everything felt absurdly normal. It was as if the ghost had once again left the building. What the heck had happened?

She glanced around the room, searching for an answer, but nothing came to her. The only thing she knew for certain was that she couldn't afford to take time to puzzle it out right now. There was a strong possibility that Gar might have sensed what happened. If he was as smart as he looked, the chances of him suspecting her involvement were high. She needed to get out before he decided to investigate.

She grabbed the hairbrush from where it had fallen to the floor and put it back exactly as she'd found it. Then she slipped out of his room and tiptoed down the hallway to her bathroom. Once the door was locked behind her, she went to the sink and splashed cold water on her face. That was one of the strangest summonings she'd ever experienced. She'd never had a ghost turn her down like that. And she wasn't entirely sure this one had turned her down, either. It was almost as if a stronger psychic force had summoned the spirit in a different direction. She shook her head. But that didn't make sense. Who else would want to call Gar's ghost? And what were the chances of them both doing it at the exact same time?

Taking a steadying breath, Em glanced in the mirror over the sink. Her face stared back at her, made more waif-like by the harsh bathroom light. Pale skin. Long, mousy hair, hollows under eyes as steel-blue as Gar's. Her six months of sobriety had added flesh to her hipbones and muscle to her arms and legs. In reality, she was looking and feeling better. It seemed like her abilities as a medium should also be strengthened. But yet, she'd failed.

Her mind went back to the first night she'd come to the complex. She'd felt like such a nothing compared to everyone else: Chloe with her stylish strawberry-blond pixie cut and chic clothes. Chandler, her sleeves of tattoos and flowing caftan, a force to be reckoned with. Midas, towering over her with his perfect dreads and button-down dress shirt. And her, a wasted thing in Goodwill castoffs, her throat tightening every time she tried to speak. She'd spent most of that night trying to blend in with the background, as well as making sure she didn't pick up the wrong glass and sip wine or a mixed drink by mistake.

Em rested her hands on the edge of the sink and gazed into the mirror again, and another detail from that night slipped into her mind, one connected to a different ghost's unnerving and untimely disappearance.

She, Chloe, and Midas had competed in an initiation test that required them to use their inborn gifts to move a ball through an iron maze. Midas had combined his knowledge of geophysics with magic to whiz the ball through. Chloe had used her energy and an athame to steer the ball. Determined to earn her place in the coven and live in the complex instead of returning to the halfway house, she had summoned a spirit to help her. That's when the orb that eventually proved to be Athena's spirit had come and been banished by Rhianna.

Rhianna. She was an incredibly skilled witch. She could be the one summoning Gar's ghost. But why? Unless she was in league with Gar and trying to help him break the attachment, which seemed unlikely.

A chill pebbled Em's arms. There was something else she hadn't thought about until now. Why would a formidable high priestess like Athena materialize in the weaker form of an orb rather than a fully materialized ghost—not to mention allow herself to be banished from her own home with her coven all around? It was peculiar, as strange as the tug-of-war she'd just experienced with Gar's seemingly powerful ghost.

Chapter 5

She never grabbed me where bruises would show.
She never left me alone too long
in the closet
or in the van with blacked out windows.
—"Alone" by E. A.

Em headed downstairs to find Devlin. She needed to tell him about the failed summoning. The whole thing was disturbing. He'd also want to know about Gar's dart gun and the labeled vials.

Lost in thought, she reached the first floor. The door to the office was open. She couldn't see anyone, but Gar and Chandler's voices were so loud and clear she could only assume they were right inside the doorway.

She slowed, unsure how to pass without looking like she was eavesdropping.

"I'm not about to let you question him," Chandler was saying. "He's just a boy."

"Exactly my point." Gar's voice was stern. "Who do you think creatures like shades are more apt to seek out? Who is easier to influence, adults or children?"

"I didn't let Merlin's Shade go near Peregrine. When things went bad, I took him to a safe house."

"Oh, so you didn't trust that the Northern Circle would protect him?"

"That's not what I said." A phone jangled, and Chandler fell silent.

Gar grumbled. "I need to take this."

Em hurried her steps, hoping to get by the office before they started talking again. But as she reached the doorway, Chandler backed out of the room and right into her path.

"Sorry," Em said, sidestepping.

Chandler latched onto Em's arm and slid a distressed look her way, as if pleading for help. "Don't be sorry. I was about to call you."

"Oh—" Em wasn't sure what to say.

Chandler glanced through the doorway to where Gar stood only a few feet away with the phone to his ear. "If we're done"—she said to him—"I want to show Em... I want to help her set up a place for the kittens before Brooklyn gets back."

Gar frowned at them. "Hold on a moment," he said into the phone. In one swift movement, he was through the doorway. His free hand closed around Em's arm. His gaze went to Chandler. "You can go. Emily is staying."

Chandler's eyes met Em's, telegraphing worry. "You okay with that?"

Em licked her lips, not as sure as she'd been earlier about wanting to be alone with Gar. Plus, while she couldn't see his ghost, her sixth sense insisted it was still attached to him—which was strange enough to make her feel deeply uncomfortable. He certainly didn't sound—or act—any more reasonable. Experience told her that the greater the distance or the weaker the attachment between Gar and the ghost, the less influence it should have over him. Then again, she'd never dealt with a person who was both haunted and part loup-garou, not to mention the addition of the whole tug-of-war thing. Still, talking with him would give her a chance to try and figure things out.

She smiled at Chandler. "It's fine. But do you mind telling Devlin I'll stop by later? He was expecting me." With luck, Gar wouldn't think anything of her comment and Devlin would figure out that something had happened during the summoning.

"Sure no, problem." Understanding flashed across Chandler's face. "After that, stop by my workshop. We can do those meditation exercises we were talking about earlier."

Em steadied her voice and kept up the ruse. "I don't think they'll help, but okay."

"Great. See you later." Chandler gave Gar one last look, then took off down the hallway toward the living room.

Gar ushered Em into the office and nudged the door shut.

The room was dark, a rich darkness that came from its thickly curtained windows and walls lined with bookcases. The only light filtered out from a gooseneck lamp, sitting on an executive-style desk. It was one of the rooms Em hadn't spent any time in. It hadn't even needed cleaning, at least before today. Now random stacks of books surfaced like skyscrapers from the desk and floor. Juice bottles, orange peels, and an empty potato chip bag littered the top of a file cabinet.

A straight-backed chair was stationed in front of the desk. Gar gestured for her to sit in it, then turned to face her with his hips resting against the desk's edge. He put the phone back to his ear. "Sorry that took so long. Like I said, this isn't a good time."

Em settled into the chair, her feet and ankles tucked safely back into the darkness beneath it. She couldn't help wondering what Gar was going to ask her. He was a special investigator, which no doubt meant he'd looked into all the coven members' pasts, including hers. Not that anyone had to dig very deep to find that information, at least not from the years she was Violet Grace.

She squeezed her eyes shut, images of tabloid covers and headlines about her reeling behind her closed lids like ads for a horror movie. Child medium does this. Child medium does that. Rumors of bad things. Rumors of hell. All trending on social media. There was little chance Gar hadn't guessed why she always wore socks and kept her legs covered in public, hadn't guessed about the scars and worse. Still, she didn't believe any of those things had been on his mind in the kitchen. The question in his eyes had struck her as more personal to him.

"All right," Gar snapped at the person on the phone. "I'll call you back later, then."

She opened her eyes in time to see him shove his phone into a pocket. He braced his hands behind him on the desktop and studied her. "So what am I going to do about you?" he said.

"Ah—" She had no idea how to answer that. She wasn't even entirely sure if he was asking her or grumbling to himself.

He shifted upright and huffed out a frustrated sigh. After a moment he leaned forward, elbows on his knees as he looked directly in her eyes. The question from the kitchen burned in his gaze. Finally, he put it into words. "You don't recognize me, do you?"

She blinked him, biting back the urge to blurt out "No." She'd never been good at recognizing people, especially not by their faces or voices like most people could. It was usually the touch or scent of someone's spirit that would strike her as familiar, when she did remember them at all.

"I think I saw you downtown," she said. "In your truck just before you arrived here." She was certain that wasn't what he meant, but it was easier to accept than the memories surfacing in the back of her mind. Moss and evergreens. She'd smelled that on his bed, and again right now, the scent of his spirit and magic, whispering in the air around him.

Disappointment shadowed his eyes. "Is that all? Are you sure?"

No, she wasn't sure. Mother of all Goddesses, he couldn't be... of all the people in this world.

Her breath caught in her throat, her eyes widening in shock. Her subconscious had tried to tell her when he'd passed in the truck. And again later in the night, when she'd been lying in her bed thinking about him on the other side of the wall... most of all when she'd sat on his bed and held his hairbrush. Tall evergreens. A river washed gold by sunset.

She swept her gaze over him more slowly, taking in every inch: shoulders matured from lean to broad and muscular over the last seven years. Long hair, just as wild and dark but a good foot shorter and held down by a camo cap instead of a knit hat. Face more rugged and worn from the frenzy of the haunting. Heavier eyebrows. No earrings.

"Johnny?" she stammered. Part of her longed to jump up and throw her arms around him. Part of her still couldn't believe it was true.

A broad smile brightened his face. "I wasn't sure you'd remember. It's been a long time. You were pretty messed up."

Her face heated and she laughed softly. "Never too messed up to forget what you did for me. But"—she gave him another once-over—"you've changed, and is Gar your real name?"

He laughed, a sound that held no hint of haunting and took her right back to how easy it had been between them for those two short days. "It is. I was named after my grandfather." He grimaced. "Would you mind doing me a favor and not telling anyone about my alias? No one in the coven, and more importantly no one from the Council. Even my superiors aren't aware of Johnny."

Em nodded. It felt right to keep that secret just between the two of them.

She shook her head again in disbelief. Johnny. Johnny Brighton. Her rebel knight. She thought she'd never see him again.

Her mind went back to that brief time. She'd been beyond sick, not only from booze and the drugs her aunt had given her, but from the hours chained in the hot van.

She vaguely remembered being in the van. The heat. Not being able to breathe. Being sure she was going to die. The door opening. The police cutting her legs from the shackles. A cop crying as he lifted her out into the fresh air. The hospital, her fleeing down the white tiled hallways, the unlocked door to the parking lot.

She'd vomited on the blacktop. But then she'd started running again—her stomach cramping, dizzy and confused—between houses and into the woods. Orbs swirled around her, their spirits urging her on and leading her to a cemetery. The sun was still blazing when Johnny found her. She didn't hear him coming and the spirits hadn't warned her. He set a bottle of water and a peeled orange a few feet away from where she was huddled, head throbbing, on the edge of delirium. He said the Council of Witches that her aunt hated had seen the news about her being found in the van. They'd sent him to secret her away from the police and bring her to them.

He gave her a backpack full of secondhand clothes. A gray hoodie and a soft pair of jeans. A blue top. A jogging bra and panties. Then he drove her to a place in the forest: tall pines and a river, shimmering gold under the sunset. The river's cool water soothed her overheated mind and body. Later, they lay in sleeping bags by a fire, its orange light flashing into the trees as she told him her dream of getting to Atlanta and Alice, and beyond that to becoming a poet and having her own place in the woods. A quiet spot for her and Alice to live. The next morning, Johnny drove to an old farmhouse somewhere just off the interstate. She waited in the truck while he went inside and returned with an envelope. Then he took her to a train station and shoved the envelope's contents into her hand: ten twenty-dollar bills, a ticket to Atlanta, and a fake ID.

"Go," he'd said, rushing her onto a waiting train. "You've been through enough shit. Live your dreams."

She'd waved goodbye to him through train's window, Johnny, her long-haired hero who thought her freedom was more important than playing safe. The guy who went against orders and let her go. She'd watched him fade into the distance as the train pulled away. When she couldn't see him anymore, she'd settled in and looked at the ID—and in that moment, she went from being Violet Grace to Emily Adams.

Coming out of her thoughts, Em took a deep breath. This was amazing. But there was one thing she'd always wondered. "Why Emily Adams? Was it a premade ID or—"

"I picked it out," he said, before she could finish. "Adams is a common last name. Good for not drawing attention. As for Emily"—he grinned—"the Council had told me a little about you. You were born in Amherst, Massachusetts, the birthplace of Emily Dickinson. You told me you wanted to be a poet."

Her chest squeezed, and tears dampened the corners of her eyes. She wiped them away quickly before he could notice, but also hoping he had.

"That's really cool. Thanks. Thanks for everything. I don't know where I'd be without you."

"You'd have had it easier if I had taken you to the Council." He sat back again, hands braced behind him on the desktop. "I assumed you made it to Atlanta. I lost track after that. Everyone did."

She thought for a second. That didn't make sense. Chloe had located her friend Keshari once by using a pendulum. "They couldn't have tried very hard. The Council must have tons of ways to find people?"

"You carried the ID I gave you for a long time, right?"

"Yeah, until the photo was outdated. What of it?"

"It was charmed against intrusion. As long as you carried it, no one—not me or the Council—could find you. Eventually, you weren't a concern of theirs." He leaned forward and touched her knee. "Em, I'm worried about you. This isn't a good place for you. The Northern Circle—"

His teeth clenched and his eyes pinched shut, as if a migraine had overtaken him. But Em didn't need her sixth sense to tell her this was no migraine. He looked exactly like Alice had when her baby's spirit took hold of her.

A ghostly hand appeared, clamping itself around his right forearm from behind, like roots grabbing hold of the earth. The misty outline of a scowling face wavered close to his ear.

Gar flung himself away from the desk, gripping his head as he retreated into the darkness by the curtained window with his back to her. The ghost spiked up behind him, spiraling like a hurricane. He wheeled back toward her, his expression grim. His eyes sparked with defensive anger, like a wolf trapped in a corner.

"Are you all right?" she asked. Her heart slammed against her ribcage. Of course he wasn't, not at all. The ghost was back.

His voice hardened. "The Northern Circle has a bad reputation for partying, and worse. They own a winery, for the Gods' sakes. You shouldn't be here, Em."

"You're wrong." She wanted to shout at him, to say how much the coven had done for her personally, how Devlin and Chloe made sure she got to meetings. How Athena had even orchestrated a ritual involving crystals that was designed to heal her emotional wounds and help her stay sober. How a lot of her current strength was due to that ritual. But the terrifying truth was she'd never met the real Athena when she was alive. Rhianna had orchestrated the healing ritual, a vengeful sociopath disguised as the coven's loving high priestess. The woman at the root of all the trouble.

"Em—" Gar paused, his voice and demeanor calming as the ghost's grip slid from his arm. "It's not just that I'm worried about you. I legally can't turn a blind eye on the coven's offenses. The Northern Circle has committed serious crimes against the witching world. They've—" He gritted his teeth as the ghost's energy strengthened. There was an audible *pop* of air pressure. The ghost vanished, and his expression eased. He puffed out a breath and rubbed his fingers against his temples. "Sorry. I'm just frustrated. Lately, I've felt..."

"Out of balance? Agitated?" She untangled his thoughts for him.

He nodded. "I didn't sleep well last night. I haven't for months."

Em ran her hand over the outside of her jeans pocket, feeling the outline of her six-month medallion and thinking through what he'd just said. It didn't sound like Gar had any idea he was haunted. That was usually the case, but she found it hard to believe that no one at the High Council had noticed. It only made sense for them to have on-staff mediums. Any self-respecting medium would have noticed the situation and felt obligated to tell him, or at minimum report it to their superiors. Either way, her not telling Gar wasn't right or kind. And it couldn't go on any longer, especially now that she knew who he was and what he'd done for her. Johnny. Her Johnny. It was amazing.

She slipped to her feet. "There's something you need to know."

The office door winged open and Devlin marched in, interrupting them the way Gar had done in the kitchen only a few hours ago. "Chandler told me you were here," he said to Em.

Gar glowered at him. "Ever heard of knocking?"

"This is my home, and Em is a member of my coven. If you're done, we'll leave and give you all the closed-door time you need to research or whatever."

Unsure what to do, Em glanced from Devlin to Gar. She needed to tell Gar about the haunting, but she wanted to break it to him gently, certainly not with anyone else around, or in the middle of an argument.

Gar watched Devlin unwaveringly. Then he flagged his hand. "Go on. Take her. You're right. She doesn't know anything."

Chapter 6

LAKE PLACID—Teenage girl found chained inside van after police respond to a report of a dog left in a vehicle with blacked out windows. According to police, when they arrived at the New Sun Convention Center they heard whimpering coming from a van owned by the Violet Grace Psychic Medium Show...
—From *The Upstate Tribune*, August 9

Taken aback and a bit hurt by Gar's abrupt dismissal, Em didn't say a thing while she and Devlin hurried away from the office. By the time they reached the privacy of the kitchen, she'd decided to not hide anything from Devlin—except for Gar's alias, and how torn and tangled her emotions were when it came to him.

Devlin poured a glass of cider for each of them, then they sat at the kitchen island while she went into detail about the impeded summoning and the weapons she'd seen in Gar's room. The weapons only concerned him slightly, but the tug-of-war sensation worried him as much as it had her, especially after she mentioned feeling the air pressure pop in the office.

His eyes went wide when she told him about the past she and Gar shared and how he'd brought it up to her. "I'm glad I interrupted when I did," he said. "I understand why you'd want to tell him about the haunting, especially after what he did for you. But you can't say a word, not yet. It's one of the few aces we have up our sleeves."

Em gazed into her glass of cider, avoiding Devlin's eyes. The only thing in her life that she'd always taken great pride in was putting the welfare of ghosts and the people affected by them before anything else. Helping them find peace wasn't always easy, but it took away some of the guilt she had about the outrageous amount of money her aunt had milked out of clients. Not to mention her guilt over disrespecting the spirits by being drunk at readings.

Years ago, she'd even snuck out of a hotel room to meet a woman who couldn't afford a ticket to a group reading. At twelve years old, she'd known it was a dangerous thing to do in a city and all by herself. But the woman had sent her a note by way of a bellhop, explaining that she couldn't afford to pay and was certain her dead teenage son wasn't at rest. Em knew the woman was telling the truth. She could sense the teenager's spirit without even trying. So, when her aunt went to the hotel bar to meet some guy, Em slipped out to the hotel parking lot and met the woman. Standing right there under a streetlight, she'd summoned the boy's spirit and helped it cross over. The whole situation had brought Em a lot of comfort, even later that night when her aunt hauled her back to the room, pummeling her with threats and taking what little money Em had in her purse to pay for the ticket the woman hadn't bought.

The touch of Devlin's hand on her arm brought Em back from her thoughts. "I want you to stay out of Gar's sight for now," he said. "But keep your senses tuned in for the ghost. See if you can figure out anything about it. I'll see if I can uncover something about this air pressure, tug-of-war sensation."

Em nodded, glad he wanted to continue to move toward helping the ghost. Now that she'd had time to think about it, she agreed that staying away from Gar was probably wise, and not only for the less personal reasons Devlin had in mind.

As it turned out, Em didn't have to intentionally avoid Gar. For the rest of the afternoon he remained sequestered in the office, interrogating Brooklyn and then Midas. The ghost's energy also remained there, fluxing and entangled with Gar's spirit, faint but omnipresent.

When early evening came, Em threw on her peacoat, put in her earbuds, and took off for an A.A. meeting. The coat was too warm, so she left it unbuttoned as she strolled along, grateful for good music, and for getting out of the house and away from the stressful emotions for a while. The Monday meeting was her favorite. It was a beginners meeting, earlier in the evening than most and close enough to the complex that needing a ride or taking the bus wasn't an option.

Once Em got there, she helped make coffee and talked to some of the regulars. Then she took an aisle seat about halfway back. Her therapist would have been pleased with her actions—if she'd dealt with the sponsor issue.

The first speaker turned out to be a guy her age. He'd started drinking by stealing beers from his father, after getting sips from the time he could walk. Later he got a prescription for painkillers after dental surgery and moved from beer to drugs. Em could relate to most of his story, though the drinks her aunt had given her had started after she'd begun doing readings for people. She'd been around ten when she'd first stolen liquor. Not long after that, she'd tried her mother's prescriptions pills, but they made it impossible to feel the ghosts, and helping the ghosts was what made her feel the best—even when it was terrifying.

The speaker talked about ending up in treatment and having a slip after getting involved with someone at rehab. As he launched into the usual suggestion about avoiding new romances in the first year of sobriety, Em frowned. Waiting a year seemed excessive, especially when it came to casual hookups.

Her mind wandered to sitting on Gar's bed, then to Johnny. A wave of ill-timed tingles stirred low in her body. She squirmed in her chair. Maybe it was better if she didn't think about Johnny, now or anytime soon. It made more sense to put a skull and crossbones over his image in her mind, label him poison and stay away like Devlin had suggested.

As everyone began to applaud the speaker, Em's thoughts of Johnny, and Gar, dissipated. She bolted from her seat, but instead of joining the crowd around the coffeepot, she beelined outside for fresh air.

A couple of old-timers and a group of guys from the correctional center were hanging out on the front steps smoking cigarettes. Lengthening her strides, she hurried past them into the parking lot and took refuge in an isolated spot between two cars. She hooked her hands behind her neck and gazed upward, drawing a deep breath to cool her heated body.

The buzz of her phone reverberated from her coat pocket. She pulled it out. There were only a couple people it could be, someone from the coven or—

Her therapist.

"Hey." She was glad the nightly call would soon be over but puzzled why her therapist/sponsor had instigated it. Calling was supposed to be the sponsee's responsibility.

"I hope I didn't interrupt anything," her therapist said.

"No. I'm at a meeting, but it's break time."

"Great. I—um..." Her voice trailed off into uncomfortable silence.

"What's wrong?"

"Ah—I owe you a huge apology."

A chill went through Em and her heartbeat slowed to a labored, hard rhythm. The therapist sounded shaken, as if it were a life or death matter. But nothing could be that bad, except—

"Your aunt... I'm so sorry. I took a long weekend. I hadn't checked my e-mail since the middle of last week."

"What is it? What happened?" If her aunt died in jail, that wouldn't be a bad thing.

"She's been paroled."

Em couldn't believe it. "When? How could they?"

"The parole board meeting was last week. The notification didn't go into details. All I know is they found her suitable for release. They let her out this morning. I'm so sorry, Em."

Em closed her eyes, her body going numb. "You're sure there isn't any way for her to find me?"

"I promise. It's been seven years. You've changed your name."

Em nodded, but her hands were shaking and more than anything she wanted to get off the phone and be alone. Given a minute, she'd get over the shock of this. Her therapist was right. This wouldn't change anything. She'd always known her aunt would be released eventually. Her mother had been released years ago and was now living in a supervised group home somewhere, talking to her psychiatrist and taking her medications— rotting, for all Em cared.

"Em, I am truly sorry I didn't tell you sooner."

"That's fine. Like you said, it's not like she can find me—or that she'll want to."

"Remember, you can call me any time. I'm here for you."

Em glanced back toward the building, to the steps where the old-timers and guys from the correctional center were lighting up their cigarettes. "I've got to go. The meeting's about to start again. Thank you. I'm glad to know."

"Take care. One day at a time."

"Yeah. Thanks again."

Em tucked her phone away, then hunched down with her back against the side of a car. She rubbed her hands over her face, cooling her heated eyelids and wiping away the seep of tears. *Dear Goddess, why can't my aunt and mother vanish from the face of the earth?*

The crunch of footsteps against pavement came toward her from less than a car-length away.

Em jumped up, startled, though she wasn't shocked that someone had followed her. That was the thing about the A.A. crowd: they kept an eye on each other. Undoubtedly someone wanted to make sure she was okay.

She plastered on a smile and turned to greet them.

Gar was striding up to her, camo cap squished over his wild hair. Ripped jeans. Worn Carhartt jacket over his broad shoulders. He looked... like he was part of the A.A. crowd.

He took off his cap and shoved it in his hip pocket. "I didn't know which meeting you'd be at. I hope you don't mind if I join in on this one."

It took a second for the full meaning of what he'd said to register. Shocked didn't begin to describe how she felt. "You're a—"

"Two years sober," he said, briskly

"Oh. Ah—that's great. I didn't see you—" She put on a smile and tilted her head to indicate inside the building. Her stomach jittered and burned with conflicting emotions. She was unsure how open she should be with him. Stepping over the line between his job as a Council employee and opening up to her like a close friend didn't seem to faze him in the least, but she wasn't so sure it was a smart thing to do. It wouldn't have fazed Johnny either.

"You probably didn't notice me because I was standing in the back of the room." He narrowed his eyes, studying her face. "Did something happen? Are you okay?"

She glanced past him to the ghost, rippling under the streetlight a few yards away, as lustrous as cellophane. "It's nothing. The speaker, his story kind of got to me."

He stepped closer, and for a frozen heartbeat she thought he was going to offer her a hug. But he stopped short, his gaze intensifying. She couldn't imagine what was going on in his mind. Finally, he said, "You were in my room earlier, weren't you?"

She felt her eyes widen. She should have expected this, but she'd totally forgot. "Ah—yeah. I put clean towels on your dresser. Didn't you see them?"

"You sat on my bed." He took another step toward her. "You touched my hairbrush. You touched a lot of my things, Em."

Her mouth dried. "I don't remember. I might have. I didn't know if you wanted me to straighten up your room."

His expression darkened. "You shouldn't lie. You're better than that."

"I—ah." She froze as he reached out, the air between them pulsing with the heat of his energy.

His hand stopped an inch from hers. His voice lowered, as if he didn't want anyone to overhear. "You wanted to tell me something earlier. Was it about the coven?"

She shuffled her feet, not sure if his stepping over the line was his rebel nature or a ploy to get information out of her. But she was certain he wasn't prepared for the truth. She glanced toward his ghost—

Her mouth fell open in surprise.

The ghost was no longer a rippling outline. It was a fully materialized figure.

One she recognized instantly.

Chapter 7

One day at a time? How about one hour or minute.
—Journal of Emily Adams
New Dawn House. Albany, New York.

Em gaped at the figure standing behind Gar. An older woman. Statuesque. Stylish coat. A silk scarf flowing out from around her neck. Her hair piled atop her head, curly tendrils flying free, as if in defiance. Em may have been bad at recognizing people, but she knew with certainty that this was the ghost she'd seen from the back of the police car 191 days ago. The witch.

The ghost leaned in close to Gar and whispered in a voice so low that Em could barely hear it, "Listen to me. Listen for once in your damn life."

The ghost's gaze flashed to Em, her eyes widening with sudden recognition. But before Em could acknowledge their mutual familiarity, her sixth sense shrieked that something was wrong—or about to go wrong.

The air pressure skyrocketed, sending Em's head reeling. Dizziness pulled in around her. Her ears rang, and the ghost's face morphed from frustrated to horrified, then her entire being—face, body, even the air around her—exploded into glimmering black-diamond grains and vanished in a *pop* of air pressure.

"No!" Em screeched.

Gar seized her by both shoulders and gave her a shake. "What's wrong? Snap out of it."

"Hey! Leave her alone," one of the old-timers shouted from the other side of the parking lot. He and another guy sprinted toward them.

Em gulped a breath, trying to regain her senses.

"Everything okay?" the guy asked as they reached her and Gar.

Gar glared at them. "Everything's fine."

"Yeah, sure," the guy said sarcastically. His eyes went to Em. "The meeting's about to start again. You want to come inside with us?"

Gar widened his stance. "I said, she's fine."

"Gar, it's all right." Em rested a shaky hand on his forearm, to steady herself and calm him. She looked at the other guys. "Thanks. But, really, nothing's wrong. We—were goofing around."

The guy frowned skeptically. "If you're sure, Em."

Though Em could hardly believe it herself, she managed to laugh lightly. "You might want to worry about Gar, though. He'll be in serious trouble if he tries to tangle with me."

The guy and his friend laughed and waved her off, then headed back toward the steps. As they disappeared inside, along with the group from the correctional center, Gar swung to face her. "What the hell's going on?"

She lifted her gaze to his. The blue of his eyes simmered with magic as bright as a wolf moon. His energy smelled like rain against evergreens. It left the taste of wilderness on her tongue. So many sensations roiled off him, unfamiliar to a girl who'd spent the majority of her life inside hotels and conference halls, and in the back of a van with blacked out windows. Familiar to a girl who'd been saved by a river's cool water and a night in the pines. By Johnny.

He skimmed his hands down her arms, pausing where he'd grabbed them only a few minutes earlier, touching tenderly now, as if to make up for the roughness. "Tell me, what's wrong?"

She drew a breath, calming herself. She'd promised not to confront him about this. But she had to. It was only fair and right. "You need to know, I wouldn't lie to you about this."

"I trust you, Em."

There was no way to sugarcoat it, so she said it flat-out: "You're haunted."

He backed away from her, shaking his head. "You're wrong. I couldn't be. The High Council watches out for things like that."

"I've seen the ghost around you before, and I just saw her fully materialize." Em's confidence set in. "My telling you this has nothing to do with the Northern Circle or your investigation. This is about your well-being, and a spirit who deserves to find peace."

His lips tensed. "You're—"

Before he could call her crazy or full of crap—two things she was used to hearing from non-witches—she fired her questions. "Have you heard whispers? For how long?"

He stood stock-still, hands clenching at his sides. After a moment, he grumbled, "Since early last spring."

"One voice, right?"

He nodded.

She didn't want to say what had to come next, to risk losing the openness that he'd offered. But to help the ghost she needed to get to the root of the problem. "Your anger toward the Northern Circle is misplaced."

He scowled. "I thought this wasn't about the coven."

"It's not. There's something strange going on with this ghost, and I suspect your misplaced anger and frustration is the result."

"I admit, I'm angry at the coven. But it has nothing to do with a ghost. I was trying to warn you before—in the office. You've had enough trouble in your life. I don't want to see you hurt again. For the Gods' sakes, I admire you for having the guts to take life by the balls and start over, not just back then but now, by staying sober." He folded his arms across his chest. "Devlin and his family aren't as innocent as you think, Em. They're guilty of murder."

She gaped at him. "I don't believe it."

"It's a fact. They murdered a relative of mine."

She shook her head, trying to begin to make sense of what he'd said. It couldn't be. But Gar's energy, his stance... everything about him said he believed it to be the truth. "Who? When? Why would they do such a thing?"

"Her name was Saille Webster. She raised my mother like her own child." He unfolded his arms and rested a hand on her shoulder, as if to let her feel his sincerity. "She was the high priestess of the Northern Circle, an older woman. Devlin's grandfather—Zeus Marsh—got sick of waiting to take over control of the Circle. He decided to speed things up."

"If it's true, why isn't Zeus in jail? For that matter, why would the High Council send you to evaluate the Circle? Isn't your connection to the coven a huge conflict of interest?"

"I don't know why they chose me. But I didn't ask for the assignment, if that's what you're implying." He paused, raking his hand through his hair before relenting. "But I didn't refuse it."

Eerie thoughts began to link together in Em's head, like the whispers of faint spirits growing closer. *A ghost she recognized. A ghost haunting him. A dead high priestess.* "The coven wasn't always in Vermont, was it?"

"No. When Saille was high priestess, the Northern Circle was in Upstate New York."

"In Saratoga?" Now that things were coming together, Em knew she should have realized it earlier. The first night she'd come to the complex,

Devlin had told the initiates an abbreviated history of the coven, including where it was located before moving to Vermont.

"Actually, it was Saratoga Springs," Gar said. "Why?"

Em closed her eyes. In a hushed voice she said, "The night I bottomed out, I was in Saratoga Springs. I saw a ghost from the back of a police car. She told me I was at a crossroads." Her throat choked with emotions at the memory of that moment. She let the feelings subside, then continued. "Just now, before I screamed, I saw that same ghost behind you. I think it was Saille."

"You don't know how much sense that makes. Saille wasn't just a high priestess. She was a recovering alcoholic. Her reaching out to a witch who was in trouble is exactly what she would have done when she was alive."

Em bit her bottom lip, her belief wavering even as she could sense his growing. "I don't think Saille could have realized I was anything more than a medium. Before I came here, I barely practiced the Craft. Truthfully, I don't have any other abilities."

Gar scoffed. "Don't say that. You're outstanding, Em. Your energy is powerful. Amazing." His gaze met hers, filled with deep sincerity. "Saille was a medium, like you—and she was an incredibly formidable and respected high priestess. You are exactly the kind of woman and witch she would have wanted to take under her wing."

Emotions jumbled in Em's chest, and the words she'd kept to herself since she joined the Circle came bubbling out. "Truthfully, I feel like an outsider when I'm around the coven. They're all so experienced and educated. Chloe with her spells. The Lady of the Lake gave her a sword of light to drive Merlin's Shade back into the otherworld. The amount of energy Devlin can control is unbelievable. Chandler welds metal with magic. Midas, Brooklyn, even the coven's satellite members have a multitude of skills. All I can do is communicate with the dead, that's it."

Gar chuckled. "You want to know what it feels like to be an outsider? You should try being me. I feel like the devil incarnate around them. Not that it's a feeling I'm not used to, being an investigator, among other things."

She smiled. In a debate about who was more of an outsider, he'd win hands down. "You have kind of been… an ass to everyone," she said teasingly.

He stared at her as if taken aback by her comment. She instantly regretted having been so cavalier. But saying it had felt normal, like an extension of how easy it had been between them so long ago. Besides, he had opened up first. He'd joked about himself. He'd stepped over the line.

He grinned, then leaned close to her and whispered, "I come by it naturally."

The tension in her chest eased and she longed to reach out and entwine her energy with his. But that wasn't a smart idea. She cleared her throat, glanced around the parking lot to make sure they were still alone, then steered the conversation back a step.

"The thing is," she said, "maybe I'm not trained in other areas of the Craft, but I am an expert on hauntings. No matter how logical and kind Saille was in life, that doesn't mean she's the same now. She could be asking you to help uncover the truth behind her death, and might be frustrated because you haven't done that. On the other hand, she could be mad at you because of your investigation into the coven. She could see you as a threat to something she built and loved."

"I'm assuming the rest of the coven knows about the haunting?"

"Yeah, I told them this morning." Em wet her lips. "I'm sorry I didn't tell you first. But I don't think you should be worried about what they could do with that information. There is a larger issue with the haunting. There's something unnatural about it."

He glanced at her. "Unnatural?"

"Saille reached out to me several times today. Every time, our connection broke before I could speak with her. It was like something was pulling her away from me—and you. Something powerful. That, combined with the haunting, is causing your headaches and mood swings."

His face went slack, his bravado falling away. "Fuck."

"We need to talk to Devlin. Get everything about this out in the open."

He shook his head, but there was resignation in his frightened eyes.

"Come here," Em said, spreading her arms out to offer a hug. She couldn't stop herself.

"Em," he murmured as he stepped into her arms and let her hold him tight.

She rested her head against his. It felt like something they should have done long ago.

Chapter 8

Rich ladies like little girls with pink bows in their hair.
They feel sorry for skinny girls and give them chocolates
and money, while they cry over messages from dead husbands and sons.
—Journal of Emily Adams
Memory from the beginning. Eight years old. Massachusetts.

Devlin did an about-face and paced back to Gar. "So, you admit to being biased against the Northern Circle?"

Gar's rigid expression didn't waver. "That doesn't mean the Circle isn't guilty of other violations—or that I believe Athena was murdered."

"What you believe doesn't change a thing." Devlin folded his arms across his chest, refusing to give an inch. Still, even from where Em stood, with her back to the living room's tall windows, she could sense a ceasefire building. Devlin unfolded his arms and held out his hand. "I guess the only solution is to agree to disagree?"

Gar gripped Devlin's extended hand in a firm shake. "Fair enough. For now."

When Em and Gar got home from the meeting, all the coven's full-time members were already gathered in the living room: Chloe and Devlin, Brooklyn and Chandler. Peregrine was on the floor, teasing the kittens with a feather. Midas leaned against the side table, listening intently as Em related what she'd told Gar about the ghost. He was a burly guy, always immaculate in his colorful button-down shirts and gold-rimmed glasses. Em doubted he ever dribbled coffee or failed to make high honors in anything. For the most part, Midas acted like she was invisible, which was probably for the best, since most of what he liked to talk about went right over her head.

"To tell you the truth," Devlin conceded to Gar, "I'd like to know what happened to Saille myself. Rumors have resurfaced lately that make me suspect my grandfather Zeus might have been involved in her death after all."

A knowing smile played at the corner of Gar's mouth, but he smothered it with a tightening of his lips. "From what my mother said, the Circle was beyond reproach. They were a power to be reckoned with back then—almost as influential as in the early days when they worked closely with the fae."

Em crept away from the window to stand behind Chloe and Chandler, seated in a pair of matching artsy chairs. She rubbed her hand across her throat, building up her nerve. It seemed smart to act fast, while there was tentative peace in the air. "We should try to contact Saille soon, to ask her how she died and what keeps pulling her away."

Chloe glanced over her shoulder at Em. "If you want to lead a séance, I could ask Keshari to help." Chloe's friend Keshari wasn't a coven member, but she had inborn magic and was trained in communicating with spirits. But Keshari had been hurt in the club fire and was only released from the hospital a few days ago.

"Do you think she's feeling well enough?" Chandler asked.

Chloe took out her phone. "I don't know, but it won't hurt to message her."

Brooklyn appeared from the lounge with a pair of beers in her hands. "Even without Keshari's help, I doubt any spirit could resist our conjoined presence." She passed a beer to Midas, then smirked at Gar. "I mean, everyone who is a coven member. Your presence would probably kill the vibe."

The remark didn't seem to bother Gar, but anger flared through Em. "That's a load of crap," she said. "Gar's the one Saille's haunting. Besides, we could use the protection of his added magic in case something goes wrong. And that's a strong possibility, considering we're dealing with an unknown element."

"The only unknown element we need to watch out for is your new best friend," Brooklyn snorted. "You do remember who he works for—as in, not us."

Chloe's phone jangled. "Damn it," she said, taking a look. "Keshari says maybe tomorrow. She's not feeling that great right now." Her voice cracked. "I feel so awful about her. If it weren't for me—"

"Her getting hurt wasn't your fault," Devlin interrupted. "If anyone deserves the blame, it's me. I should have realized something was wrong with Athena."

Gar raised his voice. "Can we get back to the subject? Em's right about the extra protection. Saille was a powerful witch, she would have no problem fully materializing after death. Whatever is preventing that has to be formidable."

"There is another red flag," Em said, realizing she'd failed to mention an important detail. "We can't forget that Athena materialized as an orb. That makes two powerful witches manifesting in weaker forms than they should be."

Gar gave a cursory nod. "Good point."

Midas cleared his throat. "Am I the only one seeing another connection? Saille. Athena. They were both high priestesses of this coven."

"I'm not willing to say definitively that Athena is dead," Gar said, "but the seriousness of these connections is the one reason I'm willing to consider any possibility." Em felt the weight of his gaze. "The High Council gave me a week turnaround time for this investigation. I don't think we can afford to wait for this Keshari to feel well enough to help, do you?"

As his gaze lingered on her, a chill traveled the length of Em's spine. She couldn't see Saille or sense her attachment to him. That should have been a good thing, but the circumstances around it were worrying her more with each passing second. Her sixth sense told her the haunting wasn't over. She nodded. "We should do it right away, tonight."

"Perfect." He looked away from her, addressing everyone. "There is one other thing you all need to understand. Brooklyn is right. I don't in any way feel obligated to protect your coven. I work for the High Council. If this séance reveals that Zeus murdered Saille, I will tell them."

Devlin dipped his head. "As high priest, I'm willing to accept that risk for the coven. Perhaps his guilt can destroy us, but proof of his innocence would redeem us."

Em nodded, and so did everyone else. Then a heavy silence settled over the room. Zeus had become the coven's high priest and financial overseer as a direct result of Saille's death. Since then, members of his family had been in charge and benefitted from their positions, right down to Devlin. If Zeus was guilty, the High Council not only had a right to punish him, they could also disband the coven and seize everything that had resulted from his crime—namely, all the Northern Circle's assets. Including the complex. They could penalize individual coven members as they saw fit, as well.

Em hugged herself and stared down at the floorboards beneath her feet, scarred and refinished, honey gold and warm. She closed her eyes and sent a prayer out to the universe. *Please, don't take away something so good.*

Em was glad everyone cooperated, and no one talked about the possible dark side as they rushed around getting ready for the séance. No need to attract any extra bad energy—there was enough of that already.

She helped Chloe and Brooklyn cleanse the dining room with sage, then she fed the kittens and carried their box to the downstairs bathroom for the night. The kittens were pretty spent after their day's activities and eager to go to sleep. She cuddled the white one to her chest, letting the vibration of his purr soothe her. What would happen to them if the coven lost the complex? It wasn't like the halfway house would let her have them there....

No negative thinking, she admonished herself. She couldn't afford it right now. Besides, Brooklyn had told the vet where they found the kittens, and he'd offered to report the incident to the police. For sure, once the story about the garbage bag hit the news, people would line up to adopt the poor things. Still, it would be nicer to let them grow up in the complex with lots of room to play and gardens to hunt in, safe and protected.

After one last cuddle, Em set the kitten into the box with the others and sauntered back to the dining room. Everyone was seating themselves around the table, except for Chloe, who was busy sending bursts of energy out to light the dozens of votive candles that decorated the sideboard.

A wave of dread came over Em as she looked at the unoccupied chair at the head of the table, the chair intended for her. She hadn't mentioned it to anyone yet, but if Saille was having trouble communicating they'd need more than just conjoined energy for the séance to succeed. Saille would also need a conduit to communicate, something more stable and stronger than a haunting. That meant one thing: Em needed to leave herself open to possession. Not one of her favorite things, not in the least.

She pasted on a smile and settled into her chair. Gar sat to her left and Chloe's chair was on her right. She brushed her hands across the linen tablecloth, getting a feel for the atmosphere around her before taking a sip of ice water from the goblet that had been set in front of her. The coolness soothed her throat, relaxing her a little. She couldn't remember the last time she'd done a séance sober. Perhaps never.

Her chest tightened as her mind went back to the water bottles her aunt had filled with "special" sodas and Creamsicle-flavored drinks, back before the conference halls, when they'd only done private readings at people's homes. Her aunt had called them treats, and they'd helped her relax, but even as a child she'd known using them was disrespectful to the spirits she summoned. They also made it nearly impossible for her to block out aggressive ghosts, like one woman's sadistic ex-husband who had possessed her without being welcomed.

Sweat trickled down Em's spine. Sometimes in her nightmares she relived flashes from that séance. Darkness and anger all around her. Such hate. Such venom. The overwhelming pressure of the sadistic spirit roaring into her. The coppery taste of blood and the tang of stomach acid in her mouth. The unbidden voice rasping from her throat, cold and masculine, "I'll kill you, bitch. Kill you and your bastard children!"

Em clamped her eyes shut, forcing the awful memory from her head. There was no way to undo the past. The only thing she could do was respect the spirits now—and respect herself by playing it safe.

"Before we start," Em announced. "I want to make it clear that I'll be opening myself up as a channel to Saille. Other spirits could step forward—perhaps even Athena, if we're lucky." She slid her fingers across the tablecloth to where Gar's rested on the stem of his goblet, then spoke directly to him. "I'm relying on you for two things: First to mentally reach out to Saille and ask her to come to me. After all, you're the person she's been trying to communicate with. Secondly, if someone or something undesirable comes through, you have to end the contact by shaking me or doing whatever you need to snap me out of the trance. You're comfortable doing that, right?"

His hand left the goblet and slid over hers, warm and steady. "Of course. I won't hesitate."

Em turned and smiled at Chloe. Even though Chloe wasn't a medium, the night Athena had first appeared as an orb she'd chosen to whisper a secret to Chloe. "Same goes for you and Athena. If you sense her, ask her to use me as a conduit."

"Of course," Chloe said.

Em looked at everyone else. "If anyone senses something is wrong at any point, please speak up."

Once everyone agreed, Em rested her hands on the table and bowed her head, breathing in through her nose and out through her mouth. She drew up her magic from deep inside her, letting it flow outward as her mind drifted free from her body.

In the background, she sensed the touch of Chloe's fingertips against hers, the electric sizzle of conjoined magic flowing into her and outward into Gar's hand, magic moving clockwise around the table, from one witch to the other, cycling faster and faster. Warmth flooded her face. Cold chilled her shoulders and back. Her pulse thumped as slow and steady as a pendulum in her ears. She longed to demand that Saille appear, but forceful summoning had failed the last time. She needed to be patient, drift peacefully, with her soul open. Toward Saille. Toward Athena. Toward any spirit who knew the truth about either of their deaths.

Em heard the faint mew of a ghostly kitten. A paw batted at her ankle as if to urge her to keep going. She floated farther into her trance, calling out softly, "Saille, we want to help you. Reach out. Tell us. Was your death innocent?"

Be careful, a child's ethereal voice whispered.

A distant ghostly chorus murmured, *Watch out.*

Em's sixth sense prickled. Saille was in the room, a wisp of energy rippling toward Gar. "I welcome you. Use my body if you must," she murmured. "I beseech you. Speak through me."

Without warning, the air pressure in the room skyrocketed and the tug-of-war sensation swooped toward Saille, reeling her backward, away from Em's reach.

Em pulled her shoulders back, spine straight. So much for the gentle approach.

She focused on the flow of conjoined magic, letting it flood her bloodstream until her hands shook from the power. She mentally yanked against the invisible tug-of-war force with every ounce of energy that she had. *Saille, come to me. Tell us. Was your death innocent?*

The tug-of-war sensation snapped, releasing Saille and sending Em's mind careening into unconsciousness. She was nothing. She was nowhere. But at the same time, she was aware of her bowed head rising to stare blankly at the people gathered around the table.

Em's lips formed words and Saille's voice rang out, "Poison!"

Chapter 9

Boston. Atlanta. Tampa. Anywhere. Anytime. 362-895-9908.
I'll be there for you, Violet. The two of us against the world.
Love, Alice
—Old note, taped into the Journal of Emily Adams

"Poison," Em murmured.

She lay on her bed in the dark, staring up at her bedroom ceiling. It was several hours after the séance and she still couldn't relax. Why couldn't Saille have used her to relay more than that single word? It proved nothing, other than that Saille had in fact been murdered. It neither cleared nor condemned Zeus. It only deepened the mystery.

Em rolled onto her side, hugging her pillow. Its softness against her cheek reminded her of coming out of the trance with Gar's hands cradling her face. He'd backed away when Chloe appeared with a cool cloth for her forehead. Still, Gar had been there for her first, like he'd promised, protecting her and bringing her back to her senses with a firm shake and soft words.

She breathed deep, taking in the scent of her pillow. Only the aroma of her. Not a trace of lavender and sage spritz like she'd used on Gar's sheets. No moss and evergreens, either.

Tucking the pillow under her arm, Em raised herself up and strained to hear if there were any noises from his room. No shower running. No headboard squeaks. Apparently, stress hadn't affected his ability to sleep tonight—or maybe he'd had a cup of chamomile tea before bed, or the lavender and sage had helped him relax.

Em burrowed under the blankets and stared into the darkness. She needed to shut off her brain and get some sleep, or she'd feel like crap in the morning. She closed her eyes, breathing slowly and deeply.

A yawn built inside her. She pressed her hand over her mouth, covering it until the yawn passed. Some people believed yawns invited demons into the body, or were demons escaping. That wasn't true. They were nothing more than the body balancing itself. A sign of the crossroads between wakefulness and sleep, and... *dreams*, was the last word she thought as she fell asleep.

Everything is dark. Rich burgundy darkness.

"Are you listening?" Saille's voice reaches Em's ear.

She's asleep. She knows it. But she's too self-aware for it to be a normal dream. She also knows when and where she is. It's a month before her sixteenth birthday. Only an hour, or maybe two, before Johnny found her in the cemetery. She's in an emergency ward, after the police discovered her in the back of her aunt's van. She's naked except for a disposable gown. But the child services crisis worker has made a mistake: her clothes lie on a nearby chair.

In an instant, she dresses. Pants. Shirt. Socks. If she's wearing socks no one will recognize her. No one looked in her eyes when they took her from the van. Not the police. Not the news people. Not the social worker. They'd all stared at her ankles and feet.

She's fleeing through the hospital now, down tunnels of glistening white tile, corridor after corridor. She throws open a door and the eye-burning flare of unimpeded sunlight blinds her. She blinks, struggling to regain her eyesight—

Saille drags her from that moment.

It's more than a year after Johnny and the train. Em stands in the wings of the Royal Palm Theater in Tampa, where she and Alice used to hang out behind the scenes, Alice reading tarot cards for the actors, Em giving them messages from deceased mentors and grandparents—the two of them theater mascots, her, a seventeen-year-old on the run.

"Listen," Saille whispers. "I don't have much time."

Gar's voice comes from center stage, speaking Prospero's lines from The Tempest, *"... poisonous slave, got by the devil himself upon thy wicked dam, come forth!"*

A stranger appears on stage. He's dressed elegantly in black, more like a cross between a cliché vampire and a ballet dancer than Shakespeare's deformed Caliban. Still, Caliban is the part he's playing.

"As wicked dew as e're my mother brushed with raven's feather from unwholesome fen drop on you both," Caliban says.

Em doesn't listen to the rest. Caliban isn't important. She needs to find a place where she and Alice can see and hear Gar better. But when she turns toward Alice, her gaze catches on a soft tendril of hair that has fallen across Alice's face, sticking to the corner of her ripe plum lips. Em bends to wipe the tendril away, but Alice holds up a tarot card between them, blocking the view of her face with Death.

A heartbeat passes. Alice lowers the card. She isn't standing anymore. She lies in the center of the spotlighted stage with her baby's ghost in her arms. Her beautiful lips are now shriveled. Her once glossy dark hair is ashen. Caliban glides over to Alice and draws a triangle around her body, bearing down hard with his pencil until the graphite line is thick and sparkles in the harsh light. He places a yellow diamond in one corner of the triangle. The stone is as large as a fingertip, glistening but full of cracks and flaws—Em can see the imperfections even from where she stands in the wings.

Em's sixth sense screams that something awful is going to happen. She knows for certain that she can't let Caliban finish whatever ritual he's preforming. If she does, then that's when the horrible thing will occur.

She races onto the stage to stop him. But no matter how hard she pushes her legs, the distance between her and Caliban widens, growing greater and greater.

She's not running across a stage anymore. She's in a cemetery with lots of trees and roads braiding through it. Alice and her baby are rising out of a grave. Caliban stands over them, waiting for something.

"Stop!" Em screams.

Caliban reaches into a pocket of Alice's sweater. As he takes out a diamond, Alice's head turns toward Em, vacant eyes staring directly at her—

But she's not Alice anymore.

It's Saille. Her lips move. "Listen to me. Poison."

Em jolted awake. Her pulse hammered in her chest. The theater. Graveyards. Poison. Triangle. Diamond.

She swung her feet off the edge of the bed, braced her head in her hands, and took a deep breath. *What the hell was the dream about?* She was good at figuring out symbols, but these had been all over the place.

Goose bumps prickled her arms. She got up from the bed, rubbing the chill from her skin as she paced to the window. A half-moon hung low in the sky, its light glistening on the gardens and the complex's front gate. In the surreal light, it was easy to imagine the three remaining flying monkey sculptures had come to life.

Em wiped her hair back from her overheated face. In retrospect, she shouldn't have been shocked by the dream's oddness. It wasn't unusual to have threads of a spirit's consciousness linger after a possession. But what had Saille been trying to tell her, beyond repeating the mention of poison?

Diamond. Triangle. *The Tempest.* As Em picked up her hoodie and shrugged it on over the T-shirt and leggings she'd slept in, she went back through the elements of the dream. She got out her journal and jotted them down, then reread the words, attempting to make heads or tails of them. Totally stumped, she decided it only made sense to go downstairs, make a cup of chamomile tea, and think everything through one more time before she tried to get back to sleep. She could check on the kittens, feed them again if they were interested.

Kittens first, she decided. If they were awake, she'd heat her tea water and their formula at the same time.

She padded downstairs in her stocking feet and headed straight for the bathroom. She opened the door—

She stopped mid-stride.

Under the soft glow of the overhead light, Gar sat on the edge of the bathtub with a nurser bottle in his hand and the white kitten on his lap. Bare feet. Jogging pants. Faded T-shirt. No trace of Saille. As he looked up at her, a tendril of dark hair fell across his forehead. He smiled, eyes brightening, lips parting as if seeing her was the best thing that could have happened.

"Great minds think alike?" he said, giving the nursing kitten a meaningful glance.

Her heart clenched, and heat flushed her from head to toe. Big guy. Little kitten. It was like a scene out of a hot-guy charity calendar. No way could she pretend it didn't turn her on—doubly so, since he'd been the object of her fantasies for years.

She glanced away from him to the kittens' box. "It was partly that I couldn't sleep. Have they all eaten?"

"This is the last one." He picked up a towel from beside him and wiped stray milk from the kitten's mouth, then got up and set it in the box with the others.

He sat back down, studying her. "What's bothering you? Bad dreams?"

She hooked her hair behind her ears and shrugged. "You could say that. I think Saille was trying to tell me something else."

He gestured at the floor. "Have a seat. I'm all ears."

"Ah—" The floor was sparking clean, the bath mat immaculate. She'd cleaned them herself. Still, a bathroom felt like a strange place to discuss anything, weirder yet at three in the morning. But somehow it also felt perfect, bright and warm with the inviting sense of him all around her. Just the two of them, without anything or anyone to remind them of the coven or Council.

Gar moved down from the edge of the bathtub, situating himself with his butt on the floor and his back against the tub, knees bent. "Are you going to stand there all night?"

Em settled cross-legged in front of him. Tingles rushed across her skin when she realized just how close they were, his feet within touching distance of hers.

His naked feet. Perfect toes and arches. Clean. Strong. Leading to muscular ankles, and a glimpse of dark silky leg hair.

Her fingers itched to touch his toes, to caress his instep and kiss her way up his calves. Her thighs muscled tingled and her stomach tensed, a surge of embarrassment jumbling with desire. Could he sense what she was feeling?

She untangled her legs and repositioned herself with her stockinged feet tucked under the corner of the bath mat. Out of sight. Out of mind.

"So?" Gar prompted. "Your dream. Was it about Saille?"

The tension eased from her stomach. "Not at first, but yes. It started with Alice." Em bit her bottom lip. Gar couldn't have forgotten that she and Alice were lovers. But he'd said that he'd lost track of her after she got on the train. "Alice was haunted by a baby she'd lost." Her voice cracked. "Alice died from an overdose."

Gar shifted closer, resting a hand on her knee. His touch was gentle, but strong. "I'm sorry. That must have been incredibly hard for you. Was that what the dream was about?"

"That and Saille…" Em told him the dream in detail, careful to not miss anything. When she was done, she met his eyes.

He fired a question, hard and fast. "What are you thinking right now? The first thing that comes to your mind. Don't think about it."

"Where is Saille buried?" she said without hesitation.

Gar frowned. "Are you asking me or answering my question? I was looking for your intuitive answer."

"That was it. Where is Saille buried?" Now that she thought about it, that question had been in her mind when she first jolted awake.

His expression grew more serious. "I had the same thought while I was listening to you. It makes sense. Graveyards. Bodies rising from the dirt. Poisons. Murder."

Em felt her eyes widen as she caught his train of thought. "You think Saille's saying she wants someone to exhume her, to test her body for poisons?"

He nodded. "The High Council's skills in that area have improved greatly in the last few years. Someone could have screwed up her original autopsy."

"You think the Council would really do another examination if the Circle requested it? We aren't exactly on their favorites list."

"Technically, they couldn't refuse." He studied his lap for a second, his mouth working like he was deciding whether to speak his mind or not. He raised his head, brow furrowed. "Devlin claims Rhianna admitted to being involved in Saille's death. But he has no proof of her claim. Rhianna was a young teenager back then, hardly experienced enough to pull off murdering a seasoned witch. Again, it comes down to his word against Rhianna's—just like with Athena's disappearance."

Em swallowed hard. She could read between the lines. He was trying to be nice for her sake. Clearly, though, he believed the coven didn't have a leg to stand on. "But you still think the Council would be willing to have Saille exhumed?"

"Yes—and nothing would make me happier than to have her murderer brought to justice. But there are normal-world laws about exhuming bodies. Non-witch judges and lawyers could get involved…. Exhumation isn't a fast process."

Excitement rushed through Em. She leaned forward, resting her hand on his knee. "Then we have only one choice. We'll cut through the red tape by digging her up ourselves, then take her body directly to the Council for testing." Now that idea was in her mind, she knew it was the best plan. "There's another benefit to doing it ourselves. If I can touch Saille's body, I'd have a direct connection to her spirit. Whatever is holding her back wouldn't be able to interfere."

A rebellious glint sparked in Gar's eyes, and he laughed. "I take back what I said about you being amazing. You're amazing *and* crazy."

She puffed out a breath, trying to curb her eagerness. "I'm not talking about us exhuming her alone. Devlin, Chloe—"

He raised his hand, gesturing for her to stop. "I still intend to finish my investigation of the coven's latest transgression: interrogations of outlying members, the impact on the local community…. Once I'm done with that, I'll help exhume Saille. That way, I can present both issues to the Council at once. I have a week to finish up here. That should be plenty of time to do everything."

"I suppose you're right," Em conceded. As much as she suspected Saille wanted them to move faster, taking time to plan carefully and not ending up in jail for grave robbing did seem smarter. Either way, she and Gar were in this together—standing on common ground somewhere between the coven and the Council.

Her gaze found his again. His shoulders tensed, and the room grew breathlessly heavy with the crackle of his energy. Moss and evergreens, the scent of his spirit, seeped into her skin. She inched nearer, but not as close as the butterflies in her stomach begged for her to be.

"Em," he said, his voice low and gravelly. A warning for her to be sure before she made another move.

She slid her fingertips across his foot, moving toward the temptation of his leg.

He locked a hand around her wrist, stopping her. "You need to understand something. I'm good at my job, Em. I can't deny that I'm attracted to you—I am, a lot. But if Devlin's family or the Circle are guilty of anything, I won't lie to the Council about it. Not for you. Not even for myself."

She got where he was coming from, and his frank honestly made her want him even more. If Zeus was guilty of poisoning Saille, she had no doubt that Gar would shout it from the rooftops. But as for the Circle's more recent crimes? Gar's one-man jury was still out on that. To him, there was a difference between swearing not to lie—and promising to tell the truth.

Now or never, Em's libido whispered.

She cupped her free hand over top of where he held her wrist. "I don't expect you to do any less than what you think is right."

He smiled, lips parting. She tilted her head, moistening her lips as she bent toward him and slid a fingertip along the neckline of his T-shirt.

"This is a bad idea," he murmured. His voice went husky. "You haven't been sober that long. Getting involved with me—with anyone, could throw you off track. I don't want to mess things up for you."

She pressed a finger to his lip, silencing him. "No A.A. talk. Just us. Just now. It's been a long time since I've been this attracted to anyone." Not through all the years of drunken hookups, not since Alice.

He scrunched forward, trapping her between his knees. His hands brushed her shoulders. "There's a good chance you're going to hate me before this investigation is over."

"There's a good chance you'll discover Athena and Saille were murdered by Rhianna." Her breath caught in her throat, anticipating the touch of his lips.

He leaned back, away from her. His voice hushed. "Um—Saille isn't here, right?"

Em swatted his arm teasingly and laughed. "That would be creepy. But, no, she's not."

She gripped the back of his head, pulling his mouth to hers. He didn't fight her. He took control instead, wasting no time with subtleties as his lips hungrily moved against hers.

"Dear Goddess," he groaned as his hands impatiently slipped under her hoodie and shirt, gliding over her ribcage to cup her almost nonexistent breasts. "I want you so bad."

She murmured, "I've wanted you for years."

Her body went liquid, bones turning molten under his touch. He kissed her neck. Her jawline. His magic hummed against her skin. Alice had brought her slowly to climax with gentle kisses and a feather-touch, but this…. Gar's magic and hunger were ferocious, a torrent, a relentless tide she wanted to get lost in.

She let her head fall back, laughing as he left off kissing, his lips teasing and sucking her nipples, taking her whole breast into his mouth. Clearly, he was a breast man, and that was fine by her. She ran her fingers down his belly, searching for the button on his jeans.

"Maybe we should take this upstairs?" he mumbled.

"In a minute." She undid his jeans.

He stopped her hand. "Condoms? I wasn't exactly preplanning."

She nipped his neck, up close to his ear. "Look in the medicine cabinet."

Chapter 10

We run naked in the darkness
caressing concrete walls,
hoping to find warmth in callous spaces.
—"Hookups" by E. A.
Memory. On the road. 20 years old.

Em was grateful that Devlin's apartment was attached to the coven's garage and that Chandler's was in her workshop. That left only Brooklyn to hear their rather loud trip up to the third floor. Well, and Midas—who Em suspected was staying overnight with Brooklyn on the second floor.

Gar carried Em the last few yards into his room and tossed her playfully onto the bed. The no-holds-barred glisten in his eyes and the exuberant sizzle of his magic shifted to something deeper and more serious. He retreated to his dresser and turned on soft background music.

"I hope you like country?" His gaze lingered on her, taking in every inch. He wet his lips.

A flush of self-consciousness crept up her chest. "Anything's fine by me."

"I've got orange juice in the mini-fridge. You want some?"

"That would be great." As he headed for the fridge, she pulled her knees to her chest. She wanted more of him. Again and again. But the mention of drinks and ebb in the fever pitch of the moment left her painfully aware that not only had she not been with anyone since she got sober, in truth, she couldn't remember ever having sex with a man when she wasn't drunk.

He returned with two bottles of juice and set them on the nightstand. He sat down on the edge of the bed and smiled at her. "Em." Her name rolled off his tongue like he was savoring the feel of it. "I'm going to be honest with you. One of the reasons I haven't slept much has nothing to do with Saille." He nodded at the wall behind the headboard. "I keep thinking about you over there, wanting a chance to talk to you."

She laughed to break the tension and scrunched forward, grabbing his T-shirt and yanking him closer. "How about we talk more later. Now let's get back to business."

He untangled her fingers from his shirt and stripped it off slowly. His body was broad and muscular, built up over the years from physical work, tattooed and scarred from unknown exploits. A soft line of black hair shadowed his chest and ran down the ladder of his abdomen, across a slight belly, and vanished into the beltline of his jeans.

A fresh surge of desire pushed aside her self-consciousness. Her mouth watered at the outline of a new erection pushing eagerly against the taut fabric of his jeans.

His hands cupped her face and he looked in her eyes. "You're not going to make me hurry this." He stroked her neck. His hand traveled south, skating down her stomach and under the waistband of her leggings. He pressed his fingertips against her clit, massaging slowly. "I'm going to make you suffer, a lot."

She squirmed, arching into the touch. He slid up next to her, still massaging as his lips found hers, kissing just as slowly. Lips brushing. His breath was fresh and clean, minty even. As his tongue traced the contour of her lips, her body went weak and she closed her eyes.

For a moment his touches stopped. She felt the movement of him wiggling free of his clothes. His hands pulled off her T-shirt. She ran hers over his naked shoulders and down his back, exploring his exquisite body. His erection pressed against her thigh, the tension of his need growing stronger with every deepening kiss and unhurried caress.

She trailed her fingertips downward, slowly, toward his cock. She closed her hand around it, moving her fingers up and down, matching the waltz of his lips against hers.

A growl rumbled from the back of his throat.

"Shush," she said, nipping his lip. "You're the one who wanted to take it slow."

"Screw self-control."

In one swift motion, he was straddling her, pinning her arms to the bed. His magic rushed over her, bathing her until her skin quivered and buzzed from the sensation. She curled her fingers, aching to drag them through his hair. His scent enclosed her. Her mouth filled with the sharp tang of his magic.

She wriggled underneath him, struggling to free herself from her leggings. He pulled them off for her, kissing her belly before moving lower to cup her buttocks as he deftly removed her panties with one hand.

"Your magic smells like autumn," he murmured. "Like fire and air. Like everything wonderful."

He kissed her upper thigh, his tongue and nibbling teeth driving shockwaves of pleasure through her entire being. He rolled his knuckle against her clit, pushing inward, a rhythmic pressure spiked with magic. She rocked against the sensation, arching in pleasure and groaning as the ecstasy surged inside her, building toward climax.

"I want you," she moaned. "I want to feel you inside me."

He shifted away from her, the sudden coolness raising goose bumps on her skin as he reached to the nightstand. The rustle of the condom wrapper sent a fresh wave of excitement throbbing between her legs. She did want him. She wanted him so bad.

His warmth returned. His hand parted her thighs. He kissed her stomach. His mouth closed around her breasts, sucking one, then the other, until her nipples ached from pleasure. His lips came back to hers. She closed her eyes, drawing up her magic and letting it flow out of every pore in her body and into his skin. Their breath mingled. Their pulses matched. The head of his cock pushed between her legs, waiting. She writhed against it, moist and eager.

He entered her, a slow thrust, followed by a deeper one. She groaned from the pleasure. He picked up the pace, thrusting harder, faster. Sweat slicked her body. She slid against him, a hot, fast pace. He pressed his face against her neck, growling as he buried himself into her.

"Em," he moaned. "Em, I can't wait—"

His body shuddered as he came. But he didn't pull out. His cock moved slowly, keeping up its rhythm as he moved his fingers against her clit, sending a quick pulse of magic into her. She moaned as the pleasure of his touch took her up and over into her own orgasm.

She collapsed, totally spent. He belly-crawled up next to her and pushed her hair back from her face, kissing her cheek and forehead. She stroked her fingers across his mouth and smiled. "That was incredible."

"I'm just getting warmed up." He grinned.

She shoved him away teasingly. "Who says you're going to get any more?"

A mischievous twinkle brightened his eyes and he lunged playfully at her as if to hold her down again.

She scuttled away, laughing.

"You're not getting away that easy." He grabbed her by the ankles and flipped her over—

A fierce memory shot into Em's mind:

Her aunt held her down by the ankles on a bed with a scrolled headboard. Handcuffs bit into her wrists. Her ankles. Her feet. The vibration of a tattoo gun echoed into her bones. Words driven into her skin: *Family is forever.*

Em wrestled against Gar's grip and slammed her foot forward. The kick connected with his face. Blinded by panic, she kicked again as hard as she could. The force sent him scrambling backward as pain shot up her leg.

"Fuck!" Gar clamped a hand over his nose. Blood flowed from between his fingers. "Fuck, fuck."

Em vaulted from the bed and backed against the wall. Sweat soaked her skin. Her pulse jackhammered in her throat. Her legs, her arms, her whole body quaked. "I'm sorry. So sorry." Tears flooded down her face.

She grabbed her T-shirt from the floor, throwing it on as she fled to the bathroom. She shoved a towel under the faucet and turned on the cold water. She'd broken his nose. And he hadn't done anything wrong. She shouldn't have come up here with him. She should have left well enough alone.

Gar stumbled into the bathroom, pinching his nose shut. Blood smeared his hands. It glistened on the dark stubble under his nose and chin. His upper lip was split. He dropped down on the toilet and leaned forward.

Bile crawled up Em's throat. Her hands trembled as she squeezed out the towel and handed it to him. "Oh my God. I'm so sorry."

He glanced up. "It's all right, Em." His voice sounded awful. He looked awful.

"It's not all right, Gar. I broke your nose."

He let go of his nose for a moment, blood trickling down as he positioned the wet towel. "It's not broken. Only bloody."

"I kicked you. I meant to hurt you. I'm so sorry."

"No," he said firmly. "I'm the one who's sorry. I knew better than to grab you like that."

Knew better? She opened her mouth to argue, but of course he knew. He hadn't even needed to see the tabloid covers and headlines or the photos of her shackle-scarred ankles and the tattooed tops of her feet, leaked to the public by someone in child services or at the hospital. He knew firsthand. He'd carried her into the river to cool her overheated body and mind, still clothed except for her shoes and socks.

Gar tapped her on the thigh. "You mind getting me some ice from the fridge?"

"Of course." Pulse still hammering, she started for the bathroom door, then turned back. "Gar? I enjoyed being with you. Seriously, it was a lot of fun."

He nodded. "Same here. Now, can you get the ice? This does hurt." He stopped talking, his gaze lingering on her as if he had more to say.

"Yeah?" She had to know what it was.

"I know you were upset earlier—at the meeting. You said the speaker got to you, but"—he lowered the towel from his face—"I didn't believe you."

She looked down at her stockinged feet. A chill worked its way across her skin. She swallowed hard. "The parole board released my aunt."

His mouth fell open. "You've got to be kidding me. She doesn't know where you are, right?"

Em faked a smile. "I think looking for me is the last thing she'll do."

Chapter 11

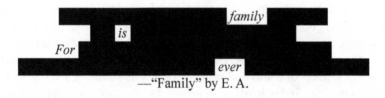

For *is* *family* *ever*

—"Family" by E. A.

Em spent the balance of the night in Gar's bed, with him holding her close. She was surprised he wanted her there after she kicked him in the face and revealed the unromantic detail of her aunt's parole status—and she wasn't surprised when she woke up alone.

However, after a second, she realized he wasn't altogether gone. His hushed voice drifted out from the bathroom. "That's ridiculous. Who is responsible for this asinine idea?"

As quietly as she could, Em scooched across the bed to where she could hear and see better.

Gar stood with his back to her, phone to his ear. No ghost in sight. "A journalist? Do you know where he is? Send me what information you do have." His voice deepened. "And tell Chancellor Morrell I plan on talking to him as soon as I get back to headquarters. This is ludicrous."

Em picked up her leggings from the floor. She was tugging them on when he walked out of the bathroom. "That didn't sound good," she said.

"It's worse than that," he snapped. He grimaced. "I don't mean to be an ass, but I need to get cleaned up and talk to Devlin as soon as possible. Do you mind?" He glanced toward the door to the hallway, a less than subtle hint.

A hollow feeling filled her. So much for fantasies about this being more than a get-your-rocks-off hookup—topped with a smidge of unwarranted kindness after the whole triggering of her past and her mention of the parole thing.

"Em." His voice remained tough, but worry wrinkled his brow. "Meet me in the hall in ten minutes. I want you to go with me to see Devlin. You need to hear this too."

"What's going on?"

"I'll tell you then. Get dressed." Gar turned, disappeared back into the bathroom, and slid the door shut.

Em stared at the closed door, heartbeat racing. Dear Goddess, what had happened?

Seven minutes later, she met up with Gar as planned. As they hurried downstairs, she had to jog to keep up with his hard strides, out the living room's glass doors and into the coven's gardens. It had rained in the night and the garden's autumn-faded spires and branches sagged, dark and bleak from the weight of the storm. Devlin's skill as a landscape architect had created the maze of plants and stone, normally as stunning and bright as a fairy kingdom. Today it looked more suitable for dark elves and wraiths.

When they neared the footbridge that went over a brook to the coven's teahouse, they veered down a narrower path. In a second, they were in a graveled parking area, and at the front door of Devlin's studio apartment.

Gar barely had time to thump his fist on the door before Devlin's golden retriever bounded around the corner, tail wagging. The dog hunkered down, squirming up to Gar, whining and quivering all over.

"Hey, big fella." Gar's voice lightened and he crouched, letting the dog lick his hands.

Em smiled, amused by the dog's overenthusiasm and relieved to have Gar look happier. "Henry likes everyone, but that's extreme, even for him."

Gar straightened back up and glowered, as if to put an end to the change in mood. He glanced sharply at the dog, whose eyes widened with understanding. He took off at a gallop, straight for the garden path.

As Em watched the dog disappear, she couldn't help but wonder if Gar was some sort of secret dog-whisperer. The truth was, he knew a lot about her and her abilities, but she knew almost nothing about him—other than his heritage. "Was that some kind of loup-garou communication thing?"

Gar's eyes narrowed. "Why? Does what I am bother you? Are you regretting sleeping with someone like me?"

"That's not what I meant," she said, retreating a step. She certainly hadn't expected that reaction. She hushed her voice. "What you are has nothing to do with whether I'm attracted or turned off."

He harrumphed. "Sure you aren't lying to yourself?"

"I'm not like that. Maybe it's something to do with me being a medium, being so in touch with spirits. I don't know." Her hands clenched into fists. She'd thought he got her—obviously she was wrong. "It's not who or what your parents are, whether you're French Canadian or Polynesian, or a guy or woman.... It's your spirit that attracted me."

"I'd like to believe that. But you wouldn't be the first to regret—" He shut his mouth as the door to the apartment swung open and Devlin appeared.

Devlin glanced from Gar to her. "Am I interrupting something?" His eyes went back to Gar, giving his bruised face a scan. "Rough night?"

"We're fine," Gar said, striding forward. "However, the coven has a new issue."

Concern lined Devlin's face. "Come in. We can talk in my living room."

He led them past his galley kitchen to his sitting area. The aroma of freshly brewed coffee and French toast hung in the air. Piano music tinkled in the background. The whole atmosphere felt at odds with the gravity of the situation—whatever it was.

Em perched on the edge of the leather couch. She glanced around. "Chloe's not here?"

"She had an early class," Devlin said. He murmured something else under his breath. In response, the music silenced, and the apartment's soft lighting rose to sharper brightness. Em would have assumed the changes were the work of a voice response system, except she'd noticed all the other coven members offhandedly whisper commands or use gestures to do lesser magics, like the way Chloe had lit all the candles at the séance with hardly any effort.

"So," Gar said, loud enough to get everyone's attention. "The High Council called me this morning. They want me to drive back to Connecticut and deliver my final report at noon tomorrow."

"You mean the report on the coven?" Em gawked at him. He was supposed to be here for another week.

"What happened to a careful and thorough investigation?" Devlin asked.

Em nodded. "That's barely twenty-four hours."

"A couple hours less than that, if you take into account how long it'll take me to drive to Connecticut." Gar's lips tensed into a grim line. "They're also sending me information about a freelance journalist they want me to interview before I leave. Do either of you have an idea what that's about?"

Devlin scrubbed his hand over his face and groaned. "Unfortunately, I do. The journalist attempted to infiltrate the coven, so he could write an article from the inside and expose the world of hereditary witches and magic. Rhianna caught him, threatened to curse his family, and took blood, hair, and fingernails from him in exchange for letting him go."

Em got up from the couch. It felt weird to be seated while everyone else stood. "Devlin's telling the truth. Rhianna's plan was to use the stuff in a ritual we thought was going to awaken Merlin and return him to this world. We had no idea she intended on bringing Merlin's Shade into this realm." She thought for a second. "The night of the club fire, after Chloe drove the Shade back into the otherworld, the journalist was on TV ranting about witchcraft. The Council might have seen that."

"You're probably right," Gar said.

Devlin shook his head. "That doesn't explain why the Council wants you to waste what time you have talking to him. Rhianna's magic messed with the journalist's mind. No one who saw the TV show could have taken him seriously. He sounded insane."

Gar dismissed the idea with a wave of his hand. "That doesn't matter. I've been ordered to talk with him. And when I do, I suspect the journalist isn't going to tell me it was Rhianna who screwed with him. He's going to say it was Athena. That's who he thought he was dealing with, right?" He looked at Devlin steadily. "That's assuming your story about Rhianna using your sister's skin to impersonate her isn't a lie."

Angry red patches tinged Devlin's neck. "I'm not lying, and you know it."

"Then find a way to prove it. I need hard evidence to take to the Council." His tone turned more casual. "Em and I were discussing exhuming Saille's body and presenting it to the Council for testing."

"Really?" Devlin swiveled, his shocked gaze falling on Em.

"I had a dream about it last night. If we exhume Saille and prove Rhianna poisoned her, that would throw doubt on all of Rhianna's other claims of innocence."

Gar spoke up. "The problem is—thanks to this ridiculous new deadline—I don't have enough time now to exhume Saille. If you want to shine a good light on the coven, you need to come up with a different plan. Solid proof. Before tomorrow morning—something like Athena's body would help."

Devlin dropped down on the arm of the couch and covered his face with is hands. "Last night, after the séance, Chloe used her pendulum to try and locate Athena. We used Athena's personal Book of Shadows for added connection. But we got nothing. Same as the last time we tried."

"Do you have something that can prove Rhianna was here the night Merlin's Shade was awakened? Even something mundane, like a local traffic cam or security recording showing her undisguised or transforming into Athena," Gar said.

"No." Frustration hung in Devlin's voice. "Between Midas and the Shade's magic, there was a citywide electronic blackout. There isn't anything, except that TV show, and that happened after Rhianna left."

Em hooked her hands behind her head, thinking back through what she remembered from that night. She hadn't been around for a lot of it, but she'd been there at the very end, when Merlin's Shade had commanded Athena to take off the skin choker she was wearing. She'd done as he asked, instantly revealing she was in fact Rhianna. But Devlin was right: nothing electronic was functioning at that point.

"Did Rhianna work any spells while she was masquerading as Athena?" Gar asked. "What tools did the coven use to awaken Merlin's Shade? Is there something Rhianna might have left a trace of her magic on? Her DNA. Hair? Blood?"

Em shuffled his suggestions around in her head. *DNA. Hair. Blood.* An image of all the coven members cutting their palms and pressing them against a peach-size amethyst came to her. "Merlin's staff crystal!"

"The—what?" Gar said.

Devlin leapt to his feet and pulled her into a hug. "You're right." He turned to Gar. "When Rhianna fled, she took the crystal with her. We all put our blood on it—including her."

Excitement gleamed in Gar's eyes, but his voice was succinct. "I'm not familiar with this crystal. What is it?"

"It's the crystal from the head of Merlin's staff," Em explained. "From his first staff, before he even met Arthur, long before Nimue—the Lady of the Lake—imprisoned him. Rhianna convinced us all to use the crystal as part of a blood oath. We thought we were rededicating ourselves to awakening Merlin, so he could help us rediscover cures that have been lost to time. We believed we were doing something that would help humanity."

"I was such an idiot," Devlin muttered.

"No, you weren't," Em said. "You trusted her because you thought she was your sister."

Em's mind went back to that night, reliving it as Devlin told Gar the story in detail. They'd all been in the teahouse. She, Chloe, and Midas had just passed their initiation tests. A circle was cast, then Athena started the ceremony to officially welcome the three of them into the coven. Of course, it wasn't really Athena, but none of them knew that.

"Chloe, come forward," Athena had called out. "Come forward, Emily and Midas."

Em approached the altar with the others and held her hands out with her palms up.

Athena dipped her fingers into a bowl of water, touched Chloe's palms, then her forehead. "Blessings and welcome to the Northern Circle, Chloe," she intoned.

A sense of peace stole over Em as Athena welcomed her the same way. Athena moved on to bless Midas, then she raised her hands and voice. "Tonight, we are not only blessed with new members. We are also on the cusp of a new beginning." The pitch of her voice dropped, each word becoming concise and rhythmic, as steady as the hypnotic pulse of a metronome. "We step out. As the Fool off his cliff. As the Wizard from the dark of the winter solstice. A new beginning. A new path for the Northern Circle." With a flick of her wrist, a slender silver knife appeared in her hands. With another flick, she slit her palm with its blade.

Em gasped at the depth of the cut and cringed at the thought of how much it must have hurt.

"Athena?" Devlin said in a hard whisper. "What are you doing?"

Ignoring him, Athena held up her hand and turned in a slow circle, revealing the stripe of welling blood on her palm. "I welcome you all to pledge like I am. Rededicate yourselves. To a new age. A new way. A new path." She turned to the altar and rested her bloodied hand on Merlin's crystal. White and purple light exploded outward, followed by a wave of surging energy. The walls of the teahouse rattled. Bright light flashed again, and Athena's voice roared, loud and powerful as a thunderstorm. "I offer myself. I rededicate myself. To a new path. To Merlin's return."

The strength of the magic had sent terror rushing through Em, followed by a sense of excitement and wellbeing. She'd come to the coven hoping to find a safe place to live during her first year of sobriety. This amount of power was far beyond what she'd expected, and exactly what she needed.

Em's thoughts returned to the here and now.

"The last time I saw the staff crystal," Devlin was saying, "was at the circle of stones, right after Chloe drove Merlin's Shade back into the otherworld. Rhianna had it."

Gar rubbed his chin. "Are you talking about the circle of standing stones in the park down the street? I saw it when I was out running."

"Yes. But the crystal isn't there now. I'm certain Rhianna took it." Devlin looked Gar square in the eyes. "Chloe might not have been able to locate Athena's body with her pendulum, but I bet she can find the crystal.

It has blood from all of us on it. If we can prove Rhianna has the crystal, would that help our case?"

"It would help convince me," Gar said. "And my opinion does carry weight with the Council."

Em's pulse picked up. With Gar on their side, maybe they could do this.

Devlin took out his phone. "I'll text Chloe right now and tell her to come back as soon as she's done at the university."

"There's one more thing: the matter of the journalist. I can't track him down and witness Chloe's divination at the same time."

A smile flickered across Devlin's lips. "Midas is our resident computer wizard. I'll have him locate the journalist for you and round up any information he can. I'm guessing that will help?"

"That would be perfect."

Relief washed over Em and she settled back down on the couch. She looked up at Gar, catching his eyes. Warmth flushed her skin as he smiled back.

She swallowed hard. There was something else she hadn't stopped to think about. Whether they found the proof they needed before tomorrow or not, one thing wouldn't change. In less than twenty-four hours, Gar would be walking out of her life, again.

Chapter 12

LAKE PLACID—MISSING TEEN: On Monday, a fifteen-year-old who had been found chained in a hot van bolted from the Adirondack Medical Center. She doesn't have a phone, cash, or connections in New York State. Police ask anyone who saw a hitchhiker or picked one up to please call them.

—From *The Upstate Tribune*, August 10

A half hour later, Gar had closeted himself in the office to do additional research and Em was in the kitchen, washing the kittens' bottles. She would have offered to help him—in fact, she was dying to know what he was looking through: daily logs of the coven's activities, financial records, or perhaps Athena's Book of Shadows. Unfortunately, when it came to reading, she was painfully slow. Not that she was illiterate—she'd gotten her GED at the halfway house, thanks to her therapist's support. Still, she was far from a bookworm.

Her fingers clamped around the nurser bottle. She crammed the cleaning brush into it and scraped the bristles against the sides extra hard. She'd been cheated out of so much. The chance to go to high school, most of junior high, and lots of grade school. She'd loved grade school. Riding the bus. Her desk. The aquarium filled with fish. Painting. She really liked art class. She remembered struggling to read, but she'd loved books and the library. And poems… she had always loved them best of all.

"School's a waste of time for special people like Em," her aunt had said to her mother. "It's inappropriate and hurtful. She's meant for bigger things: to provide for her family. Why else would she have been given such an exceptional gift?"

Em remembered reading in front of the class in fourth grade, stumbling over her words. She remembered crying about that. But years later, she'd sat in the front row of the Royal Palm Playhouse, listening to *The Tempest* over and over until she memorized every line. At night, she'd recite it aloud with Alice while they pretended to be shipwrecked instead of homeless.

An ache pinched in Em's chest, growing sharper and pushing outward until it screamed to be released. No one had heard Alice's cry that night. No one had stopped her from putting that needle in her arm.

Em squeezed her eyes shut. *Let it go. Let it go*, she repeated to herself. She stuffed her hand into her pocket and clenched her A.A. medallion. *Gods and Goddesses, grant me the power of water, to accept what I cannot change. The power of fire, for the courage to change the things I can. The power of air, for the ability to know the difference. And the power of earth, for the strength to continue on my path.*

She counted to ten, extra slowly. Then she shoved the memory back and forced her feet to walk to the fridge. She reached for the kittens' formula but changed her mind. It hadn't been that long since the kittens had eaten, but the smell of the French toast in Devlin's apartment had made her stomach growl, reminding her that she hadn't had breakfast. No doubt Gar was equally hungry. She hadn't seen him eat anything since... now that she thought about it, she couldn't remember him eating at all.

Em nibbled on Swiss cheese and ham as she assembled two sandwiches for him. She piled them on the tray with mustard and mayo on the side, along with chips, pickles, an apple, and a couple of Brooklyn's cinnamon sugar cookies, plus a glass of organic milk. Saille had remained oddly absent since her last encounter with the last tug-of-war sensation. However, hauntings—and loup-garou heritage—weren't the only things that could make a person edgy. Not eating was almost as bad, especially for someone like Gar, who wanted to stay sober and needed to keep his head on straight.

"What's this?" Gar said when she toed the office door open and walked inside with the tray of food.

The room was as dark as it had been yesterday. Once again, the only light came from the gooseneck lamp on the desk, shining down on an open book and reflecting up onto Gar's face. He looked scholarly, except for the camo cap and the bruise under his eye and up the side of his nose.

"I thought you might be hungry," she said.

He closed the book and set it to one side, giving her room to put the tray down. "Thanks. I didn't want to take time to make something, but I'm starving."

He took the top slices of bread off the sandwiches and slathered them with mayo and mustard. He glanced up at her. "Sorry if I came across as rude earlier, when you asked about the dog's reaction to me. I'm not used to talking about my family, especially the loup-garou aspect. Comes from my job, I guess."

"Don't worry about it. It wasn't exactly the right time to ask."

She sank into the chair beside the desk, watching as he added chips and pickles to the sandwiches. He mushed the top slices of bread back on, then devoured a huge bite.

She crossed her legs at the ankles and hid them under her chair, wondering if he'd rather eat in private. It wasn't just his family and past she knew nothing about. She really didn't know much about his preferences either, outside of the bedroom—or for that matter, inside the bedroom. She really wanted to, though.

He set the sandwich back on the plate. "Did you eat?"

"I had a slice of cheese, and some ham. I should go check on the kittens, leave you to eat in peace." She glanced at the book he'd been reading. It had Northern Circle's emblem on the front cover and "Athena Marsh" embossed on the spine. "Is that Athena's Book of Shadows?"

"No. It's a record of the coven's activities she kept while high priestess. I have to say, her details about the Craft are some of the most insightful I've ever read. And I've read hundreds of high priest and priestess journals." He took a sip of milk, wiped his mouth. "I wish I had enough time to read the whole thing. Nothing about this twenty-four-hour deadline makes sense."

"It does seem screwy." Before Em could get another word out, Gar's phone buzzed.

He glanced at it. "It's Devlin. Chloe's back. He wants everyone to gather in the teahouse."

The teahouse was a simple one-room structure with a translucent sliding door. Woven-straw mats covered the floor. A brazier filled with glowing coals gave off light and warmth. Em loved the unassuming beauty of the place. Totally serene. It was also the perfect place for Chloe to use her divining skills to locate the staff crystal, especially since it was where they'd performed the blood swearing with Rhianna.

As they went inside, Em watched Gar's face out of the side of her eye. He had a smile in place, but he didn't immediately take off his cap. Instead he kept it tugged low over his eyes, surveying the room from under the shadow of its bent brim.

Devlin and Chloe were already kneeling on the floor, talking quietly as they situated a laptop in front of a low altar. Brooklyn was placing candles on the altar, along with a chalice and fingerbowls filled with water and stones.

Brooklyn turned to glare at Gar, then elbowed Chloe. "Sure you're going to be able to focus with him here?"

"I'd be more uncomfortable if he wasn't," Chloe snapped. She smiled at Gar. "Join us. We're almost ready."

Em touched Gar's elbow to urge him forward and let him know she understood how awkward the situation was for him. He pulled his arm away, as if the public intimacy bothered him, then strode forward. Her stomach sank, but she guessed she understood where he was coming from. She technically was part of the coven, and he technically was their enemy, even if they'd stepped across those lines more than a few times already.

"I'm assuming you're going to use an aerial view on the laptop instead of a conventional map for this," he said to Chloe and Devlin.

Devlin nodded. "We've done it before. Worked well."

Gar crouched, looking closely at the laptop's prone screen. "You're starting globally. That's smart."

Em folded her arms across her chest and stood behind them, feeling useless as they talked about how Chloe would dangle her pendulum over the map and focus her magic. When the pendulum stopped swinging and started circling in a general location, Devlin would enlarge the map. She'd focus again, narrowing the location down from continent to country, then to city or town until they pinpointed a building. Em tucked her hands in her pockets. Of course, they wouldn't be able to get a super exact location of Rhianna if she had cast a cloaking spell or heavy-duty ward around the crystal.

"What kind of security measures do you have in mind for us?" Gar asked.

A confident gleam brightened Chloe's eyes. "Chandler and Brooklyn created an anonymity ward. Even if Rhianna senses our intrusion, there's no way she'll be able to track it back to us."

The teahouse door opened. Midas strutted in with Chandler. He flicked his dreads over his shoulder and thrust out his chest proudly. "Good news. I located the journalist. He's staying at a motel, just a little ways down Route 7."

"That's fantastic," Chloe said. She raised her voice, addressing everyone. "If you all will take a seat around the altar, we'll get started."

"Do you want me to get the robes?" Chandler jerked her chin in the direction of the supply cupboard.

"Not tonight," Devlin said. "After Rhianna, I think we can all use a break from that sort of formality."

Em looked down, hiding a grin. Apparently, it was common for members of covens to wear matching robes. Some even had different colored robes for special events or types of spellwork. But Rhianna had taken it to a manipulative extreme, very much the way her aunt had controlled what she wore for public appearances. Always dresses. Lacy and girlish. Tights with ankle socks. Cardigans with pearl buttons. It was empowering to wear what she wanted, even if her clothes were Goodwill castoffs.

She took the empty spot between Chloe and Chandler. She would have preferred to sit next to Gar, but he'd settled beside Devlin, and Midas had immediately claimed the place on Gar's other side.

"Before we begin, there are a few things that need clarifying." Chloe paused, waiting for everyone's full attention. Her gaze went to Brooklyn. "Gar's not only here as a witness. He's here to lend us the strength of his magic. If we are to succeed, we must all accept him as if he were a member of the Circle. Understood?"

Brooklyn rolled her eyes. "I get it."

Chloe turned to Gar. "I'm counting on you to do everything I ask without question."

He nodded. "Within reason."

Em hid a smile behind her hand. Yup, still the rebel. He'd follow the rules and commands of the pack. But, when it came right down to it, he was as self-guided and wary as a lone wolf—something she definitely related to and admired.

Chloe blinked at Gar like she was trying to decide how to react to his answer. After a second, she plastered on a smile and continued as if his comment hadn't bothered her. "Now that we have that settled, let's get going." She picked up a brass-bound box the size and shape of a toaster from beside the laptop. It was the box that had previously housed Merlin's crystal. "I've decided to incorporate an extra element and step in this search, to strengthen the link between the coven and the crystal." With a flick of her fingers, Chloe used her magic to open the box's lid. She took out the nest of dried grass that had served for centuries as packing material for the crystal. Cupping the nest in her hands, she intoned, "Gods and Goddesses, we beseech you, reveal to us the location of the crystal that once called this home. Reveal to us the crystal that bears the blood pledges of our coven. Show us where it is, so that we might bring it home."

Chloe held out the nest to Em. She stared at it blankly, uncertain what to do.

"Take it." Chloe thrust the nest toward her again. "Channel your magic into it. Repeat my words."

The nest felt weightless as Em cradled it in both hands. She brought up her magic as if she were readying to reach out to a spirit. She let her mind relax. The room faded and all she sensed was the delicate texture of the nest against her palms. Her magic hummed in her blood, flooding up her body and into her arms, down toward her fingertips.

"Gods and Goddesses, we beseech you, reveal..." Chloe prompted.

Em released her magic into the nest and joined her voice with Chloe's. "Reveal to us the location of the crystal that once called this home. Reveal to us the crystal that bears the blood pledges of this coven. Show us so that we might bring it home."

A warm whirl of energy eddied in her hands, her magic combined with Chloe's. Another, fainter magic stirred to life, radiating from the nest: Merlin's magic, a lingering trace of the spells he'd fused into it the day he had placed the crystal in the grass for safekeeping.

Em trembled as Merlin's magic prickled her skin, quills of his energy liquefying and flowing into her veins.

Dazed by the rush, her mind whirred. Her body hummed. Wavering on the border between consciousness and delirium, she turned to her right and placed the nest in Chandler's waiting hands. She and Chandler repeated the entreaty. Then the nest moved into Brooklyn's hands, then Midas's. As Midas passed the nest to Gar, Em's mind stopped whirring and her senses became surreally sharp. The shadowy light cast by the charcoal fire appeared as brilliant as the midday sun. The noiseless sound of mist drifting in the garden beyond the teahouse walls murmured and swished, as audible as a river. She sensed the press of each seam in her jeans and the rub of her shirtsleeves against her arms. Whether she was right to think Merlin's magic had left its imprint on her, or if the sensations were the result of some god or goddess who had come to their aid, the effect was profound.

Chloe reverently set the nest on the altar. Then she sat back on her heels, took off her ever-present charm bracelet, and held it so a pendulum charm dangled freely from the length of the chain. "Now, if everyone will remain silent and channel your magic toward my hand, I'll begin the next step." She took a deep breath, then held the pendulum an inch above the laptop's prone screen and closed her eyes. "Show me where the staff crystal is," she murmured. "Guide me to it."

Em focused her magic and sent it out, ribboning toward Chloe's hand. The more she concentrated on the ribboning flow, the more she could feel everyone else's magic meeting, joining, and flowing down into the pendulum. There was no sense of resistance as the pendulum began to swing, fanning over the laptop. It started to circle. Devlin bent forward, his fingers gliding over the touch pad as he enlarged the map from revealing the entire globe to only displaying the continent of North America.

Once again, the pendulum swung, back and forth. It took longer this time, but eventually it circled, and Devlin adjusted the image on the laptop to reveal a northern portion of the east coast.

The pendulum stopped circling and hung dead.

"Show me," Chloe intoned. "Where is the crystal?"

Em fisted her hands on her lap. She took a long breath, pulling up what magic she had left. A headache throbbed behind her eyes. Her throat was raw. She could barely sense the power of anyone else's magic now, except for Gar's. His magic still burned strong and unrelenting, as steady as a heartbeat, pulsing in time with hers.

She relaxed her shoulders and hands and closed her eyes, focusing only on the pulse of his magic, letting her energy flow down into the pendulum in time with his.

After a moment, she sensed the pendulum swinging once more, back and forth, fanning the screen. No resistance. A smooth gentle sway.

It began to circle.

"Got it!" Devlin shouted.

Em's eyes flashed open, the sense of magic now totally gone.

She leaned forward, closer to the laptop. An aerial view of a city spanned the screen. A circular parking garage. An alleyway. A flat-topped building.

"I lost track after we narrowed it down to New England," Chloe said. "But the building looks familiar."

Devlin nodded. "I feel the same way."

Everyone squished in closer to the laptop, gathering together.

"It looks familiar to me too," Chandler said.

"The last thing I saw was the seacoast. Maybe it's in Maine," Brooklyn suggested.

Gar sat back. His voice was deep and full of certainty. "I know the building. Your crystal is at the High Council's New Haven headquarters."

Chapter 13

For you, my sons and daughter, I offer a challenge and a quest.
Conquer your mother's people, be a master and ruler in her domain
before the fae can get a foothold, and you shall be crowned royal in mine.
—Challenge set forth by Magna Drilgrath, *pater daemonium*

Devlin brought up a street-view of the building. "Oh, man. I can't believe it." He turned to Gar, his voice hardening. "You want to call me a liar now about Athena being murdered?"

"This does raise questions. However, it doesn't prove anything."

"You've got to be kidding," Brooklyn scoffed.

As everyone jumped to their feet and began to argue, Em folded her arms across her chest and kept her thoughts to herself. Why couldn't Gar just accept that they were telling him the truth? For that matter, why couldn't everyone else be nicer to him? He might feel less defensive and give in if they did.

Gar glared at everyone, the bruises on his face making him look even tougher than usual. "The crystal being there isn't foolproof evidence. It's still your word against Rhianna's."

"Dear Goddess." Chandler slapped her hand against her forehead in frustration. "You're one of the most infuriating people I've ever met."

"Don't underestimate how concerned I am about this. I agree, something fishy is going on at the Council."

"You can say that again," Chloe said. "And Rhianna is the one pulling the strings."

A small smile twitched at the corner of Gar's mouth. "Fortunately for us, Rhianna isn't the only one with friends on the High Council—and neither am I." He raised his eyebrows at Devlin. "I believe someone's grandfather isn't without connections."

Em tucked her hands in her pockets, struggling to resist the urge to expose the flaw in Gar's logic. But it had to be said. "If you're so sure about these so-called friends and connections, then why didn't any of them mention your haunting or object to you being sent to investigate the Circle?"

"That is strange," Gar admitted. "It's also one of several questions that I should be able to answer once I find out whose office the crystal is in."

"You mean when *we* discover where it is," Chloe said flatly.

"It's better if I do this by myself. I'll look for the crystal right after my meeting."

"Unlike you"—Chloe's voice toughened—"I can locate it in a second, as long as you get me inside."

Gar turned to Devlin. "My plan is to ask the Council for more time to finish my investigation. If Chloe comes with me, it'll be one more thing I have to explain. Not to mention that the Vice-Chancellor will be there."

Chloe stiffened at the mention of the Vice-Chancellor. It was the lowest blow Gar could have dealt her, but Em agreed that it was an important point to bring up. Five years ago, when Chloe was sixteen, the Vice-Chancellor and his wife hired her as a babysitter. That night, because of Chloe's carelessness, their son had fallen into a pool and nearly drowned. But that wasn't the end of it. The near-drowning had left the boy brain damaged and in an essentially vegetative state. The Vice-Chancellor and his wife hated Chloe. But the tragedy had left Chloe determined to find a cure for the boy. It was a large part of why she wanted to go to medical school, and the Northern Circle's interest in exploring ancient cures had enticed her into joining.

"I'm very aware the Vice-Chancellor is likely to be there." Chloe lifted her chin. "But I'm done hiding from my past. No one ever accomplishes anything by doing that."

Em admired Chloe's determination and wished she could agree with her philosophy. It wasn't so much that she disagreed, but avoiding the past was one of Em's top priorities, especially when it applied to Violet Grace.

Midas stepped forward. "Won't it look strange if no one from the coven goes to the meeting to object to this sketchy investigation?" His eyes narrowed on Gar. "If you don't talk them into an extension, it's all over for us. We get disbanded. The Council takes ownership of the complex. They strip Devlin of his magic. Isn't that the general gist?"

"It doesn't necessarily happen like that. The Circle can file an objection, draw it out longer."

"How long?" Chandler said. "A week? A month? I've lived here since before Athena became high priestess. My business is here. This is the only home my son has ever known."

Devlin spoke up, silencing everyone. "If Gar says he can buy us time, then that's what we need to focus on. I also agree with Chloe. She needs to go to headquarters, so we can get proof against Rhianna." His dimples showed as a devious smile crossed his lips. "I also know how to get Chloe inside without raising suspicion. Legally—as the Northern Circle's high priest—I have the right to attend any meeting or hearing involving the coven. With Athena gone, the coven is currently without a high priestess, but if we had one…" He quirked an eyebrow meaningfully and let his voice trail off.

Gar tilted his head. "That's not a half-bad idea."

"Are you suggesting that the coven name me its new high priestess?" Chloe smiled tentatively, a grin slowly growing.

"Temporarily," Devlin clarified. "We do need a new one. But the position involves a lot more than overseeing rituals. Athena ran the complex. She oversaw our businesses and charitable works. I'm not sure a permanent commitment of that kind would mesh with your med school plans."

Brooklyn raised her hand. "I vote Chloe for high priestess."

"I second it," Midas said.

Devlin's attention went back to Gar. "One more thing: I'll be going to your meeting. If anyone is going to defend the Circle, it's going to be me. And if something goes wrong, I can hold my own in a fight."

Gar frowned, but then relented. "All right. On one condition. You let me talk first. If the Council grants us an extension, you'll say thank you and walk away. If things go bad, then you can have your say. Remember, though, the Council are powerful witches, you don't want to piss any of them off."

"Gar, I'm not a fool. I've heard stories about their ideas of just punishment, like Roger 'Armless' Long."

"Armless, among others." Gar's gaze flicked to Em, as if hinting that she was somehow related to the discussion.

She looked away from him, pushing that thought aside. *No.* She'd misinterpreted the gesture. Undoubtedly, he'd simply noticed her silence and was trying to draw her into the conversation. And she did have something to add, something that would most likely lead to a resounding "no" from everyone.

Chandler and Brooklyn made a couple of suggestions. Midas offered to loan Devlin and Gar a stash of techno-magic gizmos he'd designed, which did everything from opening locks to making a car's electronic footprint untraceable.

Em rubbed her arms, studying everyone. She wanted the coven to succeed. More than that, she didn't want to lose her sanctuary. She truly believed that deep down inside, Gar was on their side—especially hers.

Finally, she lifted her chin like Chloe had, though Chloe's proud, willowy height had made the move more impressive. She raised her voice. "I'm going to headquarters, too."

Everyone stared at her.

"Definitely not," Gar said.

Devlin nodded. "There's no need or reason for that."

Em stayed firm. "You can use me to present evidence at the meeting if need be, for the coven's defense. I may be a recovering drunk. I've done drugs and lived on the streets. I've made bad choices. But no one—not even the High Council—will question my abilities as a medium. I can call Athena once we get there. I'm assuming the Council allows the dead as witnesses?"

"They do." Gar grimaced. "But only fully manifested spirits—which is the problem, since Athena has only appeared as an orb."

Confidence pounded into Em's veins. She grinned. "I'm not convinced that getting her to materialize at headquarters is an impossibility. Even if I can't contact her, I might be able to reach Saille. The tug-of-war is affecting both their spirits. If its source is at headquarters—like the crystal is—then I'll be able use the spirits to locate it. If we could disrupt the tug-of-war even for a few minutes, it should allow them to manifest fully."

Gar's gaze reached into hers, telegraphing his worry. Em sent a wave of soothing energy out to him. She had to do this. It was their best chance.

"This problem isn't just the tug-of-war," Devlin added. "We don't know who is in league with Rhianna. This could get dangerous."

Em steadied her voice. "I can't shoot energy balls like you and Chloe"—she glanced at Gar—"or do whatever you can do. But I can hold my own. Spirits listen to me."

The vibration of her phone hummed against her leg. She froze, her pulse skittering in a million directions. It had to be her therapist. Anyone else who might call was here. But why was she calling again?

"Shouldn't you get that?" Gar said, his voice tense.

Em's mouth dried. She slid her phone from her pocket. "Hello?"

"Em?" Her therapist's voice was quiet—too quiet.

"Is everything all right?"

"I'm afraid I have more bad news." She hesitated. "Your aunt showed up at the halfway house."

Numbness shot straight to Em's core. She turned away from the group, walking stiffly to the teahouse door and outside. As the therapist explained what had happened, she gazed down at her shoes, seeing small feet, swollen and red from the tattooist's needles. When the therapist finished telling her the news, she dropped the phone into her pocket, too dazed to say a word.

Family is forever.

Chapter 14

BOSTON, MASSACHUSETTS: Two Hours of Spirit Messages for the audience from Violet Grace, the World's Youngest Psychic Medium. $65 (includes admission to Horizon's Annual Expo!) September 28, 4:00 p.m. to 6:00 p.m. Goodnight Inn & Suites. 4390 Pleasant Pkwy. Real intuitive guidance. Healing. Astounding.
     —Coming Events: *Bay State Community Gazetteer*

Family is forever. The words thundered in Em's head as she quickly walked away from the teahouse. When she got to the path that led to Devlin's apartment, she veered down it and began to jog. She needed to get away. To be by herself.

She sprinted past his apartment to the woodland trail that led to the edge of the coven's property. Her breath came in short pants. Her magic roiled inside her, a tempest of fear and anger.

A minute later, she reached the coven's back gate. The gate and accompanying chain-link fence were bespelled to keep outsiders from entering, but Devlin, Chloe, and even Rhianna could get through with a simple command.

Em drew up her magic and flung it at the gate. "Open."

To her surprise, the gate did as she asked. She ran through, and it swung shut behind her. Oakledge Park and the lake were just ahead. The perfect place to be alone. When she reached the park, the first thing she came to was the circle of standing stones where they'd held the ritual that woke Merlin's Shade and allowed him to escape from the otherworld. Under the late afternoon sky, the stones stood shadowless. Beyond them, the deserted lake stretched, steel-gray and grim.

She gritted her teeth, blocking out the hammer of her therapist's words, focusing instead on stones and the horrifying memories of that night: Chloe offering her blood to protect her friend Keshari. The surreal moment when Chloe disappeared into one of the stones. The unbearable moments that elapsed before she returned. Later, Athena taking off her human-skin choker to reveal that she was really Rhianna. The blood. The battle. The screams and exploding energy balls, her summoning orbs to come to their aid.

Em clamped her eyes shut, overcome by anguish and remorse from the fool's part she'd played in the events. She'd never known the real Athena, so she had no one to compare to the person she'd met. Still, she'd suspected something was wrong. But the lure of a comfortable place to live—clean sheets, soft pillows, quiet hallways that smelled of lavender and sage, good food whenever she wanted—had made her push aside her intuition's subtle warnings and ignore the similarities between Athena's actions and the brainwashing ploys her aunt had used. There were the required robes, of course. But there were other things. Baths without privacy. Kindness and empathy mixed with isolation and shaming. Long, hypnotic rituals. She hadn't drunk the wine or the strange-smelling teas she'd been offered, but they'd been ever-present.

A breeze rolled in from the lake. Em opened her eyes and let it blow her hair back from her heated face. She'd dealt with Rhianna's ploys by faking obedience and dumping drinks into potted plants. She'd survived that, and she could deal with her aunt's return as well.

Swinging her arms to fool herself into feeling carefree, Em swept past the stones and scrambled down the seawall to the beach. Tangled seaweed and feathers coiled along the high-water mark. Charred driftwood enclosed the remains of a bonfire. She reached the end of the sand, climbed up a series of low rock shelves, and then made her way along the ledges until she could see across the broad lake. Miles of water stretched toward the twilight-faded outlines of the mountains in New York State. Pink and gray rimmed the sky above them.

She sank down on the rocks and dangled her feet over the low cliff, waves rocking only a yard below. Before the call from her therapist, she'd been so sure that staying at the complex until next Spring was her smartest move. Now, she wasn't so sure—

The scrape of footsteps on stone came from just over her shoulder.

She wheeled around, heart in her throat. Who was it?

Gar stood less than a yard away. He dropped down beside her as casual as anything. He nudged her hip with his thumb. "Are you okay?"

"I was until you scared the hell out of me," she snapped.

"Why did you take off?" His voice was gentle, but firm. Serious. "The call was about your aunt, wasn't it?"

Em rubbed her hands along her legs. She gripped her knees. She wanted to lie, but she couldn't. Not to him. She nodded. "Yeah."

"Everyone's worried. You should have come back inside and told us."

Warmth radiated off of him. The strength of his presence. Moss and evergreens. She swallowed back a knot in her throat. "You didn't tell them about my aunt being paroled, did you?"

"That's not mine to tell."

She sat back, resting her hands behind her. She looked skyward. The clouds rolled, thick and deepening. "I really didn't think she'd come after me."

Gar's voice lowered. "We'll cross that bridge when we come to it."

Tears formed in her eyes and her voice cracked. She leaned forward again, elbows on her knees, fingers steepled and pressed against her forehead. "We're already there. Gar, my aunt knows where I am."

"That was her on the phone?"

"No. It was my therapist." She brushed her fingers over her eyes, wiping away the tears. "My aunt was at the halfway house this morning. Someone told her where I am. My—"

Gar looped his arm across her shoulder, pulling her in close. "She has no power over you. You're an adult. You've got friends."

"It's not just that." She drew a long breath. "My mother is with her. She shouldn't be. She supposed to be under supervision. At a group home."

She rested her head on his shoulder and stared out across the lake, black waves tipped with gleaming foam. The lights of houses flickered on in the distance, like a necklace of diamonds twinkling along the horizon.

"My mother—" Her voice stiffened, lurching toward the anger she'd held in for years. "I used to blame everything on my aunt. But why would a mother let someone... let a monster use their little girl? It's not like she was incapable of taking me and walking away."

"I don't know. I have five sisters. I can't imagine my mother or dad allowing anyone to mistreat them." Gar released her, then took her by both shoulders, turning her to look at him face-to-face. "When I was talking about Armless Long and the Council's past sanctions, you didn't react. I think there's something you don't know about your situation. Something that directly relates to your mother and aunt."

She flinched, frowning in confusion. "What are you talking about?"

"You and your entire family fall under the legal governance of the Eastern Coast High Council, did you realize that?"

"Of course I belong—I'm a member of the Northern Circle. But I didn't realize that affected my mother or aunt." She thought for a second. "Are you talking about before, when the Council sent you to find me at the hospital?"

He smiled, as if savoring the moment. "Do you know anything about your family history? Your genealogy?"

Em blinked at him, then laughed uncomfortably. "Not really." She began to quiver, her excitement growing. "I've always wondered where my ability came from. My aunt is intuitive, but she always seemed jealous of my talent."

"She probably is. She may also feel entitled to use your magic." Gar stroked the outline of her face, his gaze on hers. "After I met you and heard your story, I got curious. You had such an amazing amount of talent and courage for a young woman—a teenager. I didn't have to dig far into the Council records to find your heritage. Are you familiar with Winchester Arms?"

"They made guns, right? What does that have to do with me?"

"The Winchester family was from New Haven—where the Eastern Coast headquarters is. The last surviving Winchester, Sarah, died back in the late nineteenth century. Her husband and child died before her. Supposedly, a medium told her that their deaths were the result of a curse, placed on the Winchester family because their guns had killed so many people. That's a made-up story. However..."

The breeze picked up again. Waves crashed against the rocks, spraying cold mist. Em shivered but sat still. Cold or not, she wasn't going to move. Not until Gar finished telling her the truth. She'd given up asking her mother about her heritage even before the tattooing. She'd assumed no one else in her family cared about the past, considering the wall of silent indifference that her questions always ran into.

Gar's voice growled, a deep tone against the lap of the waves. "In reality, the medium was Sarah Winchester's illegitimate half-sister. She was also from New Haven, and felt entitled to a share of the Winchester wealth. I'm not sure exactly what the charges against the medium were; I didn't dig that deep into the records. But the Council used a curse to subjugate the magic in the medium's system. It was a curse designed to pass from one generation to the next. However, it seems time and nature have weakened the curse, and the gift of mediumship and magic is returning to your family."

"Are you saying my children's abilities will be stronger than mine?"

Gar smiled and nodded. "I'd assume so."

She looked out across the lake, for the first time in her life daring to visualize herself holding a baby, or maybe two. A kid. With magic, like Chandler and her son.

Gar's expression became serious again. "To get back to my original point: Because of your heritage, your entire family falls under the governance of the Eastern Coast Council. Your aunt and mother have committed serious crimes. All you need to do is petition the Council for protection against them. It'll be faster and more formidable than any mundane restraining order."

"You're serious." Em could hardly wrap her head around everything he was saying.

"Very much so." He pulled her into a hug and whispered, "You need to tell everyone about the possibility of your aunt and mother showing up at the complex. After that, we could go to an A.A. meeting. I don't know about you, but I could use one."

She rested her forehead against his chest. "I'm going to miss you when you leave."

"Shush about that. We need to deal with your aunt and mother first. But before that, we need to get through the High Council meeting." He leaned back and pushed her hair from her face. "You're right—it is important that you come with us tomorrow. I'm counting on you to help me with something particular."

"Sure. Anything."

"I need you to watch for Saille. I've been feeling more together since the séance, but I'm not convinced her attachment to me won't strengthen if she breaks loose from whatever is holding her back. I need you to make sure she doesn't influence me."

"I'll try," Em said, though controlling a spirit was a lot easier said than done, especially with the addition of the unknown element like the tug-of-war.

Chapter 15

It's summer. Ninety degrees in Jersey City.
My aunt buys me cotton socks. White and thick.
To go with my jeans and high-top sneakers.
—Journal of Emily Adams
Memory. Afterwards. 11 years old.

Em went back to the teahouse with Gar and told everyone about the strong possibility of her aunt and mother showing up at the complex. Gar was right: telling them was not only fair, it was also a relief.

"Seriously," Em said. "I feel horrible about this. If they show up when I'm not around, don't answer the door. They're my problem, not anyone else's."

Midas flourished his hand in the air, as if casting a spell with a wand. "A car accident. Brake failure. A gas leak. An explosion?"

Gar cleared his throat. "I'm going to head into the house before someone says something this investigator shouldn't hear."

"Wait a minute," Devlin said to him. "We should all go in. I'll order pizzas for dinner, if everyone's good with that. We've got a big day tomorrow, and lots of things to finish up tonight." He turned to Em. "I'm glad you told us. No more talk about your problems not being ours. We're family—more than family."

"Thanks." Em smiled, but in the back of her mind, her aunt's voice echoed. *Family is forever.* Coven or not, this problem wasn't going to go away, not ever.

An hour later, empty pizza boxes and plates littered the living room. While everyone else started to discuss the journalist, Em and Gar went to the front entryway. It was already after seven. If they waited any longer, they'd be late for the A.A. meeting.

But as Gar reached to open the door, Em snagged his sleeve, holding him back. "There's something I need to tell you."

He turned to face her. "Yeah?"

She rubbed her arms, hesitating. "Um, I know you're set on going to a meeting, but I don't really want to. I've gone at least once a day for almost seven months. I deserve a night off. I'm really tired...."

A knowing smile lifted a corner of his lips as she went on listing everything except her real reason for not wanting to go: her body had been on fire for him ever since he showed up at the park, and they might never have another night together.

"You sure? You do realize this is a bad idea?" He lifted her chin, then bent down and kissed her on the lips, soft and unhurried. She closed her eyes, a melancholy feeling spreading in her belly as she lost herself in the pleasure. His lips left hers, moving on to kiss the sensitive skin behind her ear before he whispered, "I was afraid you wouldn't ever get around to suggesting it."

She threw her arms around his neck, kissing him openmouthed. His hands slid down her back to her butt. Cradling it, he lifted her up. She locked her legs around his hips, squirming against him as he stumbled away from the front door to steady her back against the closest wall. The kiss deepened, his tongue caressing hers. Her body went liquid. His hips ground against her, rolling slowly in time with the caress of his lips and tongue.

"Upstairs," she murmured, nipping his bottom lip.

"Not yet," he growled. He leaned into her harder, pressing and rocking. One of his hands crept downward. It reached between her legs and massaged slowly. Waves of his magic penetrated the fabric of her jeans, exciting and tantalizing her. She arched and groaned, a spasm of joy tightening and readying to explode with each stroke of his hand.

His lips left hers. "Too many clothes."

"Bedroom," she gasped as he lowered her to the floor.

He took her by the hand and they rushed out of the entryway and up the stairs. Em smothered a giggle. She felt like a teenager sneaking past her boyfriend's parents and into his bedroom, or like how she imagined life might have been as a teen—if she was never Violet Grace and Gar had been her age. If her life had been normal.

They barely got his bedroom door closed before she had her jeans off and his were halfway to his knees. She grabbed a condom, rolling it onto his erection. She groaned as he entered her quickly, her coil of tension bursting instantly into an orgasm. He drove her to another peak, holding his hand lightly over her mouth as she writhed and screamed in pleasure.

"Shh," he laughed, thrusting more slowly. "You really have a hair-trigger."

She reached down, taking his cock in her hand and stroking it as his balls grew tense and hard, nearing his own peak. He thrust two more times, then shuddered and moaned as he came.

He fell against her, heat and the moist smell of evergreens soaking into her skin. "We're not very good at taking things slow, are we?"

She wove a hand through his hair, pulling his mouth to hers for a kiss. "I don't care. I'm more into quantity, myself."

He pushed up and swung off from on top of her. "How about a shower, then?" He waggled his eyebrows suggestively. "I know a lot about your magic specialties—I'd like to show you one of mine. I promise you'll like it."

She wasn't sure what he meant, but she didn't care. Curiosity prickled in her abdomen, growing even more intense when he took her into the bathroom and opened the metal wallet where he kept his mysterious vials of oil, so many labeled with skulls and crossbones.

"You're not going to dart me, are you?" she teased, eyeing his sleeve gun. Her breath caught in her throat. She could hardly believe it. She'd just joked with him about needles instead of panicking at the mere thought of them—not to mention the added danger of vials, whose contents no doubt fell in the drug category.

He picked out three bottles, one cobalt and two dark brown. "Every oil has more than one purpose. Almond, rose, jonquil, carnation...they can kill in some situations. Applied with a touch of magic, they can make pleasure even more pleasurable. Trust me?"

"To my soul," she murmured, and it was overwhelmingly true. Her faith in his good intentions when it came to her body, spirit, and sobriety was without question. She sensed it in his spirit, right now—just as it had been seven years ago in that cemetery, when he'd set the bottle of water and orange on the grass in front of her. When she'd gotten into his truck and let him take her to the river.

She finished taking off her shirt and bra while he dribbled oils into a tiny ceramic bowl and whispered an incantation. Then she helped him undress, and they both climbed into the steaming shower.

"Face me," he said, coaxing her close until the entire length of her body pressed against his. "Rest your head on my chest. Relax. Close your eyes."

She quivered with anticipation as he lifted her hair and began to massage oil into the nape of her neck. The spicy scent of carnations filled the steam and a sense of serenity washed over her. His fingers stroked upward, threading oil through her hair, rubbing her scalp. Her shoulders relaxed. Her mind drifted and she leaned into the rhythm of his touch. A trickle of oil escaped, trailing tingles over her shoulder and down her torso, winding the length of her legs to her foot.

Em stiffened. She glanced down. Water pooled around her feet. Her naked feet, toe to toe with his. Her socks long gone. Her tattoos unmissable. *Family is forever.*

His hand returned to the back of her neck, strong fingers kneading the taut muscles. "Breathe deep. Don't think. Relax."

She snuggled closer, resting her cheek against him and letting all thoughts of her feet and the past float away. He supported her with one arm. The scent of the steam transformed into almonds and roses. A warm rush spread across her skin, every cell awakening. A delicious pulse ached between her legs.

"Hmmm." Gar left off massaging her neck, his hands skimming down her back until they cradled her butt. "What do you say we reenact what we were doing a little while ago—downstairs? I liked that a lot."

Em slid her hands up his chest, fastening them around his neck. "Mmmmm...me too."

He hoisted her up and she wrapped her legs around his hips. He pressed her against the shower wall. Warm water sprayed all over. Steam enclosed them. Fresh scents of spice and flowers ignited as she squirmed against him. His hips moved in time with hers, a slow, grinding waltz that she wished could last forever.

Chapter 16

Her grandfather might have insisted Athena be named after the goddess,
a sort of in-joke based on his nickname being Zeus.
But the name fit her. From the day I met her,
Athena's wisdom and fight were something I wanted to emulate.
—Journal of Chandler Parrish

Em woke up the next morning warm and rested, but she and Gar only took time for a quickie. With the Council meeting scheduled for noon and an almost five-hour drive to New Haven ahead of them, they couldn't afford to linger in bed.

Shivering against a chill in the air, Em dashed for the hallway bathroom while Gar went into his own shower. Once she was done washing and had put on some makeup, she dressed in her best jeans and a dressy black cardigan that Brooklyn had loaned her. The sweater's sleeves hung over her fingers, but turning the cuffs under fixed that. In fact, she was surprised how well the rest of it fit. Brooklyn definitely didn't have a skin-and-bones figure like she did.

Satisfied that she looked decent, Em went downstairs to feed the kittens. They started to cry the second she opened the door, hungry and eager to escape their box. They kneaded their claws into her and purred like lawnmowers as they each took their turn at the bottle. She was almost finished when a knock came at the door.

"Hey, Em? Can I come in?" Chandler's voice asked.

"Sure." Em set the last kitten down on the bath mat.

Chandler opened the door and strolled in, carrying a paper grocery bag and looking indomitable in welder's pants and a frayed sweatshirt with

"Mama Dragon" written across it. A do-rag with flaming salamanders on its sides covered her short-cropped hair. Judging by the way she was dressed, Em figured Chandler was planning on tackling a big project, perhaps a new flying monkey to replace one of the sculptures that had been destroyed.

Chandler shoved the bag at Em. "I thought you might be able to use this."

"Thanks. What is it?" Em took the heavy bag. Fancy orange tissue poked out from the top. It felt squishy, like it contained some kind of clothing.

"I picked it up at the farmers market a while ago. I've been waiting for the perfect person to give it to."

Em sat down on the closed toilet lid and peeled aside the tissue. Chandler always gave off an artsy-but-tough big sister vibe, the sort of sister who would take out playground bullies for you in the morning and teach you how to bead friendship bracelets in the afternoon. The sort of sister Em would have liked to have.

Chandler rested her hands on her hips, watching as Em pulled out a bundle of embroidered turquoise and lavender silk. "It's from Tibet. Keshari's family makes them."

The fabric was soft, the colors brilliant. Em unfolded it. "A jacket? It's gorgeous. But it's too expensive. I can't take it."

"Don't be silly. Try it on. I'm dying to see if it fits."

Em stood up and shrugged the jacket on. The sleeves went to her wrist bones. The hem landed perfectly above her hips. She twirled like a fashion model. "I don't know what to say. It's—wonderful."

"Look in the pocket. There's something from Midas and Devlin."

She patted her side and found the hidden gift, something the size and shape of a ChapStick cylinder. It looked to be made of silver.

"The cylinder is from Devlin," Chandler explained. "It's a coven heirloom, designed to keep its contents and itself undetectable. Devlin had three of them. Enough for you, Chloe, and himself. Look inside."

As Em unscrewed the cylinder's lid, an electric tingle and a rhythmic pulse of magic sped up her wrist. The beat branched out, following her veins and chanting in her ears like the voice of a long-forgotten ancestor. She pushed past the sensation and shook the cylinder's contents onto her palm. Five wooden toothpicks.

"Midas calls them 'pick-a-roos.'" Chandler lifted a hand to silence Em. "Before you say anything, I know it's a silly name."

Em laughed. "I can't believe Midas named something that. He's always so serious."

"You should give him more of a chance. He can come off as pretentious. Underneath, he's nothing more than a little boy playing mad scientist—and a damn good mad scientist, at that."

Em poked the pick-a-roos with her fingernail. No sensation of magic this time. Nothing except wood. "What are they for?"

"I wish I could demonstrate. Unfortunately, there aren't any to spare. Midas only had enough to give a few to you, Chloe, and Devlin—with none left for Gar. They're for opening locks." She agilely plucked a pick from Em's palm. "You stick the pointed end into any lock mechanism, channel your magic into it, then give the command: 'sesame.'"

Em bit down on her bottom lip, resisting the urge to comment on Midas using yet another silly word. In truth, "sesame," as in "open sesame," from *Ali Baba and the Forty Thieves*, was simple to remember, which was probably the point.

Chandler set the pick-a-roo back on her palm. "Once you give the command, the pick will start burning. When you hear or sense the lock release, you need to open the door before the fire goes out. If you don't, the spell will fail and the lock will reset."

That sounded straightforward enough. Em glanced at the picks in her palm, then farther down, at the kitten staring up at her from the floor with intense blue eyes. It was straightforward, but the way the picks had been divided felt wrong. "Shouldn't we give Gar at least a couple?"

"He's not the one who has to worry about getting out of headquarters if the meeting goes sour. The three of you are another matter, especially Devlin and Chloe."

Fear tumbled through Em, coming to rest just below her stomach. If only there was another way out of this investigation mess. If Gar could get an extension for the coven without having to appear in person. If all of them could stay home. But none of those things were going to happen. In truth, they could lose, and Rhianna could get her way. She clearly had connections.

A second emotion mingled with Em's fear: guilt. No matter how many appalling things Rhianna had done, Em couldn't forget the healing ritual Rhianna had performed on her. The sense of well-being she'd felt afterwards, not to mention the boost in her conviction to stay sober. Rhianna was evil. A murderess. A sociopathic seductress. But there was more to her than just those things. There was an ability to do good—if it served her purpose.

Chandler's voice brightened. "Hopefully everything will go smoothly at the meeting and none of you will have to use the picks." She stooped and gathered up the kitten. Stroking it, she continued. "You don't have to worry about these little devils. While Midas and Brooklyn are off interviewing the journalist, I'll be here to watch over things."

Em did a double take. "I'd forgotten about the journalist. The Council's probably going to give Gar crap for not finishing that."

"I suspect he'll deal with it just fine. Either way, we need to find out if the journalist is still a threat to the coven."

"Sounds smart," Em said.

A devious twinkle sparked in Chandler's eyes, like dragons springing to life. She gave the kitten another stroke, slowly, all the way down to his tail. "There's another reason I volunteered to stay here. I know as much as Devlin about the coven's workings. If the meeting goes badly, I can protect our interests until all of you get back. And if a certain someone—or some*ones*—show up…"

Em knew what Chandler meant. She looked down at her feet. "I feel horrible about that. That last thing the coven needs is to deal with my problems right now."

"Don't worry." Chandler's voice gentled. "All of us witch-sisters and -brothers have baggage. It's hard not to when you're born with magic."

Chapter 17

Vine ripened. Hothouse grown. Big Girl. Early Girl.
Valencia. Carmello. Green Cherry. Plump. Juicy. Breasts and blood.
No BLT for me. Plain Jane. Bag of Bones.
Crescent Moon. Night ripened. Alien thing. Ribs and wrong.
—"Tomato" by E. A.
Memory. My body. 15 years old.

Em was grateful they made it to New Haven in time for Gar to drive around the historic downtown area to make sure they couldn't sense anything dangerous or concerning before they went inside to the meeting. They'd all been to the city before, even her—though she barely remembered it and hadn't known about the Eastern Coast Council headquarters being there.

Certain they weren't missing anything important, Gar drove into a parking garage adjacent to the ten-story building the Council called home. As he steered toward a private section on the garage's first level, an orange striped barrier arm automatically lifted to let his truck pass.

"This section is for Council employees and guests," Gar said, backing into a parking space near the sidewall. "If we get separated for any reason, we'll meet back here. I'll leave the truck unlocked."

Devlin rested his hand on the front dash and shifted to face Gar. "What if something happens to you?"

Gar produced a second set of truck keys and tossed them to him. "Don't wait, just go. Also, we're going to take the elevator up to the executive offices. But if you have to leave in a hurry, use the stairs. At best, you'll have three minutes' lead time before the place goes on lockdown. After that, all you can do is pray Midas's picks work."

Cold fear crept into Em's bones. She didn't like the sound of this, especially the part about not waiting and taking off in the truck if something happened to Gar.

She nudged Chloe's hip. "Don't you think we should have an alternate meeting place, like in case one of us gets separated?"

"That's a great idea," Chloe said. "How about the Dunkin' Donuts around the corner? The Council wouldn't dare make a scene in a public place like that."

Gar glanced over his shoulder at her. "Sounds good to me." His voice toughened. "One last reminder: If any of you suspect someone is in fact Rhianna in disguise, or if you see a man or woman wearing jewelry or anything made from human skin, or if you sense something is off, try to act as if nothing is wrong. Don't do anything."

Devlin shot a glare at Gar. "Don't worry. I can control myself, if that's what you're getting at."

"Good." Gar continued, all but ignoring Devlin's flare. "Now let's get this meeting over with."

As Gar opened his door, Em quickly reviewed their plan in her head. They'd all enter the building together. She, Chloe, and Devlin would wait outside the hearing room while Gar had his scheduled meeting. With luck, he'd get permission to extend the investigation for another week, ostensibly to locate Athena's body to prove their case. If he failed, they'd all go into the hearing room and Gar would prompt them through a series of questions designed to strengthen the case for an extension. No matter what happened, once they were done with the meeting, they'd find a private spot and Chloe would use her pendulum to locate Merlin's crystal. Its location would hopefully help them figure out who Rhianna was in league with. After that, they'd leave and exhume Saille's body as soon as possible, since that was a move the Council and Rhianna wouldn't expect them to make.

Satisfied that she didn't have any last-minute questions, Em climbed out of the truck and stuck close to Gar as he led them out of the garage and into an alley. Actually, calling it an alley was misleading—at least, it wasn't the kind of alley Em was used to hanging out in. There were no dumpsters. The pavement wasn't slimy with grease or cooking oil. No discarded syringes. No broken bottles. This was more of an artsy pedestrian walkway with potted trees and flowers. A small awning bowed across one section, sheltering café-style tables and chairs. The aroma of hamburgers, fries, and beer hung in the air. Even from where she stood, Em could tell other alleyways intersected with this one. In the distance, one of them opened onto New Haven's main street, with the park-like Green beyond that.

Sadness ached in Em's chest, and she had to look away from the Green. When they'd driven past it on their tour, she'd seen hundreds of ghosts there. It wasn't surprising, since the Green sat on the remains of a massive early cemetery. But it seemed like over the centuries the High Council should have helped more of the spirits find peace. It was truly awful and negligent.

Em pushed her thoughts of the ghosts aside as Gar herded them to a nondescript door in the back of the Council's brick building. The sign over it read: "Employee Entrance. No Trespassing."

He pressed a buzzer, then opened the door and held it to let everyone else go inside first. Chloe led the way, with Devlin on her heels. As Em started through, Gar trailed a finger across the nape of her neck. "You look amazing," he whispered.

Her face heated. Tingles rushed up her neck and across her scalp. "I figured I should try to look a little dressy."

"I wish we were going someplace private." His hand lit on her waist for a moment.

The heat in her face turned molten. She punched him playfully in the shoulder, then straightened her spine and marched through the doorway and into the building.

The entry was small, gunmetal gray, and box-like. A bank of elevators took up one wall. Another smaller door labeled "stairs" stood next to them. No windows. No alternate way out.

She tucked her hand into her jeans pocket and touched her A.A. medallion for strength—but her fingers brushed something else. Her knife.

She swallowed hard. Unlike the pick-a-roos, it wasn't in an undetectable case. "Gar," she said in a sharp whisper. "I have my knife on me. Is that okay?"

"Technically, no." He smiled and smoothed his hand down his forearm, a gesture she assumed meant he was wearing his dart gun device. Then he stepped ahead of her, a cool, businesslike air settling over him as he approached the elevator, where Chloe and Devlin were waiting.

"What floor are we going to?" Devlin asked.

"The fourth." Gar punched numbers into the keypad, announcing them one at a time. "1-0-31."

Em repeated the numbers to herself a couple of times to make sure she wouldn't forget.

The inside of the elevator was as sterile as the entryway. Faint classical music filtered in from overhead. Gar pressed the fourth-floor button. The elevator glided upward until it stopped smoothly.

Em stepped toward the door, waiting for it to open.

The music began to repeat the same droning song. A long second passed. Then a minute.

Gar stood perfectly still, staring ahead with his shoulders squared. Nervousness burned in Em's stomach. Sweat dribbled down her back. How long were they going to stand there?

She elbowed Chloe and widened her eyes to indicate her concern.

Chloe shook her head as if to say she had no idea what was going on.

The music stopped.

Em held her breath, expecting to sense the prickle of a magic scan or the choking sensation of deadly gas being pumped in through the air system. She was waiting for something—anything—to happen.

A woman's voice chirped, "Welcome Special Investigator Remillard, and guests. Your identifications have been verified. You may proceed."

The elevator door skated open. Em dashed out, grateful for freedom, and took a gulp of fresh air. But a healthy knot of worry remained lodged in her chest. She hadn't felt or seen a thing. How exactly had they identified her? At least they'd let her keep her knife.

Sticking close, Em followed Devlin and Gar into a museum-like vestibule. Floor-to-ceiling display cabinets, statuary, and paintings crowded every inch of the room. On either side, arched doorways led into wide corridors lit by dragon-shaped chandeliers.

As they passed the cabinets, Em took a closer look at their contents. One held only gauntlets and torques, studded with jewels and etched with images of faeries. Another cabinet contained bronze skulls. A glowing longbow hung in a black box. An oil painting depicted witches dancing naked under the light of a full moon. Swords. Scrolls. A summoner's bowl. Ancient things she couldn't identify.

An unusually dark watercolor in a black frame caught her eye. The background of the painting depicted a blood-smeared grave. In the foreground, demonic wraiths spun in glee, their hollow eye sockets enlarging into darkness and their elongated tongues flicking as their rotting flesh vaporized into a mass of putrid-green haze. Eyeballs were skewered on one the wraith's bony clawed fingers, like a disgusting shish kebab.

Chloe hooked her arm with Em's, snugging her close. "That's nasty."

"They're worse in person, take my word for it." Em hadn't encountered one in years, but that didn't make this reminder of their existence any less disturbing—wraiths were completely immoral and vicious.

Chloe shuddered, then quieted her voice even more. "The main museum is downstairs. It's amazing. But how they acquire items is less impressive. They *acquisitioned* a cauldron from my Aunt Holly last summer. It had been in my family for centuries."

"That would piss me off," Em said. She hugged herself and wondered if the Council had ever acquisitioned something from her ancestors. When they'd cursed the medium for what she'd done to Sarah Winchester, had they brought things like the medium's Book of Shadows here?

Gar's raised voice echoed the small vestibule. "This way," he said, leading them to the corridor on their left.

Doors lined one side of the corridor. Tall windows ran the length of the other side, with armed guards stationed between them, feet firmly planted, arms behind their backs, black shirts and pants perfectly pressed. The only other people around were two men in hooded robes, chatting a couple dozen yards down the hallway. Gar strode directly toward them, so fast Em had to jog a few steps to keep up.

As they approached, the men stopped talking and the taller one turned to greet Gar. His robe's gold-edged hood hid most of his face, but Em caught a glimpse of a cleft chin covered with a stubble of gray beard. She studied his hands, long and slender like a musician's, with dark brown skin. Gold rings etched with runes and studded with crystals encircled all his fingers, including his thumbs. A long green stole embroidered with gold constellations and other symbols of the Craft draped over his shoulders. Em's suspicion that he was a member of the High Council was based purely on the elegance of his attire, which conflicted with the basic black robe the man beside him wore.

"On time as expected," the tall man said to Gar. He brushed back his hood, his hawk-sharp eyes homing in on Gar's bruised nose. He chuckled. "Found yourself some trouble as usual, I see."

Gar ignored the comment and tilted his head toward a doorway a few yards down the corridor. "Is Morrell here yet?"

The man frowned. "Is there something specific you want to talk to him about?"

"I wanted to clarify that I plan on addressing the Council first by myself."

"That's smart. Keeping this as uncomplicated as possible would be preferable for everyone involved." He glanced meaningfully at Chloe.

Gar smiled. "She's here as the Northern Circle's new high priestess."

"That makes sense. However, it doesn't change my mind about keeping this simple."

"I feel the same way."

"I'm glad we're in agreement." The man stroked his stole, as if wiping away a wrinkle.

As the conversation switched to a discussion of protocol, Em stepped back from the group. The man didn't seem interested in her, and she preferred to keep it that way.

A prickle of magic traveled over her body and she realized that the shorter man in the black robe had his eyes trained on her. Even with his hood up, she could see his face clearly. He was around Gar's age, with tufty blond hair. His eyes were pinched and his skin had a gray-white sheen, like a damp raw clam.

Watch out for the voice of the dead. Watch out, the whisper of distant ghosts warned, voices so remote they most likely were reaching out to her from the Green.

"You're the infamous Violet Grace," he hissed. His gaze drove into her, his magic needling her skin as if reaching for her soul.

Em clenched her jaw and drew up her magic, blocking his intrusion before he could penetrate any deeper. She locked her eyes on his. "Violet Grace doesn't exist anymore."

"From what I hear, she was mostly a fraud anyway." His magic released her, the needling sensation gone in an instant. But she kept her eyes hard on his, anger rolling into fury.

Chloe's fingers clamped her arm. "We need to get to the waiting area."

"Right now," Devlin said, his voice stiff.

Em intensified her gaze, keeping it on the guy and pouring magic into it. There were hundreds of things she wanted to snarl at the jerk, but he wasn't the first to accuse her of fraud, and she was certain his probing had shown him the accusation was false. She was sure of something else as well. He might have worn a gold emblem of a cauldron encircled with leaves on his cloak, an insignia that most likely designated him as a potion master or something similar. But the ghosts had called him "voice of the dead," a term they sometimes used for mediums. He was a man who couldn't have missed the fact that Gar was haunted.

In one powerful stride, Gar closed the short distance been him and the pasty-faced guy. "Some of the most powerful witches have assumed the persona of a fraud." He loomed over the guy like a wolf sizing up a coyote, then turned his back on him and faced the taller man. His voice turned pleasant. "I'll see you shortly."

The Council member dipped his head, a smile playing at the corners of his mouth, as if the confrontation had amused him. "I'll tell the High Chancellor that you're here."

As Gar strode away from them and down the hallway, Em glued herself to his side. She could still feel the guy in the black robe watching her, which was more than a little disturbing.

"In here." Gar marshaled them through the doorway and into a reception room with windows that overlooked rooftops and buildings on the other side of a street. Upholstered chairs and potted palms ringed the edge of the room. In one corner, a computer, neatly stacked files, and someone's half-eaten sandwich sat on a desk. Next to the files, a selection of athames glistened in a glass box.

Gar steered them toward the far side of the room, to a group of chairs stationed under the windows. Em wanted to ask him about the men they'd met—especially the creepy asshole—but she kept it to herself. She didn't need another trip in the elevator to know it was wiser to stay quiet until they returned to the truck.

"I'll be right back," Gar said. "Fifteen minutes, at the most."

Though Em longed to hug him and wish him good luck, she nodded coolly and settled into a chair.

From where she sat, she had a partial view of the room Gar entered. He passed a narrow table with at least a dozen chairs along one side. In front of that, a single metal stool sat in a spotlight. It looked more like the setting for an interrogation than a hearing.

Chloe squeezed Em's hand. "Scared?"

"Kind of." Em laced her fingers with Chloe's, barely able to breathe as Gar vanished from her line of sight.

"It's going to be okay," Chloe whispered.

"I hope so." She released Chloe's hand. "You didn't happen to notice a drinking fountain? I'm so dry I can barely swallow."

"I didn't see one. I've got some mints, if that'll help?" Chloe pulled out a roll of Breath Savers and offered one to her.

"Thanks," Em said. A mint was a better idea than going back into the corridor. She took it and popped it into her mouth. It tasted spicy and clean, exactly like Gar's lips. Sick worry crept up her throat, killing the fresh taste. She spotted a bottle of water on the desk. Drinking it would help settle her stomach, but the bottle sat beside the half-eaten sandwich. Clearly it wasn't up for grabs.

Voices reverberated from the room Gar had disappeared into. Though she couldn't see who was talking, she could make out bits of the conversation.

"It's a waste of Council funds," a woman snarled.

A man scoffed. "We all know where this investigation is leading."

"The evidence isn't pointing in that direction," Gar stated flatly.

More voices joined in, arguing loudly.

One rose above the rest. "Isn't this supposed to be a closed meeting?"

A person in a white robe sprinted into view and pulled the doors shut, muting their voices so that Em couldn't understand a word.

She closed her eyes. *Please, please, please*, she prayed. *Dear Gods and Goddesses. Dear Alice, please watch over Gar. Take care of him and give him strength to get through this.*

The whoosh of a door opening brought Em from her prayers. Her eyes flashed open. The meeting couldn't be over this soon, could it?

She scanned the room, her hope dissolving when she discovered it wasn't the door to the hearing room that had opened. It was one beside the desk.

A long-legged brunette in spiked heels and a tight white dress darted out and to the desk without so much as a glance their way. She snatched the bottle of water and an athame, then retreated the way she'd come, closing the door behind her.

"Fuck," Chloe said, just above a whisper.

Em turned to see what was wrong. Chloe was hunkered down in her chair, head bowed as if she were attempting to stay out of sight. Devlin draped an arm around her. "Don't worry about it. She didn't even look your way."

Mystified, Em glanced from them to the door the woman had retreated through and back. "Who was that?"

Devlin's jaw tightened. "That was the Vice-Chancellor's wife."

"Oh, shit." Em gulped a breath. Just what they needed. She wouldn't have been surprised if they'd run into the Vice-Chancellor himself. He worked here. He was probably even in the meeting. But her? She was a cover model or something like that. "What's she doing here?"

Chloe groaned. "Whatever it is, it can't be good. The woman is a—" She stopped talking and touched her wrist, rubbing her fingers across her ever-present charm bracelet. "That's strange." She took the bracelet off and let the pendulum charm dangle down, like she'd done when she'd scried for Merlin's crystal.

The pendulum began to swing rhythmically, side-to-side.

"Did you ask it something?" Devlin said.

Chloe shook her head. "No. It started moving on its own—while it was still on my wrist."

Goose bumps crept up Em's arms. Chloe might not have intentionally asked the pendulum to locate anything, but they'd planned to use it to find the crystal later. "Maybe it sensed your intention," she suggested.

The pendulum stopped mid-swing, then lifted like a finger to point at the door the Vice-Chancellor's wife had vanished through.

"The crystal," Chloe whispered. "She has it."

Chapter 18

I bear no reflection
only rippled waters disturbed and unsettled.
—Journal of Emily Adams
Week two. New Dawn House. Albany, New York.

Chloe jumped to her feet and beelined for the door. Devlin lunged after her, seizing her arm and holding her back. "No, Chloe. We have to wait for Gar."

She wrenched from his grip. "Why do you think the Vice-Chancellor's wife is in a room next to the meeting? In the same room as the crystal."

Em looked from one to the other. Logic said waiting for Gar was smarter. Her heart told her Chloe was right.

"Quiet." Devlin put a finger to his lips. "They'll hear you."

Her voice lowered to a growl. "The Vice-Chancellor's wife is here to bear witness against the coven. That's the only explanation that makes sense."

Em shook her head. "But Rhianna put her blood on the crystal. Presenting it as evidence would only prove she was involved with us."

"I don't think we can afford to wait." Chloe whipped out her phone. "If Rhianna's in that room with the Vice-Chancellor's wife and the crystal, I'll record it. Then they can't accuse us of lying about their connection. This might be our only chance, while there still are Council members who aren't corrupt."

She stormed toward the door the Vice-Chancellor's wife had vanished through, Devlin an inch behind her. Em raced to catch up. If Rhianna was in there, proof of her presence in conjunction with the crystal could solve everything. If she wasn't there…well, it wasn't like they hadn't embarrassed themselves before.

Chloe flung the door open and they rushed inside.

The room was dark and tiny. Oil paintings of robed Council members covered the walls, leaving only enough space for one narrow window, a fireplace, and a second door that most likely led out into the main corridor. A ring of candles flickered on a desk, illuminating the silhouette of a tall, bleached blonde, who stood with her head bowed. In her cupped hands, an amethyst crystal the size of a peach sparkled, brighter than the purple jewels that encrusted the etched ring on her middle finger.

Though the woman's hair screened her face, Em recognized her in an instant. She wasn't the Vice-Chancellor's wife—she stood in the shadows behind the blonde.

The woman raised her head, her papery skin stretching tight across high cheekbones as a sneer lifted her lips. "Isn't this a pleasant surprise."

"Rhianna," Devlin snarled.

Her sneer widened into a jackal-like grin. "It's about time you crawled out from your hole." She licked her lips. "But it's too late to save your vile coven. The Northern Circle's time has run out." Her gaze sliced to a clock on the fireplace mantel. "Just about *now.*"

The Vice-Chancellor's wife tilted her head toward the door and cupped a hand to her ear. "Are those cheers I hear coming from the Council Chamber?"

"Shut up," Chloe screeched. "The meeting isn't even over yet." She flung her phone back into her pocket, every muscle tense, as if ready to draw up her magic and attack.

Devlin clamped his hand on her arm. "Don't. They're just trying to goad you into doing something you'll regret. You got what we need, right?"

"Yes, I think so," Chloe said.

A soft metallic *clink-clink-clink* sounded, as if one of them had dropped their pick-a-roo cylinder and it had rolled across the floor. A whiff of vinegar and sulfur prickled the inside of Em's nose. She glanced at Chloe. "We need to get out of here."

"What's wrong?" Chloe's voice caught on a gasp as fog surged through the room, coiling from ceiling to floor as if someone had set off a smoke grenade.

A shiver worked its way over Em's skin. It might have looked like a smoke grenade, but the chill in the air told her this wasn't the work of a mundane weapon.

BOOM! The sound echoed in from outside the building. Lightning flashed. The window rattled.

Rhianna wheeled toward Devlin, only her outline visible through the fog. "Clever distractions. But you're not going to cover your escape that easily. Time to face your judgment." A flash of magic crackled along her fingers as she whipped out a wand and pointed it at him.

"I have no intention of going anywhere, Rhianna." He gestured at the fog, toward the thunder and lightning outside the window. "None of this is my doing."

"You're damn right it's not us," Chloe added.

Em strained against the fog, reaching out with her eyesight and magic, searching for ghosts. Saille. Athena. Ghosts from the Green. Something supernatural that might have caused the havoc, if it wasn't a spell.

Another rumble boomed. Every hair on Em's body stood on end. Her instincts and sixth sense screamed for her to run. Another crack of lightning flashed. In the strobing brightness, Em glimpsed the Vice-Chancellor's wife scuttling away from Rhianna, slinking along the wall by the fireplace as she muttered, "Mote it be. Mote it be, dear Magus."

"We have to go now," Em said, as much to herself as to anyone else.

Another rumble.

Then silence. Long, drawn out, paralyzing silence.

Except for the *tick-tock* of the clock on the mantel.

Em sent her magic cautiously into the fog, looking for anything out of place. A wave of frenzied, otherworldly sensations rolled over her. Hunger. Lust. Excitement—

She slapped a hand over her mouth to smother a scream. Dear Goddess, it couldn't be…. It felt like Merlin's Shade.

A loud crack resounded, and the window shattered inward, glass exploding. Energy hissed into the room, sparking and wheeling through the fog like Chinese dragons. The air temperature plummeted further; Em's breath was now icy vapor.

"Get down," Devlin shouted.

Rhianna screeched.

The fog crackled and sizzled. Spears of window glass raked Em's cheek, razor-sharp as claws. She dropped to her knees and buried her face in her arms.

The floor seemed to buckle and shift, but Em's equilibrium remained intact, telling her at least part of the chaos was illusion, not reality.

Using her jacket's sleeve to protect her face from the flying glass, Em glanced up.

A sickly green haze braided with the fog. She could barely see Devlin and Chloe now, huddled only a few yards away. Farther into the room, the outline of the desk and the shimmer of Merlin's crystal showed under a beacon of light from Rhianna's wand. A dark, raggedy shape rose beside Rhianna, six feet tall and wider than a man.

Rhianna wheeled toward the dark shape. She thrust out her wand and shrieked, "Be gone!"

A dagger streaked from the shape and headed straight at Rhianna. Its blade glistened like liquid silver. It was shaped like an icicle.

"No!" Em shouted. Rhianna was a horrible person. She wanted the coven destroyed. But Em didn't want her—

Rhianna dodged aside. Too late. The dagger plunged into her chest, bright flashes of light blasting outward from the impact point. Sparking white. Sparking black. Rhianna exploded, a volcano of blood and flesh spraying the room. Gory dampness rained down over everything. The smell of burned cloth. Scorched hair. Rhianna's arms and legs splattered to the floor in a burbling and gelatinous mound. Her head landed on top of the pile.

"Guards!" the shout came from outside the room.

Em snapped back to her senses. Dozens of shouts flooded in from the reception room. The door flew open. A guard screeched to a halt, gaping at the gruesome sight. Behind him, robed witches streamed across the reception room toward the open doorway. Gar was pushing his way to the front of the pack.

"Help me!" The Vice-Chancellor's wife raced through the dissipating fog, waving her hands madly at Devlin and Chloe. "They killed her. They killed Rhianna."

"Are you crazy?" Devlin shouted. "That wasn't us."

"Murderers," the Vice-Chancellor's wife wailed.

Chloe swiveled toward the onrushing crowd. "We didn't do it!"

Em gestured at the gelatinous remains of Rhianna's body, preparing to tell what she'd seen. But Rhianna's equally gruesome ghost now shimmered where her living body had stood only moments ago. Her head was hairless, every vein clearly visible, pulsing and glowing bright blue against her paper-white skin. Her eyes were misshapen caverns.

Rhianna fixed her gaze on Em's, her mouth opening in a silent howl of terror as a group of tall, dark shapes and sickly haze spun around her, cocooning her until she was entirely enclosed.

The air pressure soared, cycling higher and higher by the second, singing in the air like a siren, just like the tug-of-war had the last time she heard it.

Em clamped her hands over her ears, struggling to block out the excruciating sensation. The Vice-Chancellor's wife fell to her knees, arms over her head. The guards and robed witches retreated into the reception room, squirming backward, trampling over each other as if they couldn't escape the pressure fast enough.

"Hecate, protect us," Chloe prayed, as every shard of glass and droplet of blood in the room began quivering like pudding. Just when Em thought her eardrums were going to break, there was a *pop* and the air pressure plummeted back to normal.

But the abnormal pressure wasn't the only thing gone. The cocoon of dark shapes and haze that had contained Rhianna's ghost had also disappeared, along with Merlin's crystal and the gelatinous mound of Rhianna's body parts.

The Vice-Chancellor's wife was back on her feet, screeching, "They did it! Murderers!"

"Don't let them escape," said a robed man, who flagged the guards forward toward the room.

Gar rushed through the doorway ahead of everyone. He pivoted, muscles flexed and ready to fight as he faced the onrush of guards. He glanced over his shoulder at Em. "There's a door behind you. Get out. Go."

He charged the guards, his fist catching one in the throat. Devlin was beside him, a blue energy ball blazing in his hands. Confusion boxed Em in. She couldn't think. She couldn't spot Chloe. But she had to get out. Had to run.

Em wheeled around and flew to the door. As she'd suspected, it opened into the corridor. The crack of energy balls hissed behind her. Gunshots. Screams. Smoke and the hiss of magic surged out into the hallway with her. The stairs. She had to take the stairs.

Panic crushed the air from her lungs. Where were the stairs?

Her pulse drummed in her ears. Sweat beaded on her temples. She gulped a breath. She had to relax, think. When they'd come into the building she'd seen a sign—in the entryway near the elevators.

She sprinted down the corridor toward the museum-like vestibule. *Please, please, let the stairs be there. Please.*

She reached the vestibule and spotted the stairwell sign beside the elevator. Guilt surged inside her. She glanced back down the corridor. Gar. Chloe. Devlin. She couldn't just leave them.

A flare of energy burst from the reception room's open doorway. Shouts. Screams. A guard's body flew out of a different doorway, cartwheeling backward and crashing into a window. A potted plant winged through the air, slamming into him. Robed people flooded from the rooms, swarming into the corridor. A guard appeared, running toward—

Fuck! Toward her.

She bolted for the stairwell door. Not locked. Gar had said she'd have three minutes before lockdown—or was it two?

She hit the stairs at a dead run. She'd escaped from a hospital before. She'd outrun Alice's dealer. Outrun the police. Outrun her aunt.

The soles of her shoes squawked as she slid around a landing. She skipped stairs, flying as much as touching steps. As she passed the door on the third-floor landing, the loud *click* of a lock snapping shut resounded. Other clicks echoed up and down the stairwell—locks automatically snapping shut above and below her.

Her mouth dried. Her pulse jackhammered. She raced downward, her hand in her pocket, holding onto the pick-a-roo cylinder. Second floor. First floor.

One door on the first landing went back into the building. The other door went to the entry with the bank of elevators, she was sure of that. But there wasn't a keyhole in the door. Only a keypad beside it. Damn, Midas. Why couldn't he have prepared her for this?

Em snatched the cylinder from her pocket and shook out a pick. She drew up her magic. But when she went to jam the pick into the keypad, her fingers fumbled, and she lost her grip.

The pick fell to the floor and rolled across the landing, over the edge of the stairwell and out of sight.

A sick feeling crawled into Em's throat. She gritted her teeth and willed calm into her shaking hands. She could do this. She had to.

She took out another pick, slowly wedged its pointed end into the narrow space between two keys in the middle of the pad, and commanded, "Sesame."

An electric prickle and a rhythmic pulse hummed up her wrist. She could hear the beat of magic in her head, an ancient song she couldn't quite remember the words to. Smoke rose from the pick and blue flames of magic licked outward.

She rested her hand on the door's thumb latch, head cocked as she listed closely for the lock to release. Gar had warned her the lock would reset if she waited a second too long.

The clank of a door opening reverberated down the stairwell from somewhere above her. The noise of distant voices flooded in, then silenced again as the door banged shut. Footsteps thundered on the stairs, heading down. Headed her way. *Fuck.* She had to get out now.

Click.

She flung the door open but closed it quietly behind her.

In an instant, she was past the bank of elevators and to the main door. She tried the latch. Locked, of course. But this time, her fingers knew what to do. She had the pick-a-roo out and the lock open in a heartbeat. She raced outside, the welcome chill of fresh air filling her lungs.

She glanced toward the parking garage. Gar's truck sat in the shadows. She looked in the opposite direction, down the alleyway, to the crowded street and beyond, to the city Green with all its ghosts. She could get lost in the traffic, the people, and spirits. Hide. Survive. She was a new initiate to the Northern Circle—Devlin and Chloe were the Council's priority. She was an afterthought they'd probably overlook. This mess wasn't her doing. If she ran, her aunt and mother wouldn't know where she was.

Her gaze caught on a couple sitting under the awning of an outdoor café, sipping beers and laughing. She'd be happy if she left. She'd be free.

An empty feeling took root in her chest, a familiar hollowness that twisted into an ache. Who was she kidding? That couple didn't reflect what her life would look like if she ran. Laughing and having a few beers would lead to stupors, blackouts, and throwing up every morning. Romance would lead to screwing strangers. Streets meant craziness. Loneliness. Hunger and worse. That wasn't freedom.

The door behind her flew open.

She yanked her knife from her pocket and spun to face them.

Gar rushed out. It must have been his footsteps she'd heard coming down the stairwell.

"Hurry." He took her by the arm, lending her strength as they ran for the truck.

A sense of joy washed over her, pushing aside her fears. She'd been wrong about what freedom was. Wrong for so long.

Chapter 19

Vodka. Tonic. Pickled eggs. Bags of lemons. Bags of limes. Credit. Debit.
Beer. Bud. Dirty glasses. Dirty hands. Eyes burn. Calves ache.
Burst of anger. Burst of words. Sharp. Shaking.
Stools up. Glasses dry. Go Home. Alone. Too afraid.
To peel away the loneliness.
—"Tired" by E. A.
Memory. Uncasville, Connecticut. 21 years old.

Em and Gar sprinted for the truck. As they reached it, Chloe and Devlin appeared, running toward them from the opposite direction. In another second, they were all inside, Em and Chloe in the back like before. Devlin and Gar in the front.

As Gar threw the truck into gear, Em leaned forward and clutched his shoulder. "Are you sure we should do this? Won't running only make us look guiltier?"

Gar floored the gas and the truck sped forward. "Believe me, we need to get out of here."

"But we didn't do anything," Chloe insisted.

A *crack* rang out as Gar slammed through the barrier arm, wood splintering and flying in every direction. Devlin looked at Chloe in the rearview mirror. "We don't have a choice. The Vice-Chancellor's wife has it out for you—or all of us. This was a setup."

"How could it have been?" Chloe asked. "The Vice-Chancellor's wife had no way of knowing we'd all show up to the meeting, let alone follow her into that room. That wasn't even our original plan."

"That's something we'll have to figure out later." Gar cranked the steering wheel, tires squealing as the truck shot from the garage and onto a side street.

Em glanced out the back window. No one was following them yet. "Do you think the Council called the police?"

"They'll come after us themselves. But you three should still get cleaned up, to be on the safe side. There are wipes in the glovebox."

"What are you talking about?" Chloe let out a yelp. "I think I'm going to be sick."

Em turned to see what was going on. Blood speckled Chloe's face and clothes. A fleshy string of something clung to her hair.

Nausea crept into Em's throat. She leaned forward to look at herself in the rearview mirror.

Something's coming! her sixth sense screamed.

Em gasped in anguish, the air pushing from her lungs. Her vision narrowed into a tunnel of darkness that ended in a pinpoint of light.

Uninvited. Uninvited, she shouted in her head. She raised a wall of energy to block the spirit's way. It slammed through her protection, entering her hot and fast.

Em's fingers curled into fists. Her jaw clenched. So much anger. So much frustration.

"What do you think happened to Rhianna?" Gar was asking, but his voice was remote, as if he were miles away.

"I'm not sure," Devlin answered, barely audible. "I sensed a strange energy. For a moment I almost thought Merlin's Shade was back. But that's impossible."

Impossible. Impossible. His voice echoed in the back of Em's head. She tried to open her mouth, to say she'd sensed the same thing—

Her hold on consciousness crumbled.

"Listen," Saille's voice snarls. "Listen for once in your damn life."

Em stands backstage at the Royal Palm Playhouse. In the wings.

Gar's voice comes from on stage, reciting Prospero's lines from The Tempest, *"... poisonous slave, got by the devil himself upon thy wicked dam, come forth!"*

Caliban appears. He swaggers to a mound of Rhianna's body parts in the middle of the stage. He draws a triangle around them, bearing down hard with his pencil until the graphite line is thick and sparkles gold. He places a yellow diamond on one corner of the triangle, another diamond on the second corner. He takes a third from his pocket, studying it. It's cracked and flawed but glistens faintly under the spotlight.

Three diamonds. Yellow diamonds. Triangles.

Em struggles to hold the symbols in her mind. She needs to remember them. Symbols are important. Triangle. The symbol of the Goddess. Solomon's Seal. Her aunt gave her a book to study symbols. It's important knowledge for psychics. Triangle. The symbol of fire. The symbol of earth, of air, of water. Pentagram. The valknut.

As Caliban bends to place the last diamond, he turns and leers at her.

Em's stomach tenses. Something awful is going to happen. She can't let him finish the ritual.

She races on stage. She pushes her legs to run, but the distance widens, growing greater and greater. She's not on stage anymore. She's in a cemetery, and Rhianna's spirit is rising out of a grave. The veins on her hairless head pulse and glow bright blue against her paper-white skin. Her eyes are misshapen caverns. Caliban towers over her.

"No!" Em screams.

"Listen to me," Saille's voice whispers in her head, a soft echo, as if she's withdrawing, like a runaway child sneaking home before their absence is discovered. "Caliban."

"Caliban," Em mumbled as she swam out of the vision, her consciousness creeping back. "Caliban. Triangle. Diamond."

Strong muscular arms surrounded her, scooping her up and clutching her close. Gar. His chest was warm and sizzled with magic. His neck smelled like moss and evergreens. His camo cap sat low over his eyes. He was cradling her close and walking quickly, like he had back when he'd helped her into the river to cool her overheated mind and body.

He nudged the bill of his cap up, then stroked her hair back from her face. "Are you okay?"

"Caliban," she slurred. It was important that she didn't forget.

She blinked her eyes open and her surroundings wavered into focus. Gar was carrying her away from the truck and through a small garage. The walls glowed with chalked sigils. Two tarp-covered motorcycles sat next to a wall. The outline of metal lockers darkened a corner. But it wasn't exactly a garage. Corrugated tin walls. Concrete floor. She'd spent the night with people who lived or had illegal businesses in places like this, people who could change their identities and vanish at a moment's notice.

"Storage unit?" she asked, to be sure she'd guessed right.

"We're changing cars." Gar toted her out of the unit to an older passenger van with windows all around. It was covered in dust, like it had been in storage for a while. The rear was jam-packed with duffel bags, pillows, a sleeping bag....

"Johnny?" she mumbled, her tongue still barely able to form words. She had a vague memory of a similar pile of stuff in the back of Johnny's truck all those years ago. Back when he'd given her his pseudonym instead of his real name.

"You never know when a rock-solid alias will come in handy," Gar whispered close to her ear. Then he kissed her cheek gently, and it struck Em that he was oddly relaxed—even more confident than usual, despite the dire situation they were in. Saille's current absence might have played a part in that, but she suspected it had more to do with his loup-garou and rebel sides being set free.

As they neared the van, Devlin came around from the other side to meet them. "We were all worried about you, Em," he said. "Do you know who possessed you?"

"Saille. There were symbols. Caliban from *The Tempest*."

"*The Tempest?*" Devlin scratched his head.

Gar shifted his grip, lowering her to the ground. "Can you stand?"

"I think so."

"Good. You can tell us all about the possession once we're back on the road. We need to get to Saratoga Springs or we'll never get Saille exhumed."

"The exhumation?" Em said. That was what they'd planned on doing after the hearing. It was part of what Saille wanted, too. But how far were they from Saratoga now? More importantly— "How long was I out? Where are we?"

"We're just north of New Haven. It's been fifteen minutes, twenty at the most."

Em's legs wobbled like a ragdoll's as Gar helped her into the back seat, where Chloe was already belted in and ready to go.

"We were worried about you," Chloe said, rubbing Em's leg. "Are you doing all right?"

"A little shaky. I'll be fine." She slid her hand across the woven seat cover. A pentagram made out of braided grass and small crystals dangled from the van's rearview mirror. Bundles of bay leaves and moss scented the air. There were even symbols painted on the floor mats. No doubt these things were intended to provide protection, and hopefully make them harder to track. Whatever their purpose, the magic they emitted warmed the air, radiating a sense of security very similar to what she'd felt when she was in Gar's arms.

Gar locked up the storage unit, leaving his truck inside. As he and Devlin jumped into the front seats, uneasiness shuddered through Em. She hugged herself against the feeling and cautiously reached out with her magic to see what was causing it. There weren't any nearby spirits—not even Saille or Athena.

She shook her head and dismissed the feeling. Of course she was on edge. She was exhausted, and dozens of the most powerful witches on the East Coast were hunting them—or soon would be.

"When you were out of it"—Chloe glanced at her and grimaced apologetically—"I hope you don't mind, but I cleaned up your face. But you might want to take off your jacket."

"Huh?" Em frowned in confusion. Then she remembered the blood raining down when Rhianna was killed and the speckles all over Chloe. She touched her face. Her skin felt smooth and clean. Not sticky at all. Now that she thought about it, she vaguely recalled the sensation of someone wiping her chin and forehead. But her jacket?

She wiped her hand down the sleeve of her beautiful new jacket. Her fingers came away tacky. Her stomach lurched. Now that she was paying attention, she could smell it too. The entire coat was splattered with blood, and worse.

"That's one of the jackets Keshari's family sells, isn't it?" Chloe asked. "Maybe her mother can get it clean."

"I couldn't ask her to do that. It's too…stained." Em peeled the jacket off and dropped it on the floor. It had been gorgeous and expensive, one of the nicest things she'd ever worn. But it was totally ruined, and Chandler was going to be pissed.

"Chloe?" Gar stopped talking as he drove across traffic and onto an interstate ramp. "Why don't you show Em the video."

"Video?" Em took the burner phone Chloe held in her hand. It was similar to her phone, not at all like Chloe's high-end one.

"It's Gar's secure phone," Chloe explained. "I transferred the video I took of Rhianna onto this one. We didn't want the Council to be able to track us, so we left our phones in the truck. Ah—including yours." An apology shone in her eyes and she swiftly added, "I didn't take anything else of yours."

Now that Em thought about it, she didn't recall feeling the weight of the phone when she'd taken her jacket off. She smiled at Chloe. "Don't worry about it. My therapist is the only person who might call. I'd rather not answer than lie to her about what's going on."

As she thought about her therapist and the halfway house, her aunt passed through her mind. If her aunt had managed to get her address from someone at the halfway house, her phone was probably compromised as well, and a call from her aunt was another one she'd just as soon miss altogether.

"Look at the video." Chloe poked her hand. "Unfortunately, I stopped recording before the worst stuff happened."

Gar spoke up. "Watch carefully. Tell me if you see anything familiar, from real life, dreams, visions, or whatever."

Em angled the phone so she could see the screen more clearly. A ring of candles flickered on the desk, just like she remembered. Rhianna stood with her head bowed, her thin blond hair screening her face. Merlin's crystal sparkled in her cupped hands, even brighter than the purple jewels that encrusted the etched ring on her middle finger. Behind her, the Vice-Chancellor's wife stood in the shadows, her hands at her sides and her lips unmoving, nothing to indicate she was working a spell. Rhianna lifted her head and a sneer crossed her lips.

"Rhianna," Devlin snarled.

Her sneer widened into a jackal-like grin. "It's about time you crawled out of your hole." She licked her lips. "But it's too late to save your vile coven. The Northern Circle's time has run out just about"—her gaze went to a clock on the fireplace mantel—"*now.*"

The Vice-Chancellor's wife cupped her hand to her ear. "Are those cheers I hear coming from the Council Chamber?"

"Shut up," Chloe screeched.

The video ended.

Em rubbed her lips, thinking back through what she'd seen. She was sure her answer wasn't what they were hoping for. "Um, I hate to say it, but I didn't see anything strange. Merlin's crystal is there. I think Rhianna was wearing the Northern Circle's signet ring. Is that what you wanted me to see? She's wearing the ring turned around backward, hiding the Circle's insignia."

Devlin whipped around in his seat, looking at her with undisguised shock. "I hadn't noticed that. I assumed the high priestess ring was at the complex, in Athena's jewelry safe."

"If you're right about the ring, that's pretty damning evidence." Gar glanced at Em in the rearview mirror. "But it's not what I wanted you to look at."

Em thought again. "I remember the Vice-Chancellor's wife muttering something like, 'mote it be, dear Magus.' It was odd, but that was after the video ended. It was probably just a prayer to her guardian angel."

"Could be," Gar said. "We should keep it in mind, though."

Chloe leaned closer and pointed her finger at the phone's screen. "Watch it again. This time, focus on the window behind Rhianna."

Em rolled her shoulders, giving herself a second to regroup. Gar was driving faster now, speeding north on I-91. Once they turned onto I-90, they'd drive right past Westfield, where she'd helped the police find a little girl's body, skyrocketing her to fame at ten years old. She'd seen wraiths for the first time that day.

Em grimaced and shook her head, freeing it from that terrifying memory. Why was she thinking about that right now? It was hardly relaxing.

Taking a deep breath, she started the video again.

The Vice-Chancellor's wife stood in the shadows behind Rhianna, just to one side of the window. Outside, something fog-like materialized, the size of a large hand with bony clawed fingers, creeping upward.

Em stilled the video and stared at it, unblinking. It couldn't be.

She touched her cheek, feeling the cut she'd gotten during the craziness. She'd decided it was from a piece of flying glass, but it had felt like claws had scratched her. Bony fingers. Nasty smells and haze. Her subconscious had been trying to tell her. She was looking at a video of a wraith—and she wasn't far from where she'd seen a pack of them that day when she was ten years old.

"You see it, don't you?" Chloe asked.

A chill shuddered through Em. She nodded, though she wished with all her heart that she could say no. "It's a wraith's hand. Fully materialized."

Chloe snatched the phone from her, studying the stilled video. "You're sure it's a wraith?"

"I've seen them before. Technically, a demonic wraith. Like in the painting at headquarters." Her breath caught on a gasp as a connection formed between the technical term for the horrifying entity in the video and the vision she'd had during the possession. Wraiths. Demons. Caliban.

"What is it?" Chloe asked. "Was that what killed Rhianna—a demonic wraith?"

"Maybe. But there's more to it."

Devlin turned to face her. "I sensed something else in the office. But before I say anything, I want to know what you're thinking."

As disoriented as Em had felt only a short time ago, now her thoughts were clear and confident. Spirits. Wraiths. The dead. These were things she understood. "The thing is, wraiths are filled with bloodlust. But they don't have the brains or the skills to create even the smallest spell, let alone orchestrate the complex things that happened in that room. But I think I know who—or more precisely what—is controlling them. I'm not talking about the Vice-Chancellor's wife. Her involvement is secondary."

"I'm assuming this has something to do with what Saille's been showing you?" Gar asked.

"Exactly." Em looked toward Devlin. "I know what you sensed. Before I totally blacked out, I heard you say that you felt something that reminded you of Merlin's Shade. I did too. But it didn't feel precisely the same."

Gar prodded for her to go on. "And the visions?"

"At one point, I pretty much lived in a theater. I saw *The Tempest* so many times that I memorized it. There's one line from the play that Saille keeps repeating: '… poisonous slave, got by the devil himself upon thy wicked dam, come forth!' That line is about the character Caliban's parentage. His mother was a witch and his father a demon. He was a cambion."

Chloe shook her head. "Maybe I'm being dense. I know the play. But how does that connect to what's going on?"

"Of course you know." Em grinned. "Merlin's father was a demon. Merlin is a cambion, same as Caliban. That's why the energy Devlin and I sensed felt like Merlin's Shade. It was cambion magic."

Devlin groaned. "I'm willing to bet there's some connection between this one and Merlin's Shade."

"A connection like Rhianna?" Gar suggested.

"And how about the Magus that the Vice-Chancellor's wife mentioned?" Em said. "Magician and Magus are similar titles—as in, Merlin the Magician and Cambion so-and-so the Magus?"

Chloe paled. "For the love of Hecate, I think you're right."

Em rested back in her seat. Despite how terrifying the situation was, a warm sense of satisfaction settled over her. One thing was for sure: They were headed in the right direction going to Saratoga Springs. Saille wanted someone to prove she was poisoned, and she was warning them that a cambion was somehow involved in the whole tangled mess—perhaps a cambion who went by the title of Magus.

She turned, looking out the side window at the passing fields and hills. Houses. A church. A gazebo. A park…

Another car ride surfaced in her mind, one she'd taken over six months ago, in the back of a police cruiser. That night, she'd made a choice to take a new path. Until now, she'd assumed that meant living clean and sober. But it had been more than that. It was also a choice to face what was in front of her instead of running away from it. She'd known it wouldn't be easy, but she'd also understood it would make all the difference, for Saille and others as well, the living and the dead.

It looked like Saille hadn't lied. Not at all.

Chapter 20

I am left crippled by your words,
an animal cut open and flung to the side of a road,
discarded to spoil and bake in the sun.
—*"Mother" by E. A.*

"Tell your grandfather to bring his dog," Gar said, taking his gaze off the interstate to glance at Devlin.

Devlin shifted the phone away from his ear and covered it with his hand. "His dog?"

"That's what I said. One hour. Just south of Albany. Ten Birdland Road. With his dog. He has one, right?"

Em frowned, as puzzled as Devlin about the need for a dog. They'd all agreed that the only way they were going to pull off exhuming Saille and getting her body to the Council for retesting was to have outside help. Zeus was the obvious choice. They could trust him, and the lingering rumors against Zeus would be outweighed by the vested interests the High Chancellor and others had in his business ventures. In turn, Gar had recommended 10 Birdland Road as a secure meeting spot.

"It's a veterinarian's office," Gar clarified. "The Council could be monitoring Zeus. Just in case, the dog will make his visit look less suspicious."

That made sense. However, when they got to Birdland Veterinarian Clinic an hour later, Em found herself puzzled once again. The clinic was in a rambling farm house that looked disturbingly familiar to her. It wasn't a sense of déjà vu; it was more like how she'd felt earlier, when she'd seen the sleeping bags and supplies piled in the back of Gar's van. A hazy, almost imagined recognition.

As Gar pulled up in front of the building and parked next to a silver Volvo, she studied the old building. It probably resembled a house she'd done a reading at as a child.

"That's Zeus's Volvo," Devlin said, opening his door. "He must already be inside." He glanced at Chloe. "Are you coming?"

She shook her head. "You guys go ahead. I'm going to stay here and email copies of the video, along with an explanation, to the Council and everyone in the coven."

"Good idea." Gar undid his seatbelt. "Come get us if you see or sense anything suspicious."

"Will do."

As Em climbed out of the van and followed him, another reason she might remember the house came to her. She caught up with Gar and snagged the back of his coat to slow him down and allow Devlin to go into the building ahead of them. Then she lowered her voice. "Should this place look familiar to me?"

He nodded. "She wasn't a vet back then, but yes. This is where your ID came from." His voice turned wistful. "She's done a lot for me over the years."

"That's cool," Em managed to say, despite a twinge of totally unjustified jealousy toward the unknown woman. She had no right to feel that way. She didn't even know her. Still, it was hard to hear Gar talk fondly about someone who was everything she wasn't: educated and smart, and a humanitarian as well. It made Em feel like a total lowlife, especially since Gar had known this woman back when Em was homeless, drunken jailbait.

Em felt the press of Gar's hand against her waist. He bent closer to her and whispered, "Can you still sense Saille around me? I'm feeling…almost too good. Sharp. Together."

The jealousy subsided, overtaken by worry. "Honestly? I'm not sure. Sometimes I faintly sense a thread of her attachment to you, then it's gone. But hauntings don't vanish until the ghost is at peace, and Saille definitely isn't at peace. It's strange."

Gar released her waist and opened the office door. He laughed nervously. "Feeling good shouldn't be a bad thing."

"Let's hope it isn't," Em said.

The reception room was sunny, the floor tiled, and the walls decorated with children's crayon drawings of birds and strange, wolfish dogs. A teenage girl in green scrubs sat behind the counter.

"I'm looking for the man who just came in," Devlin said to her. "White hair. Beard."

The girl got to her feet. "He's waiting down the hall. I'll take you to him." As she came around the counter, her gaze went to Gar. "Your sister wanted me to apologize for her. She was called out on an emergency. She said I should give you whatever you want."

"We don't need anything, except maybe shovels—two if you can spare them," Gar said.

"Sure. I'll put a couple in your van."

Sister? Em glanced at the framed credentials that hung on the wall, some for a Dr. Charles Birdland, and others for Dr. Lea Remillard-Birdland. "This is your sister's office?"

Gar slapped his forehead. "Oh, shit. I'm sorry. I meant to say something. Yeah, she and her husband are both vets. My family's super proud of them and everything they do for the pack."

"That's understandable. I wish I could have met her."

"Me too," he said.

As the girl led them down a hallway with closed doors on both sides, Em smiled to herself, feeling as unjustifiably relieved as her jealousy had felt earlier. Gar was not only amazing: his family was too.

The girl steered them into an examination room at the end of the hall. Most of the space was taken up by a steel-topped exam table. There was a metal chair and a window with magazines on the ledge. Zeus stood by the window. Between the beret that topped his styled white hair, his trimmed beard, and his expensive leather jacket, he looked like he'd stepped out of an advertisement for top-shelf cognac. Beside him, a sleek Doberman sat statue-still, the perfect companion. Zeus nodded a brisk greeting.

"Would you like coffees, or something else to drink?" the girl asked.

"We're fine." Gar shooed her out. He shut the door, then turned to face everyone. "I believe we can skip the introductions?"

Zeus dipped his head. "I know who you are. And, of course, I'm quite familiar with everyone else. Let's get down to business. What exactly is going on?"

Devlin gave him a rundown of what had happened at the Council headquarters, about what Em had seen while possessed, and Saille haunting Gar. Basically everything Zeus hadn't known already, plus their current plans.

Em tucked her hands into her pockets and stepped behind everyone else, listening and glancing at the dog while Devlin went on. Despite his statue-like pose, the dog's ears twitched, and his eyes widened and narrowed as if he had something important on his mind. He whined, and Em wondered if he was as uncomfortable about the cell-like feeling of the room and lack of a second exit as she was.

Zeus took a firmer grip on the dog's collar. "If I'm hearing you correctly," he said to Devlin, "you intend to risk being caught grave robbing so someone—I assume me—can take Saille's body to the Council and make sure a more thorough exam is done, one that includes toxicology tests." The dog fixed his gaze on Gar, his whine becoming an insistent whimper. Zeus gave his collar a jerk. "To reiterate what I've said in the past, disbanding the coven before the Council orders it is the most sensible and financially wise route for everyone involved. It's certainly wiser than this hairbrained, dangerous scheme."

"You're wrong." Devlin thumped his fist on the exam table. "It's time to prove the Circle's innocence—and yours—once and for all."

Gar squared his shoulders. "I'm not going to lie and say I don't have concerns about the incident with Merlin's Shade. But I agree with Devlin about exhuming Saille."

Zeus chuckled. "You would. I remember your mother, Gar."

"What exactly do you remember?" Heated sarcasm hardened Gar's voice. But Em didn't sense a rise in Saille's presence. His anger came only from the need to defend someone he loved deeply. "Are you saying there's something wrong with my mother because she was young and in love? Or is it because she married a loup-garou?"

Sweat beaded on Zeus's temples. "Your mother certainly didn't feel any allegiance to Saille."

"That doesn't mean she didn't love her." Gar narrowed his eyes on Zeus, his voice growling. "What about you, was Saille good to you? Would she have let your murder go uninvestigated?"

Zeus took his hand off his dog's collar to dab the sweat away. The dog bolted to Gar and hunkered down submissively, tail flailing in utter joy. Gar crouched, let the dog sniff his palm, and sent him back to Zeus with a flick of his fingers.

"Traitor," Zeus harrumphed, and glared down at the dog. His attention went back to Gar. He shrugged. "I suppose you're right. We—all of us— could stand to be more like Saille, and Athena, for that matter. I still don't think this is the wisest route."

"But you're going to help us?" Devlin asked.

Em crept forward a step and crossed her fingers in hopes that Zeus would agree.

Zeus took off his beret and scrunched it between his hands. Then he put it back on and nodded. "Against my better judgment."

Relief went through Em and she let out a long breath.

Devlin clasped Zeus's hand in a firm, double-handed shake. "You won't regret this."

"We'll see about that," Zeus grumbled.

Gar held out his hand. "We really do appreciate this."

Zeus got out his phone and brought up a map to show them not only which cemetery Saille was buried in, but also exactly where her grave was located. He also reassured them that her casket had been placed directly in the earth, not in a concrete burial vault as was now required by law.

"I won't play any part in the retrieval," Zeus said. "But if you meet me back here tomorrow at dawn, I'll see to it that her body gets to the Council and is examined properly." His nose crinkled as he scanned Devlin from head to toe. "I have one more suggestion. You—all of you—are a mess. Unless you want to draw attention to yourselves, I suggest you find some clean clothes. You smell as rank as a butcher shop."

Em cringed. She glanced at her jeans, and an intense awareness of the blood spray hidden by their dark color came over her. Zeus was right.

She stepped up next to Gar. "I've got a suggestion about that." They all turned to look at her, as if surprised to hear her speak up. "There's a Goodwill just north of Albany."

No sooner had the suggestion left her mouth than Em wished she could reel it back in.

Sure, she knew firsthand the Goodwill shop was nice, and that she'd be able to buy everything she needed with the cash in her pocket. But Chloe and Devlin didn't wear clothes like that. Zeus certainly didn't either. The dog's collar probably cost more than her entire wardrobe.

"That's a great idea." Devlin sounded thrilled. "I've been trying not to complain, but I feel disgusting. Not to mention that I'd glow like a lava lamp if the police spritzed me with luminol."

Gar slung his arm over her shoulder and she leaned against him, relieved that Devlin liked her idea and glad that everything was going to be okay.

But then a sinking feeling dropped into her stomach. Despite how much she wanted to pretend everything was fine, she couldn't believe it. If anything, the situation was about to get worse—and a lot more dangerous.

Chapter 21

I buy a packaged sandwich and climb three flights of stairs to my room.
The carpet smells of vomit. Water trickles from the shower.
But there is a bolt on the door and I'm only there for one night.
I tell myself a bare mattress is cleaner than sheets a stranger slept on.
—Journal of Emily Adams
Memory. Late Winter. Albany, New York. 21 years old.

Dozens of ghosts with sheets for bodies and skeleton-mask faces hung from the ceiling of the Goodwill store. Giant spiderwebs spanned bins of trick-or-treat buckets and racks of secondhand costumes. Mothers and kids and teenagers crowded every aisle. Long lines snaked from the checkout counters. Em was surprised to find the place so packed with shoppers. After all, Halloween was still two weeks away.

As she followed Chloe deeper into the store, her sixth sense alerted her. Sadness. Loneliness. The emotions—and whispers—of real, not pretend, ghosts filled her head, and a lot more of them than she'd experienced the last time she was in the store.

She tucked her hands in her pockets, guilt tumbling inside her as her desire to help the spirits find peace collided with the more vital need to get in and out without raising attention. She should have expected this. It wasn't unusual for ghosts to haunt items that ended up in thrift stores, or for them to become more active when they sensed her presence.

Gar nudged her in the ribs. "Get what you need." He shoved a wad of cash at her. "I'm going to wait in the van."

"But—" She started to argue, then noticed he'd snugged his cap on extra low, its brim hiding his eyes and concealing any emotion they might betray. That—along with the sweaty dampness of the cash—clued her into what was going on. Gar might have held his own in front of the Council, but a shopping frenzy was way outside his comfort zone. "What size do you wear?"

"Don't worry about me. I didn't get...dirty." His gaze went to a mob of teenage girls tearing through a case of junk jewelry. "Good luck."

"I'm out of here too." Devlin turned to follow Gar.

"Okay, I guess," Chloe said, clearly surprised he was leaving. "What do you want me to get for you?"

"A light coat or hoodie. Nothing fancy, just hurry. All right?"

Chloe waved him off. "Sure. Fastest shopping trip ever."

Em bit her bottom lip, holding back a smile. Then she glanced at the bundle of cash in her hand. Twenties. Fifties. Generous to a fault, like Johnny had been.

It didn't take much time to find a quilted jacket for Devlin. After that, Em led the way to the women's section. Other than the larger-than-usual crowd, the place hadn't changed since she visited with people from the halfway house.

As they started to make their way along a sweater rack, an uneasy feeling came over Em. She went up on her tiptoes and looked over the racks, scanning the crowd for someone familiar who her senses might have picked up on. Maybe her therapist, or someone else from the halfway house. Or, worse yet, someone from the Council, like the asshole medium with the pasty-clam complexion.

Em hugged herself. She couldn't be picking up on her aunt or mother's presence, could she?

She shook her head, answering her own question with a resounding *no*. If they were anywhere, they were headed to Burlington to look for her. Besides, now that she had taken more time to focus on the sensation, she realized it wasn't from the proximity of a familiar person. It wasn't about ghosts or her turning her back on them, either. This was the same creeping sense of uneasiness that she'd felt in the van earlier—a warning from her subconscious that she was missing, or forgetting, something important.

"This would look great on you." Chloe held up a charcoal-gray cable-knit sweater against Em's chest as if checking for size. "Comfy, and the perfect color for...nighttime activities."

"Yeah. Perfect," Em said, her thoughts still focused on remembering the something that refused to come to her. What was it?

Chloe frowned. "Something bothering you?"

"I've got this weird feeling something's wrong." She hushed her voice even more. "Do you sense anything? Magic or whatever?"

"No. But we have every reason to be worried." Chloe turned back to the rack of sweaters. "Let me just grab a bunch of things really fast. We'll try them on, then get out of here."

Chloe snagged a few more sweaters. Then she found an empty shopping cart, wheeled it to the jeans, and started tossing pants into it. Em hung back, letting her do it all. This wasn't a pleasure visit, and Chloe was the shopping expert.

In less than five minutes, they were in a dressing room. In another two, they'd made their choices. Em gathered up her things and was about to leave when Chloe stopped her. "Wait a minute. I know we're in a hurry, but there's something I have to talk to you about—while we're alone."

Chloe's serious expression stopped Em in her tracks. "Sure. Anything. Don't worry, I can keep a secret."

Chloe fiddled with her charm bracelet. "It's not exactly a secret. If anything, that's kind of the point. You and Gar—are you sure getting involved with him is smart? You barely know him."

Heat rushed up Em's chest and neck, flooding her face. Anger sharpened her voice. "You haven't known Devlin much longer, and you two are like an old married couple."

"I just don't want to see you hurt."

Em turned her back on Chloe. She clenched her teeth so hard her jaw hurt. "There's nothing to worry about. Gar and me, we just connected. Neither of us expect it to go anywhere."

"Don't lie to me, Em." Chloe's tone gentled. "Your magic makes little sparking noises whenever he's around you. I can see it in the way you look at him, too." Her voice lowered to a whisper. "The sex, the being with someone, it means a lot to you."

"Maybe. But I'm not naive, or stupid." She longed to tell Chloe more about her and Gar's past, about Johnny and how much he'd meant to her, but she'd promised to keep his alter ego a secret.

"You're setting yourself up for a heartache. You haven't been sober that long. You moved to a strange town, then the stuff with Merlin's Shade happened. Gar arrived—"

Em swung back around, glaring at Chloe. "If you're trying to say that Gar was horny and I was an easy mark, it's not that. He's a nice guy. If he has any fault, it's his stubborn loyalty to the Council. I wish as much as you that he'd totally believe us about Athena's death and Merlin's Shade, that he'd reject what the Council told him about what happened. But he's on our side now, because as much as he believes in loyalty, he believes in justice more."

Chloe smirked. "Now you're being honest."

Em realized she'd been baited and snapped her mouth shut before anything else could slip out.

"I'm not blaming you for getting involved with him. I'll admit, I'm starting to like him myself. But we can't forget that even before the Council sent him to investigate, he had it out for the Circle because of his family's love for Saille."

The tension drained from Em's muscles. She loosened her grip on the clothes and nodded, the truth behind Chloe's words twisting in her chest. "Everything comes down to Saille, doesn't it? If we can prove Rhianna poisoned her, or if she was murdered at all."

"It seems so." Chloe smiled. "Just remember, you can count on me. No matter which way things turn out."

"Thanks," Em said, and she meant it.

Chloe opened the dressing room door, and they tossed the clothes they wanted into the shopping cart and started for the checkout. But they only made it a few yards before Em's sixth sense began to tug at her.

Please. Can't you hear me? See me? a ghostly voice whispered.

Em blocked out the voice and stared straight ahead as they wheeled the cart toward the front of the store. Without taking time to locate and talk to the ghost, there was no way to tell what was going on, other than it was trapped in the Goodwill store. She didn't have time for that right now, and it wasn't like she was ignoring all the spirits who reached out to her. They were on a mission to help Saille, after all.

Chloe stationed the cart at the end of the shortest checkout line, behind a woman with a mound of clothes the size of a Volkswagen. Em eyed that stack, then their own. This was going to take forever.

Em's neck and scalp prickled, her sixth sense nagging at her once more. *Please. Hear me. See me.*

Chloe elbowed Em, then lifted her chin, indicating the store's front windows. Beyond the glass, in the parking lot, Devlin and Gar were climbing into the van with what looked like coffees and bags of fast food.

"That's good," Em said, unable to come up with anything more astute thanks to the ghost's voice pulling at her heart and body.

Please. Can you hear me? Lonely. Lonely.

"I wonder what they bought? I'm starving." Chloe's gaze flitted from the window to the exit door, like she was contemplating taking off.

Lonely. So lonely.

Em gritted her teeth. *To heck with it*, she decided. If she was going to do this, she needed to move before Chloe did. She took out Gar's cash and shoved it at Chloe. "Take this. I've got to go to the restroom."

Before Chloe could respond, Em sped away from the checkout and toward her fake destination. She veered into sweater alley, ducking down a little so the top of her head wasn't visible. Drawing up her magic, she focused on the tug of the ghost. It led her past the displays of socks and hats. Her vision narrowed. The smell of mildew filled her nose as she went through a doorway into the home goods section. Sagging sofas. Bunk beds. Air conditioners. Kitchen cabinets. A basket of soiled Raggedy Ann dolls.

Another room. Cramped. Dimly lit.

Hear me. See me.

Em's fingertips glided over a smooth desktop. Over the slick covers of magazines. Paperback books. The scent of an old library. A narrow alleyway, bookstacks rising like canyons on either side of her, up to a water-stained ceiling.

The tug released her.

Em shook her head, bringing herself out of the daze.

She stood in the far back corner of the Goodwill's cramped bookroom. From what she could hear and sense, no living people were in the room, only a single spirit. Close. Down low to the floor.

The fully materialized ghost huddled under a library table.

It was a woman, her straight black hair held back by a pair of tortoiseshell barrettes. Yoga pants—speckled with food stains and what was most likely dog hair—sagged over her shrunken body. She pulled her knees to her chest and gazed up at Em with limpid blue eyes, much too cavernous for a living human.

Em crouched. She needed to do this fast and quietly so as not to draw attention to herself, though talking to a materialized ghost was less conspicuous than ones who were invisible.

She hushed her voice. "Tell me. What's wrong?"

"Lonely," the ghost crooned.

"Can you see the light? A bright tunnel? It's warm there. Lots of people to talk to." As a rule, she never said family was waiting, at least not until the ghost mentioned missing them. Personally, she'd never go to any light if her aunt was waiting there.

The ghost's lips pinched into a stubborn line. Her eyes contracted into black beads. "Must stay. Books. Lonely."

Em scrubbed her hands over her face. "You don't have to stay. Let go."

"Books. Lost. Lonely." The ghost's voice roared with frustration and she leaned forward, fingernails digging into the carpet, like a cat readying to spring forward.

"Lost books? Tell me. I'm here to help." Em couldn't begin to figure out what she meant, but clearly the ghost's frustration was moving toward rage. "Tell me what you need."

The ghost sat back on her haunches, her jaw working. "Books. My books. He stole them. Kept jewels." She sprung to her feet and flagged her arms, indicating the old leather-bound books that overflowed cases on either side of the desk. "My orphaned books. Abandoned. Must find homes. Can't rest. Lonely. So lonely here."

As crazy as it was, Em got what she meant this time. Someone had stolen the ghost's book collection and kept only the best volumes, the jewels of her collection. The rest had ended up at Goodwill. The theft likely involved murder for the ghost to be so attached. But maybe not. She'd met spirits obsessed in death with things they collected in life.

Em scanned the books, taking a quick inventory. She couldn't buy them all, now or later. But she had to do something before this spirit started throwing things around and scratching people—if she hadn't already.

"Lonely," the ghost repeated.

Lonely. Em smiled and gave the ghost's fur-coated yoga pants another look. It might not work, then again... "Do you like kittens?"

The ghost's eyes returned to crystal blue caverns. "Yes. Love. Kitties. Puppies."

"I'm not promising, but let me try something."

Em closed her eyes, willing her mind to go back to the A.A. meeting when she'd first felt the sensation of the small spirit, crying for her help. She brought back the more recent memory from the séance, when she'd heard the kitten's mews and felt it bat her ankle. Kittens. So many of them, their tails glowing like torches in the darkness.

She pulled up her magic, releasing the feeling of the floor beneath her feet and the bookstacks all around her. She cast her magic out into the universe, calling out to the kittens with only one intention in her mind: offering them a home and letting them feel the lonely spirit in front of her.

Darkness closed in around Em as her spirit left her body, moved beyond the walls of the store and toward the edge of oblivion. Reaching out. Calling out...

Something brushed her ankle. Something mewed.

Em's eye flickered open. Her head still whirled, but she could see the ghost woman, now a fading haze mingling with the glowing shape of circling kittens.

Thank you. Thank you, the ghost's voice whispered.

"Excuse me," a man said tartly, jolting Em fully back to her senses. "Do you mind? I'd like to get to that shelf."

Her face heated with embarrassment and she scrambled aside to let the guy pass. She couldn't imagine what the man thought she'd been doing.

A voice touched her ear. *Listen.*

For a panicked second, Em thought it might be Saille telling her to listen again. She wheeled around, half expecting to see her. But the only ghosts were the fading woman under the library desk and the kittens.

The ghost woman looked up at her. *Listen. He has them. My jewels. Your priestesses.*

"Who?" Em asked, not caring if the man thought she was nuts. This ghost knew something. Something important. "Who has them?"

The cambion. Magus Dux. Stop him.

The ghost's energy refocused on the kittens, and Em could only watch helplessly as she fell silent and vanished.

Chapter 22

NANTUCKET, MA—Police suspect link between brutal murder and recent theft. Last month, Mary Reed was found stabbed to death and dismembered outside her Willow Street home. When appraiser Bill Ryan arrived this week to evaluate Reed's estate, he discovered her library of valuable books missing.
    —From *Antiquarian Weekly*, November 26

By the time Em raced out to the van, the security lights were flickering on in the parking lot. When she jumped in, her mouth began to water at the smell of coffee and what she guessed were submarine sandwiches.

Chloe passed a coffee cup to her. "Devlin bought some stuff for dinner too. We thought we'd eat once we get settled in the motel room."

"Motel?" Em set her coffee into a cup holder.

"Gar booked us a room at a motel that borders the cemetery where Saille is buried. I think it's a great idea. All we have to do is climb over a security fence and we're there."

"Between Devlin and I," Gar said, starting the van, "we shouldn't have a problem carrying the corpse."

"We'll need a duffel bag or something to put Saille's body in." Devlin's voice choked and pressed his hands over his face, like he'd done earlier, when thoughts of Athena's death had overwhelmed him.

His sorrow went straight to Em's heart. But she had news that might take his mind off the loss, at least briefly. She raised her voice. "Guys, I have to tell you something. You're not going to believe what happened. I know for sure a cambion has Saille and Athena. His name's Magus Dux."

Everyone turned to gape at her. It was lucky they were still parked—judging by the shock on Gar's face, he might have driven off the road.

"How the hell did you find that out?" he asked.

"I was on my way out of the restroom…" She started with a fib, then told them the rest exactly as it had happened, detail by detail, finishing up by repeating the name the ghost had used. "Magus Dux—and she said we had to stop him."

Devlin studied her face. His eyes beamed with cautious hope. "Are you sure the ghost said 'priestesses,' as in, more than one?"

"Hundred percent sure."

"But she didn't mention Athena by name?" he asked.

"No. She didn't mention Saille either. But it's the only thing that makes sense. Both of them were high priestesses, right?" Worry twisted inside her. She didn't want to mislead Devlin, or give him false hope that Athena could be alive despite everything they knew. "When I say 'they,' I mean Athena and Saille's spirits. Think about it. I felt the identical rise in air pressure and tug-of-war sensations working against me whenever I've tried to contact either of them. This Magus Dux is restraining them somehow. I'm sure of it."

Chloe picked at the lid of her coffee cup, staring off into space. "Identical air pressure. Tug-of-war. Spirits. If we only knew why or what he was doing with them. Or how Rhianna was involved, and the Vice-Chancellor's wife."

"That would help," Devlin said, his voice hard now. "A cambion named Magus Dux. I've never heard of him. Have any of you?"

"Not that I can think of," Chloe said.

"I haven't." Gar began to back out of the parking space. "But I have the strange feeling we'll all know more about him than we care to before this is all over."

The motel had a line of first-floor rooms that opened directly onto the parking lot and a second story with a balcony running its full length. It reminded Em uncomfortably of the infamous Bates Motel. The only difference was that this place had moonlit evergreens outlined behind it instead of a decrepit lawn and a creepy mansion.

Gar pulled in next to the office and headed inside to get the room key. As Em watched him disappear through the doorway, an unsettling sense of inevitability shivered up her spine. Not only did the motel border the cemetery, it also was a short walk from Congress Park and the gateway where she'd seen Saille that night from the police car window. Things had certainly come full circle.

When Gar returned, he drove across the parking lot and pulled up in front of the only room with a light on. "I told them we'd be checking out before the office opens in the morning. It's ours until then."

"I'll be glad when this part's over," Chloe whispered as they all climbed out of the van. "The whole idea of disturbing a grave bothers me."

"Don't worry. It's not like we're violating Saille's resting spot. She wants this," Em said softly.

Gar shouldered a duffel bag. "It's the living we need to be worried about tonight, not the dead."

Em was pleased to find the room was larger than she'd expected. A faint smell of new carpet and fresh paint hung in the air. A complete kitchenette. A table and four chairs. Not a hint of a ghost—which meant the room hadn't been the site of a murder or suicide. There'd been tons of times over the last few years when she'd have killed for a night in a place like it. Well, not really killed, or even prostituted. She would have liked it a lot, though.

Em glanced in the mirror over the dresser to see how messy she looked. Her hair hung limp and tangled, but the cut on her cheek from the wraith was thankfully small and scabbed over. More like a nasty scratch—

Her eye caught the reflection of a double bed directly behind her and pure terror shot straight to her core. Floral quilts. Perfectly stacked pillows. Scrolled metal headboard. Glistening white... An urge to vomit rushed up her throat. She couldn't breathe. Couldn't move.

A headboard. Metal scrolls narrow enough to secure handcuffs to. A mattress wide enough to hold a child down on.

Phantom pain ricocheted through her wrists and ankles. Across the tops of her feet. She clamped her eyes shut, fighting the memory. But she couldn't stop her mind from reeling back, way back: eleven-year-old her, ankles held down, wrists cuffed to the scrolled headboard. The buzz of the tattoo gun. A hand over her mouth. The bitter taste of hand cream. The fruity smell of Lifesavers on her mother's breath.

"You can't run away from us, Violet. You belong to us. *Family is forever.*"

Forever. Forever. Pain reverberated across the top of her left foot, up her ankle. Bone-deep pain. Her arms ached. The tattoo gun buzzed. Aching. Endless aching.

A moment of nothing. A breath. It was over—

It began again, pain shooting across her other foot.

"You need to listen to Auntie Lynda," her mother's voice rasped close to her ear. Her mother.

Sadness. Overwhelming sadness. Mother used to love her. Used to before the beginning, before the ghosts. More emotions, a new one rising with each stab of the needle. Hate, anger, fury pulsing in her veins. Freedom. She'd find it someday. Someday. Freedom.

"Em?" Gar's worried voice broke her free from the memory, snapping her back to the present.

She turned from the mirror. Her hands trembled. Her feet trembled. She straightened her spine and pasted on a smile. She didn't dare speak. If she did, words would come out, and he'd know for certain something was wrong. They all would.

His gaze darted to the bed, then back to her. Sudden understanding furrowed his brow. Of course he knew. She'd told Johnny everything that night by the river.

He dropped his duffel bag to the floor, dashed to the bed, and yanked the quilts and blankets off. In one swift motion, he threw them over the headboard, covering it entirely. He stormed to the second bed and draped its headboard the same way. Then he gathered up all the pillows and lobbed them helter-skelter on top of everything else.

Devlin folded his arms across his chest and shook his head at Gar. "What are you doing?"

Gar stabbed him with a deadly serious look. "What do you think the motel staff assumes we're doing in here? Two couples. Bags of food and drinks. Minimal luggage. Better to keep them thinking we had a good time." He took his cap off and tossed it on top of a pillow. "Too bad we don't have some liquor bottles to leave laying around."

Chloe laughed. "Gar, I'll never figure you out. You're all business, then you're—" She waved her hand, struggling to put her evaluation of his behavior into words.

"It's my nature," he said. "Loup-garou crazy, you know."

Devlin and Chloe both snickered. But warmth flooded Em's body when Gar slipped a wink her way before he nonchalantly picked up his duffel bag and pitched it onto the bed. He unzipped it and took out a black velvet satchel embroidered with a gold pentacle. "We need to get protective wards in place as soon as possible."

"Chloe and I can do that," Devlin said. His voice turned teasing. "That is, as long as you don't expect us to do anything crazy in the process, like hang from the ceiling or walk on our hands."

Gar's lips twitched into an amused smile. He pulled a jar of salt out of the bag and tossed it to Devlin. "No gymnastics required. Just normal protection wards. If you'll do that, then I'll take care of cloaking us from the Council."

Chloe smiled. "Judging by the van and storage unit, you've got that down to a science."

"It's one of my specialties." Gar took out a natural-twig wand from the bag and a pillar candle with herbs embedded in its honey-colored wax. He stopped, his gaze going from Chloe to Devlin. "If we get out of this with our whole skins, I'll show you how I prepared everything."

"I'd appreciate that." Devlin's eyes went wide as Gar took off his flannel shirt, revealing the dart gun strapped to his forearm. Devlin's smile stiffened. "Ah—are you a fan of Assassin's Creed, or is it the Green Hornet?"

"Green Hornet," Gar answered without hesitation. "Kato's always been my favorite super hero."

"I should have guessed from the moves you pulled on the guards back at headquarters. I meant to say something sooner—you were pretty damn impressive."

"Thanks. And thanks for the reminder. I need to re-dip my flechettes." Gar stroked a hand down his dart gun, stopping at the end of the arrow decoration. "Normally, I use a basic tranquilizing oil. But the chance of running into wraiths or cambions calls for a more creative potion."

"Like something deadly?" Chloe jumped into the conversation.

"Probably not. Killing doesn't help much with the already dead, or the somewhat immortal."

Warmth continued to radiate inside Em's chest, and the remaining tension from her panic over the flashback drained away as she listened to them razzing and talking with each other like old friends. It was nice—almost as nice as the more personal things Gar could do with his oils.

Em left them to create the protection ward and went into the bathroom with her new clothes. They would have told her if they needed her help, and they hadn't. She was glad for that. The last thing she needed right now was the pressure of fumbling her way through a warding spell. What she needed was a few quiet moments to regroup and ready herself for the trip to the cemetery.

As she turned on the shower, the same uneasiness she'd felt earlier came over her, like she was forgetting something, or her sixth sense was trying to get through to her.

She smiled as another possibility occurred to her. This uneasiness wasn't anything to be overly concerned about—she hadn't eaten anything since they left the complex, and then it had only been a donut. Of course she felt jittery. She was hungry, probably bordering on hangry. Fortunately, there was a submarine sandwich waiting for her in the other room.

She climbed into the shower and lowered her head, letting the hot water pound on her neck and shoulders as she thought through what lay ahead. Cemeteries were dangerous places, but not because of the troubled ghosts people feared they'd encounter there. Those ghosts were more apt to haunt places they'd lived or died, or things like books, in the case of the Goodwill ghost. The most dangerous things that hung out in cemeteries were usually alive, like messed up people who stuffed kittens in trash bags and then left them on railroad tracks. And necromancers, predators, addicts, and alcoholics with brains too pickled to tell reality from the surreal, just looking for a quiet place to be alone—she'd felt like that before, plenty of times.

There were things like the cambion out there too. Sure, they were protected inside the motel room's ward, and in the van, but they wouldn't be in the cemetery. It didn't seem like Magus Dux could have figured out what they were up to—or that he necessarily cared if they dug up Saille's body. Still, they hadn't foreseen his involvement or Rhianna's murder until it happened. He could be one step ahead of them now, or right behind them. He could have even been involved with the Circle's problems all along, even way back when Saille was killed.

Em turned around and raised her face, letting the water cascade against her skin, breathing the steam. She closed her eyes, clamping them tight. *Please Alice, watch over and protect us tonight.*

Chapter 23

You meet me at the grave. It's quiet and dark, the moon as pale as white lilies.
I look down, across the river at the drift of blue light on leaves, to their ghosts.
You foresaw them like this in a nightmare from which you woke in terror,
as if pulled by a string of children's cries.
—Memory. A client's premonition. Dalton, Massachusetts. 14 years old.

The moonlight shimmered on the chain-link fence, six feet tall and perfectly straight. Em shoved her hands into the warmth of her pockets, watching as Chloe and Devlin scaled the fence and dropped down on the other side.

After she'd showered, Em ate while Gar and Chloe left the motel room to dispose of any clothes that had Rhianna's blood on them. Between the bath and the food, her uneasiness had subsided by the time they returned. All she felt was relief that soon they'd be a lot closer to proving the Circle's innocence and helping Saille find peace.

Gar patted her shoulder. "Your turn."

She latched on to the fence. Its mesh rattled as she shimmied up. She flung her leg over the top and climbed halfway down, then Devlin grasped her by the waist and helped her jump noiselessly to the ground.

"Careful," Gar whispered as he passed the duffel bag full of shovels to Devlin. Then he vaulted over the fence like an Olympic gymnast. He gestured for them to follow, then loped under the evergreens and into the spidery moonlight cast down through their branches.

"I hope he's not expecting us to keep up," Chloe whispered.

Devlin tucked the bundle of shovels under his arm and flicked on a flashlight, brightening a narrow swath of ground ahead of them. "What do you expect? Like he said, it's his loup-garou nature."

Em bit her tongue, keeping her thoughts to herself as she followed them away from the fence and deeper into the grove of trees. Gar really was amazing, and the more she learned about him, the more she liked him.

His outline appeared ahead of them, silhouetted among the trees. He circled back, then guided them more slowly through sparser woods and into the cemetery. Under the gleam of moonlight, the cemetery's neatly trimmed bushes and weeping trees glimmered silver. They passed an angel statue that truly looked ethereal and an obelisk that cast a shadow in the shape of a hunched man.

Gar led them across a dirt drive and into a patchwork of mausoleums and slightly sunken graves. The sensation of decaying bodies beneath her feet lightened Em's steps and filled her with comfort. Dust to dust. The cycle of life completing itself. The only sounds were the soft swish of their movements and the murmur of a ghostly voice reciting poetry, too far off for Em to make out more than an occasional word. It was truly pleasant.

Chloe hooked her arm with Em's and snugged her close. "I wish Midas was here," she said. "I bet he has a gizmo for jamming security cameras. I'd sure rather be walking on a road than over these creepy graves."

"Me too," Em fibbed, though she agreed about disabling the security cameras. Those cameras had allowed them to use maps and street views to plan out the safest route through the cemetery in detail. Unfortunately, they were also the main enemy as far as getting in and out undetected.

Chloe released Em's arm and flicked her fingers to ignite a tangerine-size energy ball. It hissed and smoldered, sending sparks of brightness fanning in front of them like a flashlight beam.

As they left the older graves and crossed into a newer section, Em's sixth sense started to prickle and more ghostly voices reached her. A woman weeping. A child's cries. A tuneless whistle. The air chilled as an apparition paced past them, unaware of their presence.

Chloe hugged herself. "I may not be a medium, but I sensed that."

"There are more spirits in this part than the other section," Em said. She pulled her hands up into the insulated sleeves of her new jacket, shivering from the sudden drop in temperature.

"Anything we need to worry about?" Gar asked.

"Not that I can tell," Em said, hoping she wasn't missing something.

They hurried across a paved drive and down a row of modern gravestones. The frost on the grass thickened and icy fog billowed up from the ground.

An owl swooped past. In the far-off distance, a police siren screamed and then fell silent.

"We have to be almost there," Chloe said.

Gar bent close to Devlin and jutted his chin toward a monument shaped like a Celtic cross, ahead and off to their right. "Is that the one Zeus told us to look for?"

"Maybe. I'll go check." Devlin handed the shovels to Gar. With his flashlight cutting a path ahead of him, he jogged behind one of the shrubs that flanked the Celtic cross. A second later, he reappeared and gestured with the flashlight beam at a knee-high gravestone a few yards farther into the darkness. "It's right here."

Chloe blew out a relived breath. "Thank goodness."

"I agree," Em said, as they rushed to join him. "I was starting to wonder if we'd walked right past it." Now they just had to hope Zeus was right about Saille's casket not being sealed in a concrete burial vault. He'd been at Saille's funeral, but that was years ago. It wasn't impossible that he'd remembered that detail incorrectly.

When they reached the grave, Chloe increased the strength of her energy ball, floodlighting the headstone. It was natural rock with butterflies etched above a simple inscription:

> *Saille McClure Webster*
> *June 21st, 1908–June 21st, 1983*
> *The end is but the beginning, so mote it be.*

For a moment, everyone bowed their heads in reverent silence. Then Gar thrust one of the shovels into the ground. "Let's get this over with and get out of here," he said.

"Wait a minute. I want to try something." Devlin hurried to the foot of the grave.

Gar grinned. "I was wondering if you had some landscaping trick up your sleeve."

"It won't eliminate all the work, but it should help." Devlin knelt and placed his hands on the grass, fingers spread. He glanced up. "Everyone might want to step back. I'm going to attempt to peel the sod from the dirt."

Em retreated with Chloe to stand beside Saille's headstone. As much as she respected Gar's prowess, she was glad Devlin had taken the lead on this. He was the Circle's high priest, and he hadn't gotten to be that so young purely because he was a Marsh. She'd worked conjoined magic with him and felt the searing strength of his energy. Also, being in charge might help take his mind off Athena, at least for the moment.

Devlin closed his eyes, the hum of magic rippling out from his fingertips. His voice echoed in the air. "Leaves. Blades. Roots. Release the earth. Reveal what lays beneath. I beseech you. In the name of the Great Mother, show to me what lies beneath thy hold!"

A low rumble reverberated under Em's feet. The ground shuddered.

Chloe dropped to her knees. She pressed her hands against the earth, her energy crackling outward from her fingertips and joining with Devlin's. "Reveal what lays beneath."

"I beseech you!" Devlin demanded.

Steam hissed from the ground. The earth shook and rippled.

"Holy crap," Em said, struggling to keep her footing.

Devlin sent another wave of energy *snap-crackling* into the ground. "Release. Now!"

A ripping sound, like a tent zipper yanked open, reverberated and the grass peeled back from the grave in a single sheet, revealing the dirt.

"Wow. That was fucking impressive, though a little loud." Gar held his hand out to Devlin, offering to help him to his feet. "You don't happen to have another trick up your sleeve, like, say, one that will remove the next few yards of dirt down to the casket?"

Sweat glistened on Devlin's forehead and temples. He wiped it off with his arm. "I wish. Unfortunately, the spell is designed for gardening, not grave digging."

"Guess I better get to work, then." Gar thrust his shovel deep into the naked dirt.

A hollow *thunk* reverberated.

"What the hell?" Gar glared at the ground, confused. "That sounded—and felt—like wood. It can't be the casket. Not this close to the surface."

He began to dig furiously, excavating dirt off a wide swath. Em grabbed the other shovel and joined in. The sound could have been his shovel hitting a burial vault. But it hadn't made a *ping* like metal hitting concrete.

Thunk. Em's shovel hit something with an equally hollow sound.

"It is a casket," she said, but something was off. She didn't sense the natural peacefulness of Saille's decaying body. Instead she felt—

Her sixth sense whispered what she also felt in her heart. *Emptiness.*

Chloe brought a new energy ball to life, kneading it between her hands until its brightness illuminated the area around the grave. Devlin pinpointed his flashlight beam on the spot where Gar was working. In less than a minute, the entire top of a simple pine casket was revealed.

"This doesn't make sense," Gar said. "It was barely under the grass."

Devlin shook his head. "I should have realized something was up. The turf came free too easily, as if the grass was barely rooted."

Setting the shovel aside, Em knelt on the edge of the grave and touched the casket. She hated to tell them that the situation might be far worse than a casket buried too close to the surface. If she was right, then any chance of testing Saille's body and implicating Rhianna in her murder was gone. She didn't want to say anything, but she had to.

She got back to her feet. "I—I think the casket's empty."

Devlin's horrified gaze darted from her to the casket. "It can't be."

Gar wedged the tip of his shovel into the crease between the casket's body and lid. "We'll know for sure soon."

"Let me give you a hand." Chloe stepped up close to Gar, her forehead wrinkling in concentration as she compressed her energy ball until it became a sizzling mass of power, sparkling like a diamond and no larger than a golf ball. "On the count of three, you try to pry it open and I'll hit the same spot with my energy. Ready?"

Gar nodded. He took a fresh hold on the shovel's handle, preparing to put all his muscle and weight into popping the casket lid open.

"One. Two. Three."

Gar shoved the handle downward and Chloe hurled the energy ball.

Bang! Snap! Cracks splintered across the casket's lid. Hot air and light flashed out from the impact point. Another flash and a duller sparkle crackled, followed by the whine of magic. Then everything went dark all around them, except for the flashlight's glow and the silvery moonlight shining through the icy fog.

Everything was silent too, even the cemetery's resident ghosts.

Gar jammed the shovel into the widest crack. A loud *snap* sounded as he pried off a narrow section of the lid.

"I hope to hell you're wrong, Em," Devlin said, shining the flashlight beam into the narrow gap.

"I do too." Em squeezed her hands into tight fists, hoping and praying her sixth sense was wrong.

The flashlight beam filtered through the opening, fanning into the casket's interior and illuminating folds of white satin. And more satin. Nothing else.

A sinking feeling tumbled through Em. It was empty.

Devlin groaned. "What are we going to do now?"

"First we're going to fill this damn hole," Gar growled, decidedly unhappy. "Then we're going to get the hell out of this cemetery. We've made enough noise to wake up a lot more than the dead—like the cops."

"Wait." Chloe rushed forward and dropped down at the edge of the grave. "Even if someone destroyed Saille's body to hide evidence or whatever, I should be able to locate any remaining trace of her body with my pendulum. But the odds will be better if I have a piece of something that's touched her, like the casket lining." She glanced up. "Does anyone have a knife?"

"I do." Em pulled her knife from her pocket, opened it, and handed it to Chloe. She knew what Chloe had in mind. This was like when she'd increased the odds of finding Merlin's crystal by using the nest of grass that had been inside the packing box. It might work.

With knife in hand, Chloe stretched out on her belly and reached her arm into the narrow crack in the casket's lid.

Em slid her hand into her pocket, rubbing her six-month medallion for extra luck. "It doesn't seem like Saille's remains can be that far away. I saw her spirit in the park only a few months ago. The ghost in the Goodwill store mentioned her."

Tension burned in Em's stomach. This wasn't a dead end. It couldn't be. They'd find Saille's body. Somewhere. She could feel it was the truth as clearly as she could feel the raised emblems on her A.A. medallion, the serenity prayer embossed on one side of it, a triangle on the other.

A triangle.

In a flash, Em knew her previous uneasiness had nothing to do with her being hungry and everything to do with her forgetting something. She'd figured out that Caliban kept appearing in her visions because Dux was a cambion. But she'd overlooked the symbols. The triangle etched in graphite. The three yellow diamonds.

"Dear Goddess," she said, slapping her hands over her mouth to smother a gasp.

Chloe stopped working to glance at her. "You all right?"

"No. Not really. I just—" Her pulse hammered so hard, she could barely think.

"What is it?" Gar asked.

"When Saille possessed me, I saw a triangle. Three corners. Three—like the traditional power of three witches. That's what the ghost in the Goodwill meant. Not just priestesses—three priestesses: Saille, Athena, and Rhianna. Three Northern Circle high priestesses."

Devlin frowned. "Three witches. Three missing bodies. Three restrained spirits. Right?"

"Exactly," Em said. "We don't know if Rhianna's spirit is restrained. But the wraith took her body and I sensed the tug-of-war, so it makes sense. Whatever Dux is up to, it's big."

"I totally agree about the big part." Chloe pulled her arm out of the casket, a scrap of white silk gripped in her hand. "But you've got one part wrong. Rhianna never really was a high priestess, certainly not of the Circle."

Gar interrupted. "But Rhianna was wearing the Northern Circle signet ring when she was killed."

Em's sixth sense prickled, then screamed an alarm. *Something's coming. Run!*

"Something's here!" Em screeched.

Gar glanced toward the driveway, as if expecting to see the police. "Who? Where?"

The air temperature plummeted, twice as cold as before.

Wraiths swooped out from the darkness, flying at them from all sides. Flashes of energy exploded. Putrid green haze fogged the air. Em's breath became icy vapor.

"Son of a bitch," Devlin shouted, hurling an energy ball. It caught a wraith upside the head. Howling, the wraith summersaulted to the ground and vaporized in a spray of black sparks. The stench of rotting flesh flooded the air.

Em grabbed a shovel and swung at the wraiths closest to her. They hissed and circled. Gar was beside her, dart gun in his hand, taking out one after another. Still the wraiths kept coming, hollow eye sockets wide with glee. Their ear-piercing screams rang in Em's ears. The air was almost unbreathable from their stench.

Clawed fingers grabbed Em by the hair, yanking her to the ground. She rolled into a ball, protecting her head with her arms. This was stupid. They needed to conjoin their magic. She couldn't help like this. Not alone. Unless...

Em gulped a breath and squeezed her eyes shut, drawing up her magic fast and hard. Her vision narrowed into a black tunnel. Her consciousness wavered toward oblivion as she focused her intention on the wraiths and pushed all her energy into a single phrase. She'd seen Rhianna do it when she exiled Athena's orb from the complex. She could do it.

Em bounded to her feet and released the command, "Be gone!"

She gasped for breath, curling forward. Her body felt limp. Her energy was spent. It took her a second to fully come back to her senses. When she did, she found the air silent.

Every wraith was gone.

No claws sliced at her. No sparks of magic crackled in the air. No hissing. No horrible gaping mouths.

"Where's Chloe?" Devlin screeched.

Em whirled around, looking toward where she'd last seen Chloe, stretched across the grave. The only thing there now was a piece of white satin, fluttering slowly to the ground.

Chapter 24

WESTFIELD, MA—Child psychic locates body of missing ten-year-old. The body of a missing girl was discovered in St. Mary's Cemetery by psychic medium Violet Grace, according to her manager, Lynda Brewster. Grace is widely known as the world's youngest psychic medium. Westfield police are not refuting Brewster's claim or ready to elaborate on the circumstances of the girl's death at this time.
—From *West Mass Independent*

Devlin paced across the motel room. "It's my fault. I shouldn't have let Chloe get involved."

"We'll get her back. I promise," Gar said.

"How?" Devlin glared at him. "We have no idea where the wraiths took her, and none of us have Chloe's ability to locate things."

Em slumped onto the foot of the bed, head in her hands. "I'm sorry. If I hadn't frozen—if I'd driven them off sooner."

"You didn't freeze." The mattress sagged as Gar dropped down beside her and draped an arm around her shoulder. "The whole thing happened before any of us had time to think." His gave her a firm squeeze. "Did they feel exactly like the wraith at headquarters to you?"

Devlin slammed his fist against the kitchenette table. "Of course they did. It was the same damn pack of bloodthirsty bastards. I'm going to kill them. All of them."

Gar's tone hardened. "The last thing we need is for anyone to go vigilante. We need to keep our heads and play it smarter from here on out."

Em leaned against Gar. *Chloe.* There had to be a way to find her in time. Chloe had to be okay. She couldn't be dead already.

Devlin scraped his hands over his head. "This is so screwed up."

"I'll give you that," Gar said. His voice deepened. "And what I said about you during your interrogation was wrong—you're not a fuck-up. You're one heck of a man. Powerful. Skilled. What I need is for you to be that man right now. We all need that, especially Chloe."

Devlin turned away, facing the bathroom door. His shoulders rose as he took a deep breath. "You're right. I need to get my shit together."

"What's important is that we rely on each other." He took his arm off Em's shoulders and slid her a sly smile. "Personally, I think we make one badass team."

Em sat up straighter, hope seeping into her veins. Gar had something on his mind. Something doable. She could see it in his eyes. "What are you thinking?"

Gar raised his eyebrows and stared at her steadily. "Chloe isn't the only one who can locate things, is she?"

Unsettled by the look in his eyes, Em shied away. "I have no idea what you're talking about."

His smile widened. "Couldn't we use one of your spirit friends—like the Goodwill ghost—to find out where they took Chloe?" His gaze remained on her and her breath bottled up in her chest. He thought she could do it. He had total faith in her.

Devlin wheeled back around. "Is Gar right? Would that work?"

"It might." Em thought for a second. She brushed her hands down her legs. It might work, but— "I think there's a better way."

"Yeah? Go on," Devlin prodded.

Em licked her lips. "I haven't run into demonic wraiths very often. The first time, I was working with the police." She hated to even think about that day, let alone talk about it. She'd never told anyone the whole story, not the police, not her aunt or mother, not even Alice or her therapist. The serial killer she'd helped the police catch hadn't been working alone. He'd had helpers. Demonic wraiths. She'd seen them when she lead the police to the cemetery near I-90, to the shredded body of the last girl. The little girl the same age she'd been. The ten-year-old.

"Are you saying you think we can use the wraiths to find Chloe?" Gar asked.

"Not exactly." She thought for a second, struggling for the best way to explain. "The only way this cambion Magus Dux can control demonic wraiths is to let them feed on living people's energy—and their flesh. Dux has to be close to a source of people. Maybe in the middle of town, near where I first saw Saille."

"That's great," Devlin said, his voice brittle. "But how are we going to pinpoint an exact location?"

"This isn't the same as when we held the séance. We don't want to call a spirit to us. We want to locate one."

Devlin folded his arms, muscles taut as wire. "Chloe isn't dead. I'm certain of that."

Gar nodded. "There wasn't any blood."

"I agree. I didn't sense her spirit leave her body, or see her ghost." That wasn't to say Chloe was still alive, but it was better to stay silent on that point. "I'm willing to bet Dux is keeping Chloe near Saille, Athena, and Rhianna. If I had a personal object from all three of them, I should be able to locate them—the way I've located victims for the police by letting their spirits guide me to their own remains."

"Dux will have warded his lair against things like that," Gar said.

"That's why I'm suggesting items from all three. If I focus on the energy from all of them at once, I'll have three times the chance of breaking through whatever magical protection Dux has in place." There were flaws to her logic and she suspected Gar and Devlin realized it. But they didn't have time to second-guess everything. No one else was coming up with a better plan. She hesitated. "It wouldn't hurt to use an object from Chloe too, just in case."

Devlin's eyes went flinty, but then he nodded tightly and glanced to where Chloe had left her bag. "She always keeps a hairbrush in there, a toothbrush...lots of things." His gaze darted to Gar. "What did you and Chloe do with our bloody clothes? You didn't burn them, did you? They had Rhianna's blood on them. That's all we have of her."

"Don't worry." Gar beamed. "We bagged them and tossed them in a dumpster."

Adrenaline flooded into Em's veins. "I picked up the piece of silk Chloe cut from Saille's casket. That gives us Chloe, Rhianna, and Saille. The only person we're missing is Athena. That's not ideal, but I could make do."

Devlin stuffed his hand into his jacket pocket and pulled out a keyring. He showed her the fob: a faded piece of purple macramé studded with beads. "Athena made this for me. I've had it for years."

"Perfect." Em smiled at him, though she wasn't so sure it would work. The macramé was more of a personal memento to him than Athena. Now she wasn't feeling as sure about her plan as before. The only thing she was certain about was that they were about to attempt something beyond dangerous.

She closed her eyes to say a quick prayer for strength, but behind her closed eyes she saw a disturbing memory from the day she'd found the ten-year-old girl's body and the wraiths: the inside of a tool shed, windows and walls sprayed with blood. Blood gleefully finger-painted across the ceiling.

"You do realize"—Gar's voice drove off the nightmarish memory—"Dux will sense we're coming as soon as we step outside the protection of this room and the van's wards. He knew we were in the cemetery."

Em weighed the idea for a moment. "Maybe not. He could have had an alarm-spell on Saille's casket to let him know if someone discovered her missing body." She nodded, agreeing with her own idea. "My magic will be pinpointed on the ghosts, not Dux or the wraiths. We just need to move super fast."

She swallowed hard. More like they'd have to move lightning fast.

And even then, locating and getting into Dux's lair was only half the battle.

Chapter 25

*Blood drained from a taken life. The juice of grapes, unfermented.
Mix by the light of a conjuring fire. Serve with bread,
unleavened and black, in the basin of a summoner's bowl.*
—Gifts to Bind the Servitude of Wraiths
Translated from Archaic Welsh by Magus Dux

It was just after midnight when they pulled into a parking lot near Congress Park. Em waited in the van with Devlin while Gar scrunched his cap low over his eyes and went to dig through the dumpster where he'd left the bag of bloody clothes. A minute later, he returned with a scrap of stained cloth.

Em wasn't surprised by the sick feeling that invaded her stomach as she rolled the bloodstained scrap and the satin from the casket around strands of hair from Chloe's brush. Horrific thoughts reeled in her mind: Rhianna's blood spraying the room at headquarters, Saille's poisoning—

Em bit down hard on her lip to stop her mind from continuing down that gruesome path. *Focus.* She had to focus on the spirits' energies and not worry about the past.

Clearing her mind, Em went to work. She secured the rolled fabric with the string from Devlin's macramé fob, creating a bundle the size of cork. With that done, she palmed the bundle. No second thoughts now. No turning back. Just fearlessness and jumping in, like Chloe would.

"I'm ready to go," Em said, scrambling out of the van.

The brisk night air cooled her heated face as she and Gar walked to the rear. Despite the late hour, they were far from alone. People roamed the sidewalks, under the streetlights, laughing and talking low. Music drifted from a restaurant. A car pulled into a parking space not far from them.

Em gripped the bundle tighter and focused on the press of it against her palm as she intoned, "Give me aid. Show me that together you're greater than that which confines your spirits. Show me the way that I may free you." A prickling sensation spread across her palm. "Show me where you are."

"Do you feel anything?" Devlin whispered anxiously.

She nodded, then closed her eyes and focused only on the prickle and the ridged texture of the bundle against her skin. She let her mind move deeper, past the physical sensation of the string, fabric, and hair. Her magic and sixth sense reached out, latching hold of a faint tug: Athena's love radiating from the macramé string, Rhianna's anger and terror blazing from the blood, and Saille's fierce determination even in death. Three witches. No trace of a fourth ghost, no Chloe.

Relief swept through Em and she opened her eyes. "I don't sense Chloe. That means she's still alive for sure."

"Dear Hecate, thank you. Fucking thank you," Devlin murmured.

Gar took her arm. The bulge of several assorted weapons at his waistline rubbed against her as he drew her close. "What do you need us to do?"

She leaned into him as if they were a couple walking home from a normal date. "Just make sure I don't trip over anything. It's not like I can't see where I'm going, but I tend to get tunnel vision. A quick prayer for protection might be a good idea, too."

Saying the last part wasn't necessary—the crackle and heat of Gar and Devlin's protective energies sizzled in the air. It was astonishingly comforting to have their presences on either side of her, rather than the chill of policemen and reporters who were certain she was a fraud—and an aunt whose only desire was fame and fortune.

Em squeezed the bundle and refocused on the spirits. "I can feel you. Lead me. Guide me to where you are."

She let go of the world around her, feeling only the hardness of the pavement under her shoes as her sixth sense and the spirits led her forward. The pull was weak, which wasn't surprising considering the power of Magus Dux's tug-of-war spell or whatever was restraining them. Rhianna's pull was the strongest, faded but blistering with rage.

Em's subconscious registered moving past a concrete planter, skirting a tree. A gazebo, maybe. But they weren't in Congress Park. They hadn't gone that far from the van. They were on a sidewalk.

Gar's grip clamped her forearm, helping her step off a curb. Wet leaves in the gutter. The clatter of a discarded can rolling across blacktop. He held her back and the breeze from a passing car brushed her skin. Her mouth watered at the smell of hotdogs. Sauerkraut. Brick buildings hemmed her in. A narrow street or fancy alleyway, like the one outside the Council's headquarters.

"You're doing fine," Devlin whispered.

The tunnel in front of her eyes constricted to a speck of light. She walked toward it as if stepping into a dream. Faint awareness murmured to her, telling her what they passed. A boutique. A bookstore...

Be careful, Saille's voice whispered in her head.

Kill the fucker, Rhianna snarled.

Flash! A bright light and surge of energy jolted Em from her daze.

A red, baseball-size orb pulsated an arm's length in front of her. Blindingly bright. As fiery as a comet.

Gar released her arm. "What the fuck?"

"Athena!" Devlin stared at the orb, mouth open.

Em's sixth sense told her Devlin was right. It was Athena.

The orb streaked away from them, rocketing low to the sidewalk, up the narrow street. It slammed itself against a first-floor window. *Bang! Bang!*

Pop! The orb evaporated, and every sense of Athena drained from Em.

Em took off, pumping her arms as she ran toward the window. Gar and Devlin trailed on her heels. Athena had to be showing them the way. Nothing else made sense.

She reached a blacked-out window and froze in her tracks.

Her mind flailed wildly. She couldn't swallow. She couldn't move.

A blacked-out window, like in her aunt's van.

The day before Johnny helped her leave the persona of Violet Grace behind, someone had called the police to report a dog whimpering in a hot van. Blacked-out windows. Left chained up. Her punishment for refusing to eat lunch. The policeman had cried when he found her. She'd felt his tears on her arm. The heat had sizzled up from the blacktop. She'd shivered from the ambulance's cool air—

"...a Blind Tiger's another name for a speakeasy." Devlin's voice freed Em from the memory's harsh grip.

She shook herself the rest of the way back to her senses and looked to see what he was talking about. Next to the blacked-out window was a bright blue door, tastefully dented and scratched to mock a neglected service entrance. A drumbeat of music and voices throbbed behind it. She caught a whiff of beer and liquor, and fried food.

Stepping closer, she read the words on a fake bumper sticker that was painted across the center of the door—obviously the name of the business. Below the name was an odd poem:

The Blind Tiger
Like the blind tiger in Pergamon
I seek the unseen and feast on its words.

She reread the sign and wrinkled her nose. "Pergamon? Unseen?"

"It makes perfect sense," Delvin said. "Pergamon. Words. Half-demons."

Gar frowned. "I have no idea what you're getting at. Wasn't Pergamon an ancient city?"

Devlin waved them into a huddle. He hushed his voice. "Pergamon was a Greek city. It's also the name of an ancient library. Don't you get it? This is the reverse of a speakeasy. This Blind Tiger looks like a bar, but I'm willing to bet we'll find a secret entry to a hidden library somewhere inside."

"Are you saying Dux is a librarian? Then why is he kidnapping and killing witches?" Gar shook his head, but his serious tone said he wasn't ruling the idea out.

"Maybe not a library," Em said. The Goodwill ghost. The stolen books. "Maybe he's selling black market books about the dark arts or the Craft in general. He could be intending on using the power of three high priestess to enhance—" The words died in her throat as an image of wraiths covering priceless books in the skin of murdered high priestesses leapt into her mind, made more appalling by the fact that books covered in human skin truly existed.

She swallowed back the taste of bile. Dear Goddess, Rhianna had used necromancer magic and Athena's skin to create the necklace that allowed her to impersonate Athena. The chance of her skin-covered books theory being right was not only sickening, it was a real possibility. But no way was she going to tell Devlin this was a fate his sister might have met—and one that awaited his girlfriend. They needed him in control, now more than ever.

Gar grumbled. "Black market books is a good theory, but it doesn't explain why Dux went out of his way to take priestesses from the same coven."

Em grasped the door latch. "I don't know. But Dux has probably already sensed our presence. We have to get Chloe out, now."

"Not so fast." Gar whipped out his phone. "I'm calling Zeus."

Delvin lunged, closing his fingers around Gar's hand before he could make the call. "The last thing we need is to wait for him—or have him to show up halfway through."

"If something goes wrong, you'll be glad he did." Gar wriggled his hand free and put the phone to his ear. He frowned, then said, "Hello, Zeus. This is Agent Garfield Remillard. We're about to go into The Blind Tiger in Saratoga Springs. If you don't hear back from us in an hour, send in the troops."

"Voicemail?" Em asked as Gar put away the phone.

"Let's hope he checks his messages."

Devlin raked his hand over his head. "You do realize he'll alert the Council."

"I'm counting on it. Now, let's find Chloe."

Chapter 26

Love is small things,
a coffee shared under a blanket,
sweetened from a packet of sugar you kept in your bag
for the day when we could afford nothing else.
—Memories. Alice. Atlanta. 16 years old.

As they stepped into the dark bar, the heady aroma of whiskey set Em's senses on edge. She looked down, getting past the smell and the stares of the people who'd turned to watch them enter. She should have expected both things. But that didn't make the panic rising in her chest any less real. Walking into the bar felt exactly like stepping into an audience to give a group reading: all eyes on her, the smell of liquor filling her sinuses.

"Stay behind me," Gar said above the music.

Em nodded, more than grateful to stay in his shadow as he moved ahead of her. The only thing that made it even better was Devlin's proximity behind her.

Gar wound between the crowded tables and along a narrow dance floor, pulsing with dancing couples and the strobe of a blacklight. Suddenly he wheeled, grabbed her upper arm and steered her to a vacant table.

"What's wrong?" Devlin whispered.

Gar bent toward them. "Did you notice the bartenders?"

Unsure what he meant, Em craned her neck and looked through the crowd. Two tall women stood behind the bar, a white woman with straight blond hair cascading to her hips and a black woman with a massive afro.

She gave them a second look. Despite the obvious differences, the women appeared disturbingly similar. Oddly tall. Boyish hips. Conical Barbie boobs. Heart-shaped lips and oversize eyes. A waitress in a silver mini dress quickstepped to the end of the bar, her long Barbie legs strutting with measured precision. She had the same puckered lips. Same monstrous eyes.

Em shuddered. "That's really creepy."

"My guess is they're lesser demons, or more cambions," Devlin said.

Gar shoved his baseball cap lower over his eyes. "Whatever they are, this crowd won't shield our presence for long. We need to put some distance between us and them."

Em took a fresh grip on the bundle of cloth and drew up her magic. Her skin tingled and her sixth sense pulled at her. She swallowed her fear, motioned for Devlin and Gar to follow her, then let go of reality.

The walls of the room seemed to move in close around her; the voices and music merged into a distant roar. All Em could do was hope Gar and Devlin would warn her if she headed toward any of the Barbies—or other danger.

An arched doorway appeared in front of her. She went through it, coming partially back to her senses as they stepped into a T-shaped hallway. In front of her, a set of stainless steel doors blocked the way. A sign read: *Kitchen. Authorized personnel only.*

To her right, restroom doors shone under a bright overhead light.

Her sixth sense pulled her to the left, down an alcove unlit and empty except for a bookcase that spanned its farthest end. The books were shelved by color and size: blue across the top, and brown closest to the floor. Logic screamed that the bookshelf probably contained the secret entry to the hidden speakeasy-bookstore.

Her sixth sense urged her to turn toward the sidewall. It was upholstered floor to ceiling in blood-red leather and studded with decorative copper tacks.

"What is it?" Gar asked.

She raised a hand to silence him as she focused all her energy on the wall. Most of its surface was covered with oil paintings depicting demons dancing under various phases of the moon. The rest of the wall was simply leather upholstery and nothing else. Her sixth sense drew her closer and she spotted a hand-size place where the leather was blackened, as if stained from repeated touching.

Yes, her instincts murmured.

She also felt something reverberating up through the floor beneath her feet, a pulse like a tell-tale heartbeat. *Pump-pump. Pump-pump.*

Cold sweat slid down her spine. She didn't like the feel of that. But she couldn't afford to let anything distract her. They needed to find Chloe.

She glanced at Gar, then nodded at the black stain on the wall. "That way. It's a door."

"Great." Gar started to step forward.

Devlin touched his shoulder. "I sense magic on the other side. Witchcraft. And other things. There's something right below us, too."

"Something pulsing?" Em asked, shifting her focus back to the rhythm beneath the floor. *Suck-thump. Suck-thump.* The rhythm was slightly different than a moment ago. She recognized it for certain now: the tug-of-war.

Devlin shook his head. "It's not really a pulse. It's more like a pressure, pushing and pulling."

"We need to hurry," Gar said. He swept forward and pressed his hand against the stain. A *click* sounded, and a door silently opened. He stuck his head inside, took a quick look, then motioned for them to follow.

Em dashed after him through the doorway. On the other side, she found herself in a narrow hallway flanked on both sides by towering bookstacks. Piles of magazines cluttered the floor. Maps dangled from the ceiling. An overstuffed chair sat under a lamp, perfect for reading. All in all, the place had a cozy vibe and a gentle buzz of magic, homey like a hobbit burrow—it was a sense of safety Em didn't trust at all.

As Devlin closed the door behind them, the noise from the barroom faded and the sound of the tug-of-war increased, now thudding below them like a giant clothes dryer filled with sneakers.

Gar moved aside so Em could take the lead. She refocused, drifting back into a daze as her sixth sense guided her down the hallway past a circular staircase. Her body trembled from fear and her pulse thundered in her ears. Still, she crept forward, down the tapering alley of books and into an even narrower funneling passage.

She passed an arrow-shaped sign that pointed to an opening between two pillars. The word "Geography" was scribbled across the arrow's shaft. Another sign wavered into sight: "Romance. Ask for cost. Trades considered." It pointed up a ladder that ended at a hole in the ceiling.

"I sense Chloe," Devlin whispered as Em was pulled toward what looked like an open closet door. "We're getting closer."

Holding tight to the cloth bundle, Em came out of her daze and reached into her pocket with her free hand. The cylinder of pick-a-roos was there, and her medallion. But something was missing—

The air crushed from Em's lungs. Her knife. She'd given it to Chloe, so she could cut a piece of lining from the casket. But she'd hadn't gotten it back.

An ache tightened Em's chest. She hadn't gone anywhere without the knife, not since Alice had given it to her in Atlanta. She doubted Chloe still had it, either.

Gar nudged her forward. "Go on. I'm right behind you."

She straightened her spine and stepped into the closet. A single bare lightbulb hung high above her, illuminating the space in quivering light. On either side, shelves held volumes of children's books: *The Red Fairy Book, The Blue Fairy Book, The Green, The Yellow, The Brown....* The magic chiming off the books grated against her skin like hundreds of crickets scraping their legs. But there were other things on the shelves as well.

Dolls.

Naked Raggedy Anne dolls.

Her eyes zeroed in on the largest of them, the size of a small child. The red heart stitched to her yellowed linen breast framed two words: *Mine forever.*

Dead, cold fear sliced her to the core. She glanced down at her feet. *Family is forever.*

Her knees weakened. Her body quaked, like a child who didn't know which way to turn for help.

Get out. Hide. A voice inside her screamed for her to turn around, to push past Gar and Devlin, run back to the bar and keep running. Run and hide, forever.

Em clenched her fingers harder around the cloth bundle, squeezing fiercely. She gritted her teeth. *No.* No running. Not now. Not ever again. Why did she have to keep telling herself this?

She renewed her focus and stormed forward, out through an opening at the rear of the closet and around a corner, down another alleyway of books. She didn't know if the three witches' tug was still drawing her, but the direction felt right. She had to keep going. Devlin had sensed that Chloe was close.

Sprinting, she went down three stairs and out onto a crescent-shaped balcony that overlooked a cavernous circular room, rising two stories and down one to a sparkling black marble floor. The entire place gleamed with light, spilling from chandeliers strung with diamond-like crystals. After the confinement of the hallways, the grandness of the room made her head swim, as if she'd woken from a nightmare to find herself teetering on the edge of an amphitheater's upper galley.

"Wow," she said softly.

Gar clamped a hand over her mouth, dragging her back from the balcony's banister. The brim of his cap skimmed the top of her head as he leaned close to her ear. "He's down there."

Magus Dux. The energy tingling in the air was like what she'd felt just before and during Rhianna's murder. Cambion magic.

Devlin ducked down and crept to the banister. He took a look, then came back to join them. "Chloe's there," he whispered. "There's a pillar partly blocking the view, but it's her. The bastard cambion is with her, and two wraiths..."

He continued to whisper, drawing an invisible map on the marble floor with his finger while he explained the circular room's layout with an architect's precision. On each side of the balcony there were staircases that went down to a black marble floor. The room was enormous, with a raised platform surrounded by pillars at its center. Dux stood, and Chloe knelt on the closest edge of the platform. Behind them, the wraiths waited behind a table-like altar.

Gar nodded, and a smile flicked across his lips, as if he were feeling good about the odds. His confidence eased Em's tension, but it returned with vengeance as he swiveled his cap backward and waved for them to follow him. Three against three were good odds in theory—but not when she was on one side of the equation and bloodthirsty wraiths and a cambion were on the other.

As they began working their way along the balcony, Em shoved the bundle of cloth into her sweater pocket for safe keeping. After a moment, they reached one of the staircases that led down to the room. The stairs were marble and wide. Halfway down them, life-size lion statues crouched on ornate bases. Like Devlin had said, Dux stood in the center of the room on a platform with his back to the staircase. Chloe knelt a few yards away with her head bowed.

Magus was the perfect title for him. He was tall and had the bearing of a Russian ballet dancer, a young version of a stereotypical wizard, right down to his wild bronzed hair and flowing beard. His black pants clung to him like a snake's skin. His unbuttoned, sleeveless shirt revealed claw marks and scars shaped like ancient runes.

Sparks snapped from his fingertips as he paced to Chloe and flicked her chin up. Looking directly in her eyes, he spoke loudly, his voice rebounding off the towering walls. "I feel foolish about my mistake..."

Em caught a glimpse of something gleaming around one of Chloe's ankles, and what Dux was saying faded under a flare of cold fury. A shackle, the other end of its chain secured to the floor beside the altar.

She clenched her jaw. He would regret taking Chloe. He'd regret he'd even thought about messing with Saille or Athena. He'd even regret murdering Rhianna.

Unwavering determination beat inside Em as she crept down the staircase behind Gar and Devlin. When they reached the landing and lion statues, Gar signaled for them to duck down. Em did as he commanded, waiting tightly coiled but motionless as a brunette Barbie marched into the room with a copper basin and placed it on the altar.

"Mistake or not"— Dux gestured extravagantly at the copper basin— "there is no sense in wasting something this succulent." His voice lowered and Em had to concentrate to hear as he continued. "Mote it be, as you witches like to say."

He dipped his fingers into the basin, took out what looked like a gelatinous strip of bacon, and flung it wetly toward the wraiths.

"Mine!" One wraith shoved the other aside, snatched the strip, and shoveled it into its gaping mouth.

The other snarled, clawed fingers slicing at the first one's face.

"Now, now. There's plenty for everyone." Dux tossed a piece to the second wraith.

Em shuddered as her sixth sense picked up on the last traces of energy trickling from the meat. It was human. Worse than that, the energy was familiar: Rhianna.

Nausea surged up her throat. No doubt about it, the bacon-like flesh was Rhianna, or at least from some tattered part of her remains that had vanished from the office at headquarters. An arm or leg, perhaps.

Dux flipped a second strip to each of the wraiths, then whipped a handkerchief from his pocket. Wiping his fingers demurely, he stalked up to Chloe and squatted down, staring at her eye to eye. "My father will no doubt shame me for that simple mistake we were just discussing. A foolish lapse in judgment, as he will call it. He's much like your father. Demanding. Critical."

"Don't you dare say that," Chloe snapped. "My father is nothing like yours."

"Of course he is." Dux tossed the handkerchief to the floor. He leaned within an inch of her face and snarled. "My father is a demon scholar. He is...demanding, especially after his own failure with my half brother, Merlin. Fortunately, I have found the *key* to changing his opinion of me." He emphasized the word key, like he'd intended it to have more than one meaning.

Chloe glared at him. "I'm sorry you didn't get along with your father. Poor you."

He straightened and chuckled. "As I recall, there is a boy lying unconscious in a hospital room because of you. Your desire to learn a spell that could cure him was the reason you wanted to awaken Merlin. Am I correct?"

A chill raised the hair on Em's arms and she hugged herself against it. Dux was right about that. Terrifyingly so.

"Medicine and magic. A spell that can cure," Dux mused. He gestured beyond the platform to an open doorway and a dimly lit room. File cabinets. A desk. More bookcases. The room appeared to be an office.

A glimmer of gold in the distant room caught Em's eyes. Something a foot wide floated in midair.

She widened her eyes, straining to see it better. A triangle? Something sparkled in two of the corners. Diamonds. Yellow diamonds. She wouldn't have been sure about it at that distance, except she'd seen them, and the triangle, in her visions. Her sixth sense was confirming she was right.

Em reached forward to tap Gar's shoulder so she could point out the triangle. But she shrank back and froze as Dux abruptly wheeled away from Chloe and toward them.

She let out her breath as he immediately swung back to Chloe and continued his lecture. "Medicine and magic!" he repeated. "The desire for a cure is how Rhianna seduced you into doing her bidding. It is ironic that the search for that same cure brought the boy's mother to me—and allowed me to entice her into setting Rhianna up."

Chloe gaped at Dux. "You mean the Vice-Chancellor's wife? You're saying you have a spell that can help her son?"

"Wouldn't you like to know." Dux sighed dramatically. "I miss Rhianna already. She was such an eager little...devotee. Yes, that has a nicer ring than 'slut and liar.' Regrettably, I let her charms and that ridiculous signet ring convince me she had truly become the Northern Circle's high priestess, a *key* to my plan. In truth, her lies were many and her fidelity lay only with Merlin's dark half."

A tingle of magic feathered Em's cheek, then withdrew. Her heart leapt. Chloe's magic. She backtracked the sensation to be sure. Chloe's gaze met hers for an instant before flicking back to Dux's face.

Adrenaline rushed into Em's veins. Chloe had sensed their presence. She knew they were here—which was fantastic as long as she could keep the discovery to herself.

Dux looked away from Chloe and strolled back to the altar. He fished around in the copper basin as if selecting the perfect meaty ribbon. The wraiths squirmed low, snaking closer to him, snapping their bony fingers, itching to get hold of it. Dux dangled the meat in the air enticingly. Then he tilted his head back and sucked the ribbon into his mouth.

"That was delish," he said. He sashayed back to Chloe, belched, and wiped his fingers clean on her shoulder. He leered at her. "Luckily, an ambitious little friend at Council headquarters heard about you, sweet high priestess of the Northern Circle. Now you shall fulfill my dreams. That is, as soon as Rhianna's less delectable parts are done meeting a less satisfactory fate than the one I'd planned for."

Dux reached around to the back of his waistline. A glint flashed as he drew a large dagger. Its blade glimmered like liquid silver. It was shaped like an icicle.

"No!" Devlin screamed.

Devlin shot to his feet and ran past Gar, an energy ball forming in his hands as he raced down the staircase. Gar was a second behind him, gun in his hand. Em drew up her magic, readying to add her energy to Devlin's. But before she could, Devlin hurled the crackling energy at Dux.

Dux grinned, the flash of his blade already speeding toward Devlin's energy ball.

Boom! Crack! Dux's dagger sank into the sphere. Bright flashes of light blasted outward as the ball exploded, sparking white, sparking black. Snakes of magic hissed into the air, just like at headquarters when the dagger had sunk into Rhianna.

The wraiths hurtled into the air, green haze coiling around them. Their screams ricocheted off the walls as they circled the room, no doubt waiting for the command to attack.

Amusement flickered in Dux's eyes. He held his hands out at his sides, palms visible as if to offer peace. "Bravo! I wasn't expecting the three of you for another few minutes." A jackal-like grin crossed his lips. "My little Raggedy Ann friends warned me of your arrival."

Devlin planted his feet, shoulders rigid. "Let Chloe go."

"You don't really think I'm going to do that?" Dux stroked his necklace, a long series of chains with plastic doll legs and arms dangling from them. "The current question is, what to do with the three of you? Hmmmm… witch-skin covered Books of Shadows fetch a nice price these days." Em felt the weight of Dux's gaze settle on her. "You might be worth studying first. Your influence over the dead is fascinating. Perhaps a wee experiment involving electrodes and braincells."

Anger burned inside Em. She glanced at the shackle on Chloe's ankle to further fuel her hatred. She wasn't going to let Dux intimidate her. She had to help Chloe.

Em drew up her magic and called out for help. *Spirits bound to the earth, I command you. Come to my aid. Come!*

Only silence answered. No voices. No sensations, other than the wraiths' energy needling her skin. No Saille or Athena. No Rhianna. Not a single spirit.

She trembled. This wasn't good. Something was interfering with her ability to reach out, something nearby. A powerful spell, perhaps.

"Ready?" Gar said, under his breath.

The hum of Devlin's energy whined in the air, as if he could barely hold it back. Em gave up calling the spirits and drew up what magic she had left, sending it out to join with his.

She took a deep breath. There was only Dux and two wraiths. They could do this.

"Now!" Gar shouted.

They all charged forward—

The black marble floor shimmered, sparkling like crushed diamonds beneath their feet.

Then it vanished.

Chapter 27

I feel as old and gray as the sea
was last night,
with its shore doomed waves and mermaid tears.
—"Death" by E. A.
Memory. Merritt Island, Florida. 18 years old.

Em free fell through glittering darkness, air whipping past her.

"Gar! Devlin!" she screamed.

The temperature plummeted. Her breath fogged the darkness. The spell on the floor must have been what interfered with her reaching the spirits.

Thoughts flicked into her mind. *If I die, I'll be with Alice. I'll be happy.*

She closed her eyes, surrendering to the momentum. To the inevitability of death.

Death. Alice. Peace. That wouldn't be so bad.

Something grasped her shoulder. A hand, holding her back, slowing her descent.

Other hands closed around her waist. Orbs brightened the darkness, sparking with energy.

Emily. Emily, we're here. We're here for you, ghostly voices echoed. Saille. Athena. Rhianna. The Goodwill ghost. Others she only faintly recognized. The act of her, Devlin, and Gar passing through the floor must have consumed the spell's power. With it gone, her connection with the spirits had returned.

Violet, children murmured. Hold on. *We're coming.*

Ghosts crowded in, choking the air below her with their filmy bodies, slowing her passage. Slowing, but not stopping it. *We're here. We're here for you.*

Em. Alice's voice brushed her ear, as fast as a summer love—as cool as Alice's fingers had felt when Em found her in the bathroom. *You have a new life. New love. Live for both of us.*

Em reached for Alice, arms flailing in the void. She hadn't heard that voice since the day Alice died. "Alice, I love you. Where are you?"

Silence answered, every ghostly touch, every whisper and murmur, now gone.

No light. No orbs. Just darkness, falling, and deafening silence.

"Alice!"

Em hit bottom. Her knees buckled. Her body somersaulted, shoulders and hips slamming hard-packed earth and concrete until she slammed into an iron grate.

Too stunned to move, she lay still. Cold ground. A faint, flicking light, coming from somewhere. Pain pinched her neck and shoulders, but she could move her legs.

She crawled onto her hands and knees. One hip throbbed. Her hands stung. But nothing felt broken. No blood, other than the scrapes.

Em blinked her eyes to adjust them to the dim light, then scanned what lay around her. The grate she'd landed against was thick iron, its crosshatched bars so close together that nothing larger than a tangerine could pass through. Beyond it, light flickered down from an old-style florescent fixture that hung haphazardly from the ceiling. She'd landed in a cell in a small, dungeon-like chamber. A single door led in and out of it.

Her gaze went deeper into the chamber, to a white enamel table covered with creepy-looking surgical implements. A black rubber apron hung over a standing lamp.

"Dear Goddess." Terror spiked through her when she spied what sat beside the table: a dentist chair with leather restraints attached to its arms and clamps on the headrests.

She scuttled away from the grate into the farthest corner of the cell. What did Dux do in here? Torture? The experiments he'd eluded to a moment ago—the ones he wanted to do to her?

"Gar. Devlin," she whispered hoarsely, though she knew no one else was in the dungeon. All three of them had gone through the floor together. She'd seen that. But she didn't recall sensing their presence during the fall. The ghosts had slowed her descent, but had anyone gone to Gar and Devlin's aid?

Her eyes went back to the dentist chair. There was an extension cord looped over the arm restrains. *No.* She wouldn't let it end like this. Alice had told her to live. Johnny hadn't put her on that train all those years ago just so she could lose her life when they'd finally reconnected and she was getting her act together.

No. She wasn't going to give up without a fight. She wasn't going to let Dux win that easily. She was alive, and her heart said she wasn't the only one who had survived the fall.

Chapter 28

In the ▮▮▮▮▮ *darkest* ▮▮▮ *hour* ▮
▮ *there is* ▮ *hope* ▮ *more*
▮ *brilliant* ▮ *than* ▮▮ *stars or sun* ▮
—"Finding Light" by E. A.

Em crouched in the back of the cell. She had to find Gar and Devlin—if her heart was right about them being alive. It didn't seem like Alice would have said anything about finding new love if Gar hadn't survived the fall.

Her gaze went to the lock on the cell door. She slid her hand into her pocket and closed her fingers around the cylinder that held her last two pick-a-roos. From her side of the cell, the lock looked like nothing more than a solid square of iron. There had to be a keyhole on the other side. Most likely one bespelled. Still, she had escaped from the Council's headquarters. How much harder could this be?

Her leg muscles screamed in protest as she struggled to her feet. She snagged a piece of gravel from the floor and tossed it at the grate. When she'd rolled into it, she hadn't been zapped by magic or an electric charge. Still, double-checking seemed smart.

The gravel bounced off with a faint clink, then dropped to the floor undamaged. If she was lucky, it would have the same innocuous effect on naked human skin. In truth, if the holes in the grate had been any smaller or her hands any larger, she wouldn't have stood a chance at doing what she intended.

Em took a pick from the cylinder, then licked her hand and arm to lubricate them so they'd slide through more easily. She took a deep breath.

Okay, Midas, your magic works great against witches' security. Let's see how it does against a cambion's.

Cupping her fingers as close together as possible, she narrowed her hand and slid it into the hole in the grate that was closest to the lock. Her wrist bone resisted, but she managed to wriggle it through. Then she twisted her arm until she could almost get the tip of the pick into the keyhole. She jammed her arm in farther, her skin bunching against the grate as she gained another inch. Carefully, she manipulated the pick between her thumb and forefinger, extending it as far as possible.

"Sesame," she commanded, drawing up her magic and thrusting the pick forward into the keyhole.

An electric prickle and rhythmic pulse hummed up her wrist. She could hear the beat of the pick's magic in her head, a primal song she couldn't quite remember the words to. Smoke and blue flames of magic leapt outward. She'd done it.

She yanked her arm back to withdraw it from the grate—

It didn't budge.

Holy crap! Her wrist was stuck tight. Once the lock clicked open, she'd only have a second to push the door open before it relocked.

She spit on her wrist, spreading the fresh lubricating coat of saliva with her free hand. *Please, please, please.*

The locked clicked, the glare of the blue flames dimming.

She swallowed hard and scrunched her fingers as tight as she could, then squirmed her wrist like a cork stuck in a bottle. She yanked again—

Her arm slid from the grate. She stumbled backward, losing her footing for a moment before she regained it and rushed forward to open the cell door. As she scrambled out and into the dungeon, she glanced back at the dying flames in the keyhole—and a terrifying thought occurred to her. She only had one pick-a-roo left now. Once she used it to get out of the dungeon, she'd have no way to get through any future locks.

Unless... She lunged for the pick, still smoldering in the cell's lock. Heat and magic snapped at her fingertips as she plucked the half-burnt remains from the keyhole. In five swift steps, she was at the chamber's exit. She shoved the remains into its keyhole.

Flames flickered out from the lock, not that strong but flaring quickly. She worked the door's latch.

Once. Twice—

The flames sputtered. The lock clicked, and the latch released under her grasp. She hurtled out into what looked like the very end of a tunnel and shut the door behind her.

Darkness closed in. Not just darkness. It was a complete blackout, cold and clammy. But at least she'd caught a glimpse of the tunnel before she shut the door. It was narrow, with a low ceiling. Since she was at the very end of the tunnel, there was only one direction left for her to walk.

Em held her hand out in front of her, inching forward until her fingers found the damp, cool surface of a wall. Gliding her hand along it, she crept away from the dungeon door. The wall's slimy surface slicked her fingers. The rough floor crunched under her footsteps.

Her shoe stubbed against something hard. She nudged the obstacle with her toe to puzzle out what it was. Wide. About a foot tall. A step, going upward.

Cautiously, she lifted one foot, moving the other up only when she was certain she had solid footing. At this rate she'd never find Gar and Devlin before Magus Dux and his wraiths came looking for her.

She drew up her magic, let it prickle down her arms and into her fingertips. Before the Circle had woken Merlin's Shade and everything went to hell, they had gone through days and nights of intense training to strengthen their abilities. Working together, the coven had summoned fog, called the wind, and created energy balls with their minds and magic. Granted, those things had been accomplished with the conjoined magic of more than a half-dozen witches under the guidance of a disguised Rhianna. But Em had formed an energy ball during those sessions, just like the one Chloe had used to light their way in the cemetery.

Em concentrated on the space between her hands and released her magic. A pea-size spark of light broke the darkness, gyrating and growing between her hands.

It sizzled and went out.

Em focused harder and tried again. Not even a spark that time.

She wiped her hair back from her face. *This was stupid.* She needed to use her strengths, not mess with other people's. She nibbled her lip. She could call Athena and ask her to lead the way to Devlin and Gar. Her orb form would be bright enough to work. But Dux had a hold over Athena. It was likely he'd sense something was going on. She needed a different spirit, one that Dux might overlook or not even sense.

Alice. Her guardian angel. But it had felt like Alice was moving on when she'd told Em to live life for the both of them. Still, spirits that had gone into the light could return.

Em filled her mind with a single memory and sent it out to the universe: Johnny putting her on the train so she could get to Alice.

"Alice, please," she intoned. "Come to me one more time. Take me to him as he once sent me to you. Help me find my way in the dark."

Cool fingers instantly laced with hers, as fragile as mist. Alice's shimmering outline appeared beside her, a glowing pale blue in the darkness.

"Take me to him," Em whispered. "Hurry."

Alice's glow cast moonlight-pale shadows across the floor and walls as they fled up the tunnel, hand in hand. The eerie light was far better than total darkness, but Em still could barely see. She reached out with her sixth sense and prayed that it or Alice would warn her if wraiths—or something worse—lay ahead.

But they didn't run into anyone—or anything, not even doors on either side of the tunnel. No lights ahead. No burned-out torches. No other dungeons or cells. Nothing.

When they got to the top of another short flight of stairs, the crunch of Em's footsteps against the gritty floor began to fade under a louder and unnervingly familiar sound coming from directly above them. *Pump-pump. Suck-thump.*

Goose bumps pebbled Em's arms. But the sound was a good sign. It had reverberated from directly below them when they'd entered Dux's bookstore, so clearly the room she'd seen Chloe in was not that far above her. However, that made it even stranger that they hadn't run into anyone yet. Where were all the wraiths and Barbies?

She sidestepped a dark, oily puddle on the floor and caught a whiff of rancid blood. Yeah, this place definitely wasn't always deserted.

Em squeezed Alice's misty fingers. "You do know where Gar is, right?"

Alice's ghostly form nodded—at least Em thought she did. It was hard to be sure. Alice's outline wasn't as defined as it had been moments ago. Her glow wasn't as bright either. She was breezing down the tunnel faster now too, as if she was afraid they were running out of time.

Just as Em thought she was going to lose touch with Alice, the tunnel ended at an equally dark corridor that went in two directions. From what little Em could see, the walls and floor were tiled in white and spotlessly clean.

She shivered uneasily. Sterile white and tiled—just like the walls in the hospital where she'd escaped from the police and doctors.

Alice released her hand, her outline flickering brighter as she pointed to an enormous door on their right with snakes and beetles carved into its stone arch.

Go. He's there, Alice said, barely louder than a breath.

Em's heart leapt. But she hadn't needed Alice to tell her. A flutter in her chest said Gar was behind the door.

She turned back to Alice, readying to thank her with a hug—

Only a faint silvery wisp of Alice remained, barely visible.

Em wasn't sure, but she hoped she was right. "Can you see the light?"

Yes. My baby. Waiting.

Tears burned in Em's eyes. She reached out, her fingers passing through the wisp. One last cool touch. "I love you."

It's time to let go. Time to live. Love...

As Alice's voice faded, raised voices came from behind the door.

Em snapped back to attention. Wiping her eyes with the back of her hand, she rushed to the door. It was huge, so large it had to weigh at least five hundred pounds. The latch was three times the size of the one on the dungeon she'd escaped from. The lock was equally oversize.

She swallowed dryly. The keyhole was twice as large as her thumb, far too big to hold a pick-a-roo securely.

Crouching, she peered through the keyhole. The glaring brightness of the room beyond made it hard for her to see much. A Barbie paced through her line of sight, impossibly long legs marching with sharp precision. She held a gun—a dart gun, with a golden arrow decorating its barrel. Her flutters and Alice were right. Gar had to be in there somewhere. It only made sense.

The Barbie swiveled toward the door, her penciled-on eyebrows lowering like she sensed Em's presence.

Em snagged the last pick from the cylinder. She shoved it in the keyhole and held onto it to keep it from falling out. Maybe the door was locked. Maybe it wasn't. She didn't have time to chance it. *Live. Love.* That's exactly what she intended to do.

"Sesame," she commanded. Heat swept up her arms, as if every hair was electrified. Blue flames licked between her fingers. The beat of a primal song throbbed in her head.

A click echoed from the lock.

Em grabbed the latch, flung the door open, and tore inside. She snatched the first thing she could grab: a basin filled with surgical implements. The Barbie aimed the gun at her. Em swung the basin. It connected with the Barbie's wrist. Implements and the gun flew into the air.

"Bitch!" the Barbie screamed.

Em swung again, slamming the Barbie full force in the face.

A wet *thwack* rang out and blood flew from the Barbie's nose. Her giant eyes narrowed into dark slits. Her voice rasped, "I'm going to kill you."

A huge syringe appeared in the Barbie's hand, needle glistening.

Em's mind flashed back. Her arms pinned to the bed. The needle. The pain branching across her feet and up her legs. Her mother. Her aunt. The police had asked her about needles the night she bottomed out. Never needles.

Hatred roared into Em's veins. Her lips pulled back in a snarl. She swung again, harder yet. The Barbie flung up her arms to block the attack, syringe clenched tightly. The basin collided with the side of her head. Em swung again. And again. Blood stained the basin. Blood stained the syringe. The Barbie howled and dove for the gun. Em slammed the basin into the back of her skull. *Crack!*

The Barbie sank to the floor, motionless. Em raised the basin for another blow—

"Stop!" Gar shouted. "Em, stop. She's dead."

Em froze, the basin and her arms still over her head. Below her, the Barbie lay on her side, her eyes wide open. Blood bubbled from her gaping mouth. Her nose was pulp, her forehead split open to the bone.

The pan dropped from Em's hands, a metallic *clank* reverberating in the small chamber.

"Em, snap out of it," another voice commanded. It was Devlin, somewhere behind her.

"Hurry," Gar said to her. "Check the body for keys."

Em could feel her hands and feet, but she couldn't make them move. "I killed her," she mumbled. Her voice sounded wrong, as if it came from outside of herself. Surreal. Distant.

"The keys," Devlin said emphatically.

She turned toward the voices. Gar and Devlin stood in a grated cell, identical to the one she'd escaped from. That's what she was here for, to help them escape. That's what she was doing.

In a rush, Em's brain righted itself. She dropped to her knees and worked her hands over the Barbie's limp body. The blood on the Barbie's face had mixed with her caked-on makeup, liquefying it and revealing lizard-like skin beneath the coating. Human or not, she'd killed her. Killed her in blind rage. Em shook her head. Rage wasn't the only reason. The Barbie had a gun. And Gar in a cage. And Devlin… She checked the Barbie's pockets for a second time. No keys. And she'd used her last pick.

Cold sweat dampened her sides. She glanced at Devlin. "Do you have any pick-a-roos left?"

"I used all of them getting out of headquarters—and half of Chloe's."

"Don't look at me," Gar said. "I never got any. I vote for blowing the sucker. Between the three of us, we've got enough magic."

As Devlin argued that blowing the door would alert Dux and leave them weakened, Em searched the implements strewn on the floor for something that could be used to pick the lock the old-fashioned way. Her pulse throbbed loudly in her ears, a forceful tempo matching that of her heart. An ancient rhythm of fear, bordering on panic.

An ancient rhythm. Tempo. Em's pulse sped even faster. She bolted to the cell door.

"Let me try something," she said. She'd felt the rhythm of the spell Midas used to create the picks. She'd heard its primal song. If she could duplicate it using her own energy, maybe it would work.

She pressed her hand over the lock, closed her eyes, and focused on the sensation of the keyhole against her palm. She brought up her magic and let go of the world around her, moving into a daze like she did when reaching out to contact spirits. But this time, instead of casting out a net of magic for ghosts, she focused on the keyhole and released her energy in time with the fast rhythm of her heartbeat: the oldest song, the first song copied by ancient shamans. *Thump. Thump. Thump-thump...*

She let herself fall into a daze, her mind going back to the rhythm she'd felt when she used the pick-a-roos, the slightly different heartbeat of Midas's spell. *Thump. Thump-beat, beat.*

Heat flooded up her arms and an electric crackle tingled against her skin. Even with her eyes shut, she could see the blue flames flickering against her palm. She could feel the heat. Flares of white light, flooding outward.

"Whoa," Devlin's shocked voice said in the distance.

Click.

"Open the door," she mumbled from her fog. "Quick."

The push of the door opening threw her off balance and sent her lurching sideways. Gar caught her, steadying her until her senses returned.

"Are you all right?" he asked.

She nodded. "I just need to catch my breath."

Gar brushed back her hair. He pressed a kiss at the base of her ear and whispered, "You're fucking amazing. You know that, right?"

His voice snapped her fully back to reality. His comment sent warmth across her skin. He was the one who was amazing. Her sweet, rebel knight.

She laughed and pushed him away. "Takes one to know one."

Devlin joined them. He handed Gar the dart gun, a knife, and various other weapons. He glanced at Em. "Do you know where Chloe is?"

"No. But the room she was in is above us." Her fingers went to her sweater pocket, searching for the cloth bundle. She should be able to use it to guide them. Except—

She jammed her hand deeper in her pocket, feeling around again.

The bundle was gone.

Chapter 29

Rip it apart
Tear it to pieces,
Pull down the stars and blow them into dust.
—"Anger" by E. A.
Memory. On the run. 15 years old.

"I lost the bundle," Em confessed. "It must have fallen out when I went through the floor." She nodded toward the corridor. "I think we'll find Chloe if we keep moving up."

"Okay, then. Let's get out of here." Devlin turned on a flashlight and headed for the door.

Em stuck close to him and Gar as they hurried from the dungeon and went into the dark corridor, past the tunnel she'd emerged from and up a steep, winding flight of stairs. When they reached the top, the relentless *pump-pump suck-thump* reverberated from straight ahead instead of from above.

"You hear that, right?" Em whispered to Gar.

He cocked his head, listening, a movement that was so wolf-like it made Em's breath falter. He lowered his voice. "Yeah, and I don't like it. The only thing that bothers me more is the lack of guards."

Em nodded. "That is weird."

"Shush." Devlin raised a hand to quiet them. "I sense magic. What the—"

A high-pitched squeal of magic suddenly joined the relentless *pump-suck* sound. The noises entwined and sped up, pulsing faster and louder until it began to whistle. The air pressure in the corridor soared, screeching louder than a siren.

Em clamped her hands over her ears. Gar did the same, groaning and hunching down.

The wail of a woman—a ghost—screeched above the other ear-shattering noises, mixing with the relentless *pump-suck pump-suck*. Struggling and failing, screeching and wailing, trying to break free from the tug-of-war.

"Athena!" Devlin howled.

He streaked forward, past a stairwell flanked by torches and gargoyle statues. Gar raced after him, with Em an inch behind. The heart-wrenching wailing and ear-piercing sounds rang out from a brightened doorway just ahead of them—

"Shit." Em skidded to a stop as two wraiths swooped out of the room, claws slicing the air. A dart whizzed from Gar's hand, striking one of the wraiths. Sparks and light exploded outward. Devlin hurled an energy ball, disintegrating the other wraith. Green haze and the stench of rotting flesh fogged the air.

Behind you, Em's sixth sense screamed.

She wheeled. The corridor behind them swarmed with wraiths, flooding out from the gargoyle-flanked stairwell and streaming toward them. "Look out! Behind us!"

"Get down," Devlin shouted at her. A fresh energy ball sizzled in his hands.

She ducked, the energy ball whistling overhead as she drew up her magic. Light flashed. The wraiths screeched. She blocked out the sound, focused on the closest surging wave, and shouted, "Be gone!"

Some of the wraiths burst into haze. Others cartwheeled to the floor, snarling and thrashing like netted crocodiles.

"Nice move," Gar said to her. He tossed a grenade-like canister into the snarling mass. It exploded with a tremendous *bang* and a flash of light. Em threw her arm over her eyes, blocking out the searing brightness. The smell of moss and mushrooms overpowered the stench of rotting meat. Gar whipped out his dart gun and began taking the wraiths down one after another like skeet at a firing range.

"How many more can there be?" Devlin roared as another half-dozen hazed the corridor. He hurled a small vial at them, purple mist and salt raining from it.

"There aren't any coming from that way." Gar gestured at the bright room where the woman's wail and the tug-of-war sounds still screamed. "If we retreat there, we can ward the doorway to hold them off."

With Em in the middle, the three of them backed down the corridor and into the room. The place was as hot as a furnace. Everywhere, massive machines thumped and whined. Metal arms lifted and pounded downward. Belts shrieked. Gears clicked and ticked. The *suck-pump pump-pump*, like a tell-tale heart on steroids, didn't pause for a second. Neither did the wailing.

Turning her back on the machines, Em stared into the corridor, through the haze and purple mist. She pulled up her magic, focused single-mindedly on the wraiths, and commanded, "Be gone! Be gone!"

Wraiths fell to the ground, first one, then two more. Em stopped focusing on them and joined her energy with Devlin's as he sprinkled a protective line of salt across the threshold. Killing wraiths was a must. But helping her high priest might just keep them alive.

Despite the gravity of the situation, Em smiled as she realized she'd thought of Devlin as her high priest, and doing so had felt as natural as joining her magic with his—not just to save their lives. What she felt was deeper, something right and enduring. Something worth more than just the few months of safety she'd wanted from the coven. It felt like belonging. Like home. Like family.

"Incoming." Gar grabbed her, yanking her back from the line of salt.

Snap. Pop! Like a June bug hitting an electric bug zapper, a wave of wraiths collided with the salt ward. Light crackled outwards. Their bodies cartwheeled backward, screeching howls from their gaping mouths. They flew back down the corridor, the click of their claws echoing off the walls as they swooped between the gargoyles and vanished into the darkness of the stairwell. In a swirl of green haze, all the other wraiths followed suit, disappearing into the stairwell until even the sound of their claws vanished.

"Holy crap," Em said. "Where do you think they're going?"

Gar gave her a one-armed hug. "Probably to regroup—or tell Dux, though I can't see how he wouldn't already know. Either way, I'll guarantee you they know another way into this room. It won't be long before they use it."

"Over here," Devlin called from behind them.

Em turned, scanning the tangle of machinery. Devlin stood with his hands over his ears beside a spinning metal basin about twenty feet wide. Jointed pistons pounded into it as it spun, their metallic heartbeat muffled by the whining and wailing emanating from the basin.

A *clunk* sounded from the pistons. They stopped moving and the basin ground to a standstill. Every noise in the room winded to a halt as well.

Em shivered. The room's quiet was almost more disturbing than the sounds, especially since she could still faintly sense the ghost trying to break free from the tug-of-war.

Stop the Magus, the wailing voice called out to her from inside the basin. But the voice didn't belong to the spirit she expected. Not Athena. *Diamonds. Diamonds for the key.*

"Rhianna," Em murmured. *What key? Do you mean the triangle?* She cast her thoughts out, letting her sixth sense guide them into the machine and to Rhianna. Rhianna might have wanted revenge on the coven, but now she had a reason to want to bring Dux down as well. *Triangle. Key. Diamonds. Witches. What do they symbolize?*

No sooner had the thought left her mind than she realized her mistake. The triangle wasn't a symbol. It was real. She'd seen it upstairs. The witches were real, too.

Em's breath caught in her throat. Witches. Diamonds. Literally real... When she and Alice had lived at the Royal Palm Playhouse in Tampa, she'd made her living doing readings for the actors and patrons. One woman always wore a necklace with a single blue diamond: a stone created from the remains of her dead husband.

Em walked stiffly to where Devlin stood by the basin. No blood splatter streaked its metal surfaces. No ribbons of flesh. But those things weren't needed to transform a person into a diamond, at least not according to what she'd learned from the woman in Tampa. The only required ingredients were hair, extreme heat, and pressure. However, trapping a witch's spirit and magic in a diamond might entail something else. Perhaps the addition of a spell and bone or marrow could create that kind of living death.

Em forced her gaze to travel deeper, into the very center of the basin. She couldn't see anything other than a glistening plunger, but she could feel Rhianna's sadness and imprisoned energy pulsing within the machine's core. Rhianna might not have been the high priestess that Dux wanted, but clearly he had decided to keep her spirit and magic rather than set them free.

Gar's fingers laced with Em's, and she squeezed his hand for support. Even if he and Devlin had guessed the truth, she had to say it out loud, if only to drive the truth home in her mind.

"Dux is turning them into diamonds," she said, her voice husky. "When we were upstairs—where Chloe was—I saw a room off to the side, maybe Dux's office. There was a gold triangle floating in the air. It's a key of some sort, I'm certain of that. I'm also certain there were diamonds in two of its corners. Saille and Athena."

"No. You're wrong." Devlin gripped the edge of the basin as if protecting his sister. "I feel Athena here."

Em gentled her voice. "I'm sorry. At some point, she was in there. You're sensing that. It's not current energy."

Gar growled. "Stolen books. Now this. I can't believe this Magus Dux never crossed the Council's radar."

"I agree," Em said. "But we can't waste time thinking about the Council right now. There's still one diamond missing in the triangle."

Devlin went pale. "Chloe."

Chapter 30

closets. cupboards. hotel wardrobes.
under the bed. behind the chair. out of sight.
out of mind. close the door. close the lid.
long. dark. narrow. forever. no fear.
—"In Praise of Hiding Places" by E. A.

"What do you think the key opens?" Em asked as the three of them raced down the corridor to the gargoyle-flanked stairwell.

"Whatever it is, you can be sure it isn't good," Devlin said.

Gar hooked his arm around Em as they ran up the stairs. With his help it felt like she was flying, her feet barely touching the treads as she ran. She was extra grateful for that. The air in the stairwell was thick with the wraith's stench, almost unbreathable.

When they reached the top of the stairwell and went out onto a landing, Em bent over with her hands on her knees as she gulped fresh air. "That smells worse than skunk."

Gar leaned close to her, his voice hushed. "But it makes them easy to track."

He took out his gun, motioned for her and Devlin to get behind him, then headed down a hallway with curtained doorways on both sides. In the distance, a voice droned, growing louder and more distinct with each step they took.

Em drew up her magic, keeping it ready as Gar slowed, now inching forward, almost brushing the doorways' thick curtains as they passed.

They rounded a corner and saw the end of the hallway a dozen yards ahead of them. Beyond its mouth, pillars framed an entry to the circular room where they'd fallen through the bespelled floor, except this time they were on the opposite side of the room.

Gar tilted his head, listening, then veered toward a nearby doorway. He glanced behind its curtain. "Hurry," he whispered, waving them inside.

Em scrambled through the gap in the curtain, Devlin on her heels. No sooner were they out of sight than the fast clip of high heels on marble sounded, coming out of the circular room and into the hallway they'd just left.

"How many?" Em asked, voice hushed.

Gar nodded and held up two fingers.

Em's mind filled with images of the Barbie she'd killed. Dear Goddess, when the Barbies discovered what she'd done, they'd be after her blood for sure.

As the clip of heels drew even closer to where they were hidden, Gar flattened himself against the wall beside the curtained doorway. Em did the same, standing stock-still between him and Devlin.

A Barbie's voice filtered in through the curtain. "... I can't believe it."

The other one tsked. "What do you expect from a witch? They're all liars."

"I thought Rhianna was different."

The second woman snickered. "She is now."

"Yeah, dust to dust—witch to diamond."

"A shitty, imperfect diamond."

"Dux said we can finish her transformation once he's done with the new high priestess."

"Whatever. As long as we get that machine reset and back up here in time for the bloodletting. I bet that little blond witch will scream like a banshee."

Devlin tensed and shifted away from the wall. Em readied to grab his arm and hold him back if he headed for the door. She felt horrible for him. She couldn't begin to imagine how much he was hurting. Still, if he went off half-cocked, it could get them all killed, including Chloe.

"More like a dozen banshees," one of the Barbies giggled as they passed.

Once the click of their heels faded around the corner, Em scrunched closer to Devlin. "We're going to get Chloe out of there in time. Don't worry."

"You're damn right," he said, low and cold.

"Shush." Gar silenced them. He motioned for them to stay put, then slipped across the room to a second curtained doorway on the other side of the room. Judging by the door's location, Em figured it most likely opened into the circular room.

While Devlin nudged the curtain open a crack and peered out, Em took a moment to glance around the room they were in. The place smelled strongly of leather, and she wasn't shocked to see worktables stacked with books in need of covers and repairs. Her gaze went to a heap of tanned leather. Yeah, she really didn't want to think too hard about what sort of being it had come from. Animal. Bird. Human.

"Pssst." Gar signaled for them to come take a look.

Em hurried over with Devlin. But Gar didn't step aside instantly. With one hand holding the curtain closed, he spoke directly at Devlin, "We have to play this smart."

"You think I don't know that?" Devlin pushed Gar's hand aside and looked out. His shoulders tensed. "Son of a bitch."

"Put your anger into your magic," Gar whispered. "Keep it hot and your head cool."

Em slipped up close to them and glanced out the opening.

Wraiths swooped everywhere, blocking her view of the room as they came and went. Between their passes, she glimpsed Dux pacing along the edge of the raised platform with a phone to his ear. Behind him, Chloe lay on the altar, her arms and legs held down by Barbies.

Panic crushed the air in Em's lungs. Her gaze dropped to her feet. She could feel the hammer of the needles. Her mother's hand over her mouth. The bitter taste of her lotion. The fruity smell of Lifesavers on her breath.

Em clenched her teeth, fighting against the memory.

That's the past. It's done. Over with, she told herself. This was about Chloe. Not her.

She drew a deep breath and held it, then let it out slowly to calm herself like her therapist taught her. *Relax. Let it go.* She could do this. She had to.

Taking another slow breath, Em looked out again. Chloe was being held down. But she wasn't shackled. She wasn't fighting against them either. "Do you think she's unconscious?"

"I can sense her magic," Devlin said, sounding relieved. "She might be drugged. But she's alive and conscious. Thanks to Hecate."

Dux's voice boomed as he shouted into the phone. "Yes! I said on solstice eve." His voice sweetened and Em had to strain to hear as he continued. "You won't want to miss the celebration. I'll be revealing something truly extraordinary…"

As Dux's voice dropped out of hearing range, Gar steered them away from the doorway and the curtain fell closed. His gaze went from Em to Devlin. "Here's what I'm thinking. First, I'll use my darts to test the floor. There are a lot of Barbies coming and going across it, so I'm willing to bet the spell has been lifted, for now. Feel free to speak up if you have any suggestions."

"The spell's power was used up when we fell through it," Em said. "Before that happened, there was a moment when I couldn't connect with the spirits. Once we went through, I could again." She shuddered. "But I still think you should test it. Just to be safe."

Gar smiled at her. "That takes a weight off my mind, though I agree about playing it safe." He looked at Devlin. "We'll have to attack fast. Shock and awe. Grab Chloe and get out."

Devlin nodded. "I've got two of your light bombs canisters left, and a few other tricks."

"Good." Gar's gaze returned to Em. He ran a hand over his cap, as if hesitant to say what was on his mind.

She frowned. "You better not be thinking of telling me to wait here."

"I wish I could." Worry flickered through his eyes, but it was followed by a gleam that said he had full confidence in her. "While Devlin and I go after Chloe, I want you to get the gold triangle. You know where it is, right?"

"Yes. In an office just to the right of where we are now—twenty or thirty yards at the most." She really hadn't expected this. But it made sense. They couldn't just leave the key here, even if they didn't know what it was for.

"Stick close to the wall," Gar told her. "Use the pillars to shield you from Dux's view. Once you've got the triangle, leave. Don't stop to help us. Don't think about us or Chloe. Get out."

"I can't do that," she protested. "You might need—"

Gar raised a finger to silence her. "No matter what happens, we can't let Dux complete that key. I need you to make sure the Council gets it."

"What?" She couldn't believe he'd even suggested it. "Why? We can't trust them."

"Give it to Ignatius. He's the chancellor I talked to in the corridor at headquarters. You remember what he looks like?"

She nodded. She didn't like the idea. But this wasn't the time or place to debate it. "Just don't ask me to give it to the asshole who was with him. That guy may be passing himself off as a potion master, but he's a medium. There's no way he didn't know you were haunted." She bit her tongue to keep from going on. So much for waiting for the perfect time to debate things.

Amusement twitched at the corners of Gar's lips. "The asshole's name is Heath Goddard, and I know what he is."

"Heath Goddard." Em repeated the name, committing it to memory. "I don't like—or trust—him."

"I'm with you there," Gar said. "He's number one on my list for having been involved with Rhianna."

Devlin stepped forward. "Em, don't take any unnecessary chances."

"I second that idea." Gar pulled out his phone and gave it to Em. "Once you get outside, call Zeus. If we're lucky, he might already be in town. He'll know how to contact Ignatius."

Em stared at the phone, her head whirring from the craziness of what they were about to attempt. It was unbelievable how her life had changed since that day with Johnny at the river, and even more so since she'd gotten sober and started living at the complex, not to mention in the last few hours.

"On the count of three," Gar said, easing the curtain all the way open.

He held one finger up. Then two—

He took a dart from his sleeve and lobbed it past the pillars and into the center of the room. It landed with a *thunk*, point stuck firmly into the floor. No sparks of Dux's magic. No sense of magic at all.

"Did you hear that?" One of the Barbies swung to look in the dart's direction.

"Three. Go!" Gar sped forward, shooting darts one after another to mark a path to the platform. Devlin hurled a canister. It exploded. White light flared.

Em squinted against the brightness. She drew up her magic, focused it on an incoming wave of wraiths and shouted, "Be gone! Be gone!"

Then she bolted along the edge of the circular room, sticking close to the wall and using the pillars to shield her from view as she raced toward Dux's office and the triangle.

Chapter 31

No ghosts walk her hallways. No wraiths scream in her cellar.
Her house is haunted by boxes of scarves and postcards.
Broken earrings. Tattered ribbons. Torn paper. A carnation, dried brown.
Skeleton keys lay in a bowl. Which lock they open, she cannot remember.
—Journal of Emily Adams
Memory. Elderly client. New Haven, Connecticut. 10 years old.

Screams and explosions of magic roared behind Em as she dashed into Dux's office. File cabinets and bookcases lined one wall. Showcases packed with stuffed lizards and glass knickknacks covered another. The gold triangle floated five feet above a flat-topped desk. It was equilateral and moderately thin, like a trio of rulers glued together and spray-painted gold. Yellow diamonds glistened in two of its corners.

Em licked her lips and went up onto her tiptoes, preparing to grab it—but retreated. What if the triangle was warded with a protection spell? She didn't sense anything, but she might not. She didn't have experience detecting such things. She might not even sense if the triangle was booby trapped.

Bang! Bang! Bang! Rapid fire explosions boomed from the raging battle. The floor shook. Knickknacks rattled in the showcases. Chloe's distant scream pierced the air.

"Screw it." Em went back up onto her tiptoes and clamped her fingers around one side of the triangle. A sharp sting of magic shot up her arms and her sixth sense jolted awake. She yanked on the triangle to pull it free from whatever kept it suspended—

It didn't budge.

Gritting her teeth, she grasped it in two hands, drew up her magic, and channeled it into her clenched fingers. Sparks of magic arced out from her fists. She yanked again. The triangle resisted, then released so quickly that she stumbled backward. But she had it. Time to get out.

Her chest tightened, and a painful sense of desperation closed around her.

The books. The books, Saille and Athena's emotion-choked voices cried in her ears. *Take the books. The books.*

"Which books?" Em asked.

The other room. Other room. Hurry.

Em spun around, looking for an adjoining room. She spotted a doorway next to the largest showcase. Heartbeat racing, she sprinted to it and into what appeared to be a sitting room. There was an ornate fireplace and an upholstered sofa and chairs, cozy and welcoming. Globes spun slowly. Atlases opened, beckoning for her to take a look. Overhead, crystal-draped chandeliers twinkled invitingly. Pretty. Peaceful. The scent of violets filled her nose....

Her muscles went slack, and an urge to sit down and put her feet up washed over her.

What the hell? Em shook her head to free it from the overwhelming desire to relax. There was something strange going on in this room. Something she didn't have time for.

She clutched the triangle tighter and scanned the room. Books. Special volumes.

Just to her left, three leather-bound books floated upright in midair with their spines touching so they formed a triangle. A waterfall of black sparks hissed downward from the cluster. Shafts of light shot upward from it. Within the shafts of light, Merlin's crystal hovered.

Her gaze flicked from the triangle of clustered books to the gold triangle in her hand. There was a definite connection, but how it worked or what spells were involved was way out of her league. All she could hope was that the books would be as willing to come with her as the gold triangle had been. But how was she going to transport everything out of here, especially with all the sparks and light? Not to mention the fact that leaving Merlin's crystal behind didn't seem like an option.

A chill swept up her arms and across her scalp.

Something's here, her intuition murmured.

She drew up her magic, casting out her net as she turned in a slow circle. She couldn't see anyone. But she felt a presence. Not a ghost—this was alive. Powerful magic.

Cold sweat iced her body. It wasn't Dux, but the energy felt similar—a cambion.

"Dear Goddess," Em gasped. It was Merlin's Shade.

A tall apparition with a long white beard manifested directly behind the floating books, like mist becoming solid. How had he escaped from the otherworld? They'd just imprisoned him. The Lady of the Lake, Nimue, had pledged to keep a closer eye on him.

He held out his hands at waist level and the cluster of books floated down toward him until it hung just above his palms. Black sparks bathed his fingers and the shafts of light continued to shoot toward the ceiling.

Em shuffled backward. Every lingering trace of unnatural calmness was gone from her body and the room. Merlin's Shade. He was beyond dangerous. A master of magic. Unscrupulous. Powerful. Still, she had to get the books. But how?

His misty-green gaze settled on hers. "These books are mine to give. Years ago, I freely gifted one set to the sorceress Nimue. I give this set to you, along with the crystal from my first staff. Use them well."

Em stiffened. Her instincts whispered for her to grab the books and run. Spirits she trusted had told her to get them. But this was too easy—and easy was never good. She'd seen firsthand where trusting him had taken Rhianna.

She raised her hands, palms out as if to fend off the gift. "Thank you very much. But I don't want them."

His eyes sparkled and he laughed. "Child, you mistake who I am. I am not only my Shade." He gestured at the waterfall of dark sparks, then to the shafts of rising light. "Like my Book of Shadow and Light, I assure you that the man standing before you is my entirety."

"Ah, you're—Merlin?" Em's head spun. She had sensed a cambion. It made total sense that Merlin's energy would have reminded her of Dux; they were half brothers.

He is. Saille's voice murmured.

Em blinked at him. Merlin. The great wizard. His dark half and the light. The books and crystal were his legacy, and they belonged in the safekeeping of a powerful witch, not a messed up psychic medium like her. "I think you're mistaking me for Chloe, the high priestess."

"I know who you are. Born, Kate Brewster. Became, Violet Grace. Are, Emily Adams." He brought his hands together. The shafts of light and dark sparks vanished. The books joined into a single volume with the crystal fused to the center of its cover, then settled onto his palms. "Like you, I was born a witch with a gift for seeing the dead."

Her thoughts jumbled. Saille had been a psychic medium too, and a powerful witch. But she—Emily Adams—wasn't anything above average. She couldn't even make a decent energy ball. "That's cool—and I'll take the book to keep it out of Dux's hands. I'm sorry, but I don't want to be its guardian. I can barely take care of myself. Besides, I'd never be able to make use of it. I'm not even good with modern English, and it's written in what?" She thought about Merlin's legends and the tales of the round table she'd always loved. She ventured a guess. "Archaic Welsh?"

"There is no reason you can't learn the old language. You already possess a key." He tapped the book with his forefinger, turning it in midair so its cover faced her. The outline of a triangle was incised into the leather, a size and shape that perfectly matched the gold one clutched in her hands.

"But the key isn't finished—" She clamped her lips together once she saw the darkness hidden in his offer. Merlin both light and shade. "Forget it. I'm not going to kill Chloe so she can be turned into a stone and complete a key. For Dux or you—or for my benefit."

Merlin flicked his fingers, sending the book drifting toward her. "Chloe is not the only young witch here."

"She's the only high priestess." Em drew up her magic and flicked her fingers at the book, sending a wave of energy to shove the book away. No surprise, it didn't move a fraction. But it did come to a standstill.

A slight smile rippled across Merlin's lips. "You are not only young, you are a member of the Northern Circle."

"I'm not their high priestess." Merlin was awfully dense for an allegedly wise man. "I'm not special. I'm not any kind of chosen one, trust me on that."

All humor faded from his expression. His voice rumbled, the magic in its timbre vibrating straight into her bones. "I agree. There are others like you. But that makes you no less special. You are an aspect of the Goddess, just as Chloe is." A devious glisten sparked in his eyes. "You see, my imbecile half brother mistranslated my spell. The key does not require three high priestesses from the same coven. The requirement is the power of three witches from the same coven, each representing one aspect of the Goddess: Maiden. Mother. Crone. The reason Rhianna could not activate the key is because she is far from a maiden. You, however, are still in your youth. A maiden. Full of failure. Full of courage. Full of potential."

Em's chest tightened as the truth of what he was saying sank in. Since she'd gotten sober and joined the Circle, that was exactly how she felt. Full of failure. Full of courage. Full of potential.

Merlin flicked his fingers, his body shimmering and beginning to fade as he sent the book inching toward her again.

Boom! Crack! Sounds of the battle broke through the silence, reverberating loud in the room. The walls rattled. The chandelier over Em's head swayed, prisms clattering. The distant din of screams and shouts transformed into a loud roar as new voices joined in. Men. Women. Lots more of them joining the battle.

Em clutched the gold triangle tighter, hoping Zeus had gotten Gar's message and the onslaught was the arrival of the Council Guard. It had to be.

The thump of footsteps sounded behind her, someone running through Dux's office and toward the room she was in. She swiveled to see who had come to her rescue. Gar?

Her body went cold as Magus Dux sprinted into the room.

He swung the door shut behind him and swept his hand across it, sparks of magic fanning from his fingertips, sealing it closed. He turned to face her, amber eyes blazing with fury. Dirt and blood steaked his clothes, but other than that he looked unscathed. "That will give us some privacy. A smart idea, wouldn't you say?"

Em's legs weakened. She clutched the triangle tightly to her chest. Whether it was a losing battle or not, she wasn't going down without a fight.

Dux stepped closer. Light glistened off sweat that beaded on his temples. His chest rose and fell rapidly.

Sweat? Rapid breathing? Em pressed her lips hard together to keep from smiling. She knew those signs. She'd seen them on her aunt hundreds of times. Dux's bravado was false. In truth, he was terrified. Unfortunately, that made him even more dangerous.

She took a relieved breath. Thankfully, she didn't have to face him alone. After all, Merlin wouldn't have offered her the books if he was on Dux's side. Would he?

Em turned back to Merlin. The book still drifted between them, but he was now no more than a curl of mist, as silvery as Alice had been before she'd gone into the light.

I can do no more in this form, Merlin's voice whispered in her ear. *The book is your weapon. Maiden. Mother. Crone. Page three. The spell is on page three.* The last misty trace of Merlin evaporated, and his voice silenced.

Dux dove for book. Em reached it first. She swung it out of Dux's reach and slapped the gold triangle into the incised slot on its cover.

The book shuddered in her hands. Its vibrations branched across her skin, awakening every inch of her.

"Give it to me," Dux said, prowling toward her. "Don't make me have to kill you."

She gripped the book in two hands and lied. "Don't think I won't use this. Merlin told me how."

He snorted. "How can you? The key isn't complete." He stopped moving forward and smiled. His voice sweetened. "How about we turn this into a win for both of us? You keep the book and come with me. I'll give you sanctuary. You won't have to worry about your aunt hunting you down. You could write your poetry in peace."

Em's mouth went dry. How could he know about that? She'd never told anyone about her dream of being a poet, except for her therapist, and Johnny.

Slow, cold dread seeped into her veins. *Gar couldn't have told him her secrets. He wouldn't betray her like that. Please, not Gar.*

A memory from when she'd first arrived at the Circle's complex came to her. Rhianna, disguised as Athena, was talking softly to her, a heart-to-heart about her life and recovery, including the poetry.

Hot anger rushed through Em. She clenched her teeth to keep from shouting that she knew who had told him. Better to stay quiet. To keep him guessing.

"Well"—Dux huffed out a breath—"if you're not willing to cooperate, you'll have to die." He gestured with two fingers and an icicle-shaped dagger flew from his beltline to his hand. It glimmered like liquid silver. "Recognize this?"

Em staggered back. It was identical to the dagger he'd used to destroy Devlin's energy ball—and the one the wraith had used to kill Rhianna.

He leered, tossing the dagger from hand to hand. "One last chance. Give me the book."

Memories of Rhianna's blood spraying the room, of her head landing on the gelatinous mound of her body parts, flashed before Em's eyes. So many times she'd been ready to die: that day in the hot van, when she saw Alice dead on the floor.... But now she wanted to live. Not just today, but the next day, and the one after that.

Still, protecting the book was beyond important.

She squared her shoulders and snarled at Dux. "You want it? Come and get it."

Dux grinned like a jackal. "If you insist."

The pound of fists against wood sounded, followed by Gar's voice coming through the door behind her "Em! Are you in there?"

"Hurry!" she shouted. "Dux is with me."

Dux scowled at the door. "Pound all you want. You'll never get through in time."

He turned back to Em, sliced a look at the dagger in his hand—then hurled it at her blindingly fast. She flung the book up, shielding her body. The dagger *thwacked* into it. Black sparks erupted from the impact point, a geyser of magic exploding outward. The force of the blast sent the dagger flying from the book's cover and everything else in the room spinning. The chandelier smashed against the ceiling. Magazines circled into the air. Em tumbled sideways into the side of an upholstered chair—and the book soared from her hands.

"Come to me!" Dux commanded. He flicked his fingers, sending a wave of magic toward the book.

Em threw herself into the magic's path before it could reach its target. The magic speared her in the spine, a thousand needles stabbing all at once. She screamed as the pain jumped from synapse to synapse and rattled into her bones. Tears of anguish flooded from her eyes, but she refused to let the pain immobilize her. She grabbed the book, opened it, and sprung to her feet.

Page three, that's what Merlin had said. She looked down. There was a pen and ink illustration of three women, each holding a corner of a gold triangle. Below it was a short spell written in Archaic Welsh. She couldn't begin to understand what it meant. But maybe sounding out the words would work.

"How did you open that?" Dux snapped. "The key isn't complete."

Em's breath seized in her throat. She looked at him, totally shocked. He was right.

He flexed his fingers and an energy ball appeared in his hands, growing stronger as he kneaded more magic into it. "Give the book to me and I'll let you live."

She straightened her spine and glanced back down at the open book resting in her hands. The power of three. Maiden. Mother. Crone. Saille. Athena. And her.

The living and the dead, Saille's voice whispered the same words Em had intuitively sensed that night in the back of police car.

Sudden understanding dawned on her. The two diamonds sat in the corners, imbued with power from witches who were no longer living. The crone and the mother. The third corner was the seat for the maiden's magic, for her magic. The book had opened because she'd touched that corner, whether she'd realized it or not.

Em steadied her voice, driving all emotion from her tone as she looked back at Dux. "If I give the book to you, what guarantee do I have that you won't kill me?" If she could activate the triangle again, maybe she'd be able to read the spell. If she couldn't use the spell, then why would Merlin have been so adamant about her knowing the page number?

Dux tilted his head, amber eyes glistening as they bored into her. A wicked smile crossed his lips and Em had the uncomfortable feeling that he'd puzzled out where his translation of the spell had gone wrong. Three aspects. Not three priestesses. He wet his lips with his tongue. "Mark my word, I have no desire to kill you. Not anymore, at least."

She wrinkled her forehead, considering her options. At the same time she inched her left hand across the underside of the book, feeling her way along the shape of the triangle. Her fingertips slid over one diamond. Then a second.

Keep going, Athena's voice said.

"Em!" Gar shouted from the other room. "Hold on. We're coming."

Her fingertip found a slight dimple in the triangle: the seat in the empty corner.

"We don't have all night." Dux stepped toward her. One step closer. Then another.

She pushed her fingertip into the dimple.

Help me understand, she called out to Sallie and Athena.

A wave of adrenaline-fueled energy surged into Em, the conjoined magic of the three aspects. She swayed from the power of it, her vision going black for an instant as the power roared through her blood, her flesh, her skin. She looked at the page, her eyes seeing the words with perfect clarity, her ears hearing Saille and Athena's voices as they chanted the words. She opened her mouth and joined in.

Dux shrunk back. "Stop it!"

Em lifted the book over her head. Purple light shot out from Merlin's crystal. It illuminated the ceiling, then fountained down all around her like purple rain. She lost sense of the floor beneath her feet and rose into the air. Saille and Athena's arms encircled her. Their chant rang in her ears, words she didn't consciously understand but she knew their sole intention: *Banish his magic. Drain it. Drain it. Be gone!*

"Stop!" Dux screeched.

"Em, hold on," Gar's voice thundered in the background.

Everything in the room rose alongside her. Sofa. Toppled over chairs, magazines...and Dux.

"I'll curse you," Dux slurred. His body twitched and jerked, tremoring faster and faster as it distorted and slowly twisted upward through the purple rainfall of light and toward the ceiling.

In the back of her mind, Em heard the *slam-crack* of something driven hard against the door. An ax. Magic. Maybe both. She sensed the wood splintering. Saw Gar and Devlin race inside. Other faces too: Zeus, Ignatius…a dozen other witches, drawing up their magic. With so many more powerful witches there, it made sense for her to stop working the spell to drain Magus Dux's magic. They could take him into custody. It was over.

But Em couldn't stop. This wasn't like when she'd killed the Barbie, not blind rage. This was a spell Merlin had created and she and the other aspects of the Goddess had put into action. Once begun, it could not be taken back.

Dux's body twisted tighter and tighter. His eyes bulged. One shoulder humped. The other shrank. His legs stretched, impossibly long and skinny. Black sparks crackled up and down the length of him, flickering and fighting for a moment longer. Finally, the sparks hissed out and the sense of his magic evaporated from the room. His body dropped to the floor, still breathing but deformed. And for the time being, drained of power.

Em lowered the book and slowly drifted downward until her feet touched the floor. As she took her finger from the dimple in the triangle, Saille and Athena's voices whispered, "So mote it be."

Em bowed her head. "So mote it be."

Chapter 32

Where we travel was once our dreams.
—E. A.

Em slumped at a table in Dux's empty barroom, clutching a Dunkin' Donuts coffee in both hands. Across from her, Chloe rested her head on Devlin's shoulder. They were both covered in debris from the fight. Scorch marks and burn holes speckled their clothes. Devlin had a couple of bruised ribs. Chloe was trembling and nauseated from a tranquilizing potion Dux had forced down her throat. Still, it was beyond lucky that none of them weren't hurt any worse.

Blowing out a relieved breath, Em set her coffee aside and rested her hands on the book in front of her. Merlin's Book of Shadow and Light. She smoothed her hand along the gold triangle adhered to its cover and brushed the purple crystal at its center. The peaceful sensation of Saille's and Athena's spirits cooled her fingertips.

Em closed her eyes and reached out to them. *You're free now. You can move on.*

Their magic rippled up her fingers, caressing her hands with their conjoined strength.

No, Athena whispered. *We choose to stay. Blessed be the Northern Circle. Our circle. Your circle, Emily Adams,* Saille's voice crooned.

The weight of Em's exhaustion faded behind the soaring lightness that filled her heart. *Yes.* Her circle. All of their Circle.

"I wonder what the Council will do with Dux," Chloe said.

Em opened her eyes. "I don't care, as long as I never see him again."

"Kidnapping. Murder. Thievery. First he'll be sent to headquarters for interrogation and trial. But they'll give him a life sentence for certain. His powers will be stripped, so they can't regenerate." Devlin stopped talking and sat up straighter as Gar and Zeus walked out of Dux's speakeasy-bookshop and came across the barroom toward them.

Warmth flushed Em's body and her pulse quickened. Claw marks striped Gar's jawline, along with a fresh bruise. His rumpled black hair was a mat of dirt and plaster dust. But the blue of his unhaunted eyes simmered with magic as bright as a wolf moon, brightening even more when they met hers.

She rubbed a hand over her throat, unable to swallow because of the longing branching through every cell of her body. She wanted so badly to feel his arms around her, to taste his lips. To kiss the salt from his skin and breathe in his evergreen scent.

The warmth in her body crept across her cheeks, and she looked down as he and Zeus walked up to the table.

"Good news," Zeus said cheerfully.

Em raised her gaze. Devlin's grandfather really did fit the moniker of Zeus, and not just because of how dignified he'd looked yesterday with his Doberman. Even in the barn coat he was wearing today he had the aura of a man who held his ground, a leader.

Zeus rested back on his heels, a satisfied expression settling over his face. "The High Chancellor and Ignatius found decades of recordings in Dux's office. They peeked at a few. One showed Rhianna bragging about dipping Saille's athame in a poison that Merlin's Shade had recommended. As soon as Saille pricked herself for any ritual or spell, she was doomed to have a heart attack."

Chloe shook her head. "That sounds like something straight out of *Hamlet.*"

"Rhianna couldn't have been more than sixteen when she did it," Devlin said. He bent forward and rested his fingertips on Athena's diamond. "At least no one will be able to accuse her of deserting the Circle."

Zeus nodded. "We'll plan a memorial service once things calm down."

The sadness in their voices went straight to Em's heart. "We freed her spirit, and Saille's. They can move on or stay. It's their choice now, and that's what matters."

Gar wandered away from Zeus to stand behind Em, massaging her shoulders as he quietly moved the conversation back a step. "It's going to take months to go through all the recordings. Clearly, blackmail was one of Dux's favorite weapons."

Em looked up at him. "Shouldn't we take advantage of everyone being here and confront the High Chancellor about other witches being involved in Rhianna's plot to destroy the Circle? I mean, he and a lot of the chancellors are here now, right?"

Gar lowered his voice to a hush. "We can't afford to take chances. Whatever's going on is more invasive and complicated than we thought."

Zeus leaned forward. "Gar's right. We need to play things close to the vest for now. Bask in the limelight of the Circle's victory." He straightened back up, pride glistening in his eyes as his voice rose. "It appears my ex-coven—my grandson's coven—has been responsible for the recovery of the largest cache of stolen arcane books ever known. In effect, you four have presented the Eastern Coast branch of the Witch Councils with a library of knowledge that will be envied worldwide."

He stopped talking as a group of guards marched in from the bookstore hallway, followed closely by Ignatius and a humpbacked elderly gentleman, both dressed in tweed sports coats and trousers. Judging by the way Ignatius was kowtowing in agreement with the older man, Em assumed he was the High Chancellor.

Another man trailed in their shadow. Clam-pasty skin. Nose and lip scrunched as if he expected to smell something unpleasant at any moment.

"Heath Goddard." Em growled under her breath. She shoved her hand into her pocket and clutched her medallion to calm herself. She wouldn't let him get to her. Not like he had the last time.

The guards headed for the bar. One of them strode behind it and began searching through the cupboards and drawers. Ignatius and the other gentleman strolled toward their table. Unfortunately, Heath did as well.

"So here's where our heroes got off to." The High Chancellor puffed a little, winded by the walk up from the lower levels. "The Council wants to extend our thanks to all of you."

"Excuse me," Heath interrupted, "they haven't been cleared of the charges. They killed Rhianna. In front of a witness."

Em bit her tongue. *Yeah, right. The Vice-Chancellor's wife was as reliable a witness as Dux himself.*

Chloe jumped to her feet and pinned Heath with a glare. "That's bullshit. Her murder was Dux and his wraiths' doing. Not us."

"Chloe." Devlin put a warning hand on her arm, easing her back into her seat. "I think we should let the Council work this out."

She glowered. "I suppose you're right."

Ignatius nodded. "Wise idea." He narrowed his gaze on Heath. "Did you arrange for the moving vans yet?"

His mouth opened and snapped closed. "Ah, no—but I'll call for them right now."

"Better make them tractor trailers," the High Chancellor said. "I suspect there are things yet to be discovered in the bowels of this lair."

As Heath dutifully retreated to a nearby table to make his call, Em wiped her hand over her mouth to hide a smirk. Still, she couldn't resist ripping a hole in his plan to defame them. Besides, Chloe deserved all the support she could get. Em smiled at the High Chancellor. "Would you mind telling the Vice-Chancellor's wife something for me?"

His bushy eyebrows lowered, as if he were puzzled by her request. "Why, of course. What is it?"

"Um—" She struggled for the best way to phrase her words, since she'd only overheard the information. "Dux hinted that he might have a spell that could help her son."

Chloe's head whipped up, her eyes widening as if she'd just remembered the conversation—which wasn't surprising, since she had been drugged when Dux told her. "Em's right. Dux was evasive, but that's the feeling I got too."

A delighted smile spread across Ignatius's lips. "That is fantastic news."

"Yes, very much so," the High Chancellor said.

Heath lowered his head, scowling at his phone.

Em nibbled her bottom lip. She could top that news off by adding that Athena and Saille were now capable of fully manifesting and testifying in the Circle's behalf. She could also summon Rhianna's spirit, no doubt still attached to her unfinished diamond.

As if he had read her mind, Gar's fingers tightened on her shoulder. "Not yet," he said, close to her ear.

The High Chancellor cleared his throat. He addressed them all. "If you don't mind, Ignatius and I need to get back downstairs. These sorts of projects don't run themselves."

The two of them turned and started back across the barroom, gathering up Heath on their way. But as they reached the hallway, Ignatius broke off and strode back to the table.

"I forgot," he said when he reached them. "You're all free to leave. We'll be in touch if we need more information." He nodded at Gar. "It's going to take a few days to get everything squared away here. Once that's finished, it'll be all hands on deck in New Haven."

Gar dipped his head. "Yes, sir." He hesitated. "I do need to go back to Burlington first, collect my things. Some of the coven members were also interviewing the journalist. Even if we're calling the investigation on the Northern Circle closed, I'd like to know what they discovered."

Ignatius folded his arms across his chest. "Having others do your work? Isn't that a bit irregular?"

"There wasn't anything regular about this investigation. Wouldn't you agree?"

"That's true." Ignatius unfolded his arms and clapped Gar on the shoulder. "See you soon, then. Say, first thing Monday morning?"

Monday morning? Em glanced up at Gar as the words sank in. Gar was leaving. Soon. Really soon.

Gar smiled at Ignatius. "I'll be there."

Em clamped her eyes shut, blocking tears. *Goddess grant me the power of water, to accept what I cannot change —*

A sharp ache tightened in her chest and she couldn't bear to go on.

Chapter 33

These words do not stand by themselves.
They are Plath. They are Frost. They are the fade
of dreams. The sharp blood metal of souls.
—"Roots" by E. A.

Brooklyn had homemade corn bread and a crockpot of chili waiting when they got home. It smelled wonderful. But when Em sat down at the kitchen island to eat, the knot of sadness in her chest stole her appetite.

She toyed with her bowl, poking at the chili while stealing glances at Gar. His face was flushed from a freshly taken shower. His still-damp hair hung over his forehead as he crumbled corn bread into his chili, gulped down the bowlful, and then asked for more.

Devlin and Chloe began relaying everything that had happened to Brooklyn and Chandler. Midas arrived in the middle of the story. He scraped the last serving from the crockpot and joined them at the island.

"We owe you, big time," Devlin said to him. "Your lock-picking gizmos saved our asses. Right, Em?"

The mention of her name startled Em back to attention. "Yeah, definitely," she said, drumming up a smile. She suspected Devlin expected her to tell Midas about how she'd used the rhythm of his spell to open the cell. But she was more interested in things related to Gar, like anything that might keep him from leaving. "No one's said anything about what happened with the journalist."

Brooklyn got up from her stool and collected Gar's empty bowl. "Midas and I had a little talk with him." She eyed Em's barely touched meal. "Are you finished?"

"Sorry. The chili's great. I'm just overtired."

Chandler set her spoon down and glanced at Gar. "I didn't go with them. But it sounded like the journalist is doing okay, at least compared to the night of the club fire."

Midas scoffed. "You've got to be kidding. Sure, Rhianna's spell didn't totally fry his brain, but he's far from with it."

Brooklyn glared at him. "If you're suggesting he's not a threat to the witching world's anonymity because he's crazy, then you're nuts." The sharp tone of her voice made Em wonder if Brooklyn and Midas's hookup days had come to a swift and hot end.

Gar coughed into his fist. "I'm going to pretend I didn't hear anything about breaches in anonymity around here. What I don't hear, I don't have to relay to the Council."

"Well, Mr. Hear-no-evil," Brooklyn said, "if that's the case, then you might want to cover your ears for another minute."

Em sat up straighter. This didn't sound good.

"What is it?" Chloe prodded.

Devlin turned to Gar. "Maybe you should leave the room."

Brooklyn continued without waiting for Gar to get up. "The journalist has an additional and equally dangerous fixation."

Midas continued the story. "The night of the fire—after he was interviewed on TV—the journalist spotted a shapeshifter changing. He followed him into an alleys on Church Street." He slanted a look in Gar's direction. "He's convinced the shapeshifter was a loup-garou."

Gar's expression didn't flinch, but his eyes focused only on Midas. "Was he positive it wasn't a large dog? I can't believe any loup-garou in its right mind would change in public. That's against pack and witching laws."

"That's exactly what the journalist thought," Midas said.

"But you're positive he saw something he shouldn't have?" Em asked. She didn't need to remind anyone how easy it was to be deceived by looks. They'd all learned that lesson the hard way.

Brooklyn nodded. "No doubt about it. Whoever it was changed in public, as bold as anything."

Devlin turned to Gar. "We'd be more than happy to keep looking into this for you. After all, breaches are the responsibility of the local coven." He hesitated. "Same goes for the irregularities at the Council. We're not going to sit still."

"I don't blame you. I'm not planning on letting go of this myself," Gar said.

"Oh!" Brooklyn interrupted. She glanced at Em. "I forgot to tell you. The vet called."

Em took a sharp gulp. The first thing she'd done when she got back was check on the kittens. They'd looked good. "What's wrong?"

"Nothing's wrong. The vet called to thank you—well, both of us, actually. The vet reported how you found the kittens, and where. It turned out the police had received an anonymous complaint about someone throwing a bag of kittens in a dumpster."

"They caught them?" Em could hardly believe it.

"Not after that complaint. The bag wasn't in the dumpster when Animal Control checked. But after the vet called, they found what was left on the tracks. They searched the apartment house where the dumpster was.... It was all over the news yesterday. There were more kittens, puppies, iguanas...all stuffed in tiny cages in a dark basement. I just don't understand people like that."

Em rubbed her hand over her heart. "I'm with you on that. It's just horrible."

Bing-bong-bing. The chime of the front doorbell sounded overhead.

"That's strange," Chandler said, getting out her phone. "I'm expecting one of Peregrine's friends to pick him up for a party, but it's way too early." She checked the screen and frowned, then passed the phone to Devlin. "Someone you know?"

A chill iced Em's spine. Someone Chandler didn't recognize. Someone unexpected.

She drew up her magic and reached it toward the front of the house.

A familiar energy waited there, terrifying and real. The fruity smell of Lifesavers filled her sinuses. The bitter taste of hand cream settled on her tongue. Her toes scrunched as phantom pain shot across the tops of her feet and up her ankles.

"Are you all right?" Gar asked.

"Phone," Em rasped, holding out her hand.

Devlin handed it to her. She clutched it for a long moment, her hands shaking as she closed her eyes and braced herself. Then she looked at the security camera image.

A prim woman stood, one hip cocked as she glared at the doorbell. Her arms were folded across her chest. Dark glasses shoved up on top of her highlighted auburn hair. Fashionable jacket. Pressed jeans. A blanket scarf was tossed with careful indifference around her neck. Totally unchanged, even after years in prison.

Her aunt.

Chapter 34

There will always be haters and skeptics who doubt Violet's abilities. I'm grateful to be the one blessed with the duty of shepherding her through this minefield of negativity. She is a sensitive child. A delicate gift from God.
—*Crystal Voyage Magazine,* exclusive interview with Lynda Brewster

"Are you sure you want to talk to her?" Gar said as they reached the front door. "I'd be more than happy to get rid of her for you. Guaranteed, she'll never bother you again."

Em studied the back of the door, a single panel of oak standing between her and pure terror. "I have to do this. It's like—" She wiped her sweaty palms down the sides of her jeans, struggling to come up with a comparison. "It's like with the kittens. It isn't who or why they did it that matters. It's the accepting and moving on. The next step."

Gar moved in close behind her, the warmth of his body soothing her as he slid his hands down her arms. His lips brushed the top of her head. "I'll be right here. If you need me."

"You don't know how much that means to me," she said. Then she took a deep breath and opened the door.

Her aunt had left the stoop and now stood with one jutted hip resting against the hood of a gray SUV. Another woman sat in the car's passenger seat, head bowed as if intently studying something on her lap. Em didn't need to see that woman's face to know it was her mother, obediently staying put like she'd undoubtedly been told to do.

Em lifted her chin and scowled at her aunt, who tilted her head in a restrained greeting, then strolled back toward the front walk. Em pulled back her shoulders and marched forward to meet her. Her muscles ached from all she'd been through and pain radiated from the spot where Dux's magic had struck her spine. Still, she kept her stance tall and her face impassive.

No one can take your power away if you don't let them. Her therapist's favorite mantra rang in her head, each syllable matching a strike of her heel. *No one. Never.*

They met halfway down the walk. Her aunt scanned her from head to toe. "So, you're calling yourself Emily Adams now? A rather unimaginative choice."

"You're not welcome here," Em said, her voice as sharp as a needle driven into unwilling skin.

"Your mother and I hoped by now you would have come to your senses."

Heat rushed into Em's blood. She hardened her voice. "Come to my senses?"

"Sweetheart, you know as well as I do that you're not normal. You need to be with people who understand your special needs."

Em clenched her jaw, struggling desperately to will calmness into her body. *No one could take her power. Never again.* "I want you to leave. You exploited me. You abused me. Neither of you are welcome in my life."

Her aunt glanced over her shoulder at the gray SUV. "You're breaking your mother's heart. You—" She looked skyward, as if searching for the right words.

"Yes?" Em said, knowing full well what always came next. Damn her aunt. Damn her for all those years of pain.

Her aunt smiled down her nose at Em. "Family is forever."

The heaviness that had weighed in Em's chest for years flew from her in a rush. "You're not my family anymore. I have a new one. And if you ever dare to contact me again, I'll—"

Her aunt's eyes narrowed. "Call the police?" She tsked. "How many crimes are you guilty of? One word from me and you'll be back in that halfway house, or worse. Now be reasonable."

Em's hands snapped to her hips. She bent toward her aunt, her voice deadly quiet. "I'm not talking about the police." She paused, allowing her aunt's discomfort to grow. "I'm not the only witch standing here, am I?"

"Ah—" Her aunt flinched, her hand going to her scarf, as if confused and surprised to have her negligible intuitive ability brought into the conversation.

"I know about Sarah Winchester and the curse the Eastern Coast High Council of Witches put on our family because of our ancestor's crime. The question is, why did you refuse to tell me anything about our heritage?"

Her aunt clapped her hand over her mouth, totally stunned. "A curse? I have no idea what you're rambling on about."

Em smirked. Her aunt could pretend innocence, but the sweat beading on her temples and the fast rise and fall of her chest said otherwise. "You didn't want the Council to find out about how you were abusing me and my abilities, did you?"

"You're crazy—just like your mother. These—these witches you're living with"—she waved her hand wildly at the house—"are messing with your head."

"No one's messing with my head. Not anymore. Not ever again." Em stepped within inches of her aunt, never breaking eye contact. "I have a coven behind me, and friends on the High Council of Witches. One word from me and they will find you. I'm not alone anymore."

Her aunt paled. "But—but your mother."

"She's not innocent either," Em said. Then she turned on her heel, marched back to the house, and slammed the door shut behind her.

Gar's arms wrapped around her, embracing her tightly. She shrunk against him, resting her forehead against his chest and closing her eyes.

"Are you all right?" he asked.

She nodded, listening closely as the slam of a car door echoed in from the parking area. The crunch of gravel under tires sounded, then faded into the distance. Then nothing. Blissful nothing.

"Come on," Gar said. "You could probably use some quiet time."

Em leaned against him as he guided her upstairs to her room. It was dark and cozy and warm. The kittens tumbled out from under the bed to greet them and she sank onto the floor with Gar beside her, letting the cats crawl onto her lap.

She snuggled the white one against her face, listening to his purr. She stole a sideways look at Gar and found him watching her. The world slowed to a stop as a heavy sense of sadness gathered between them.

"Gar?" she finally said, because she'd regret it if she didn't. "You were right."

His voice stiffened. "About what?"

"About you and me—and sobriety." Tears dampened the corners of her eyes, but she lightened her tone and tried to sound teasing. "How many A.A. meetings have we missed?"

"We can go to extra tomorrow to make up for them." He said it blithely, but his eyes filled with concern. "What's really going on?"

"I'm going to miss you something awful," she said, because it was the truth, even though they'd only known each other for less than a week.

Feeling so strongly about him was ridiculous. But that was how it had happened with Alice, too. They'd met one afternoon on the loading dock at a conference center, two souls perfectly aligned.

Gar slid close to her and touched her cheek, looking in her eyes as he slowly stroked the outline of her face. "I wanted to talk to you about that."

Her breath stalled. "Yeah?"

"I don't want to make you uncomfortable. I don't want to push or rush anything. But Devlin said—if I wanted to—I was welcome to join the Circle for celebrations. The full moon. Rituals... I come to Vermont to see my mother quite often. I could stop by, if you want."

She flung her arms around him, pressing her face against his neck. Tears flowed from her eyes, exhaustion, happiness, so many emotions flooding out all at once.

He hugged her hard against him, rocking her. She closed her eyes, feeling the warmth of his body and magic washing over her, strong and protective. Loving. Her Johnny. Her rebel knight.

"Em, there's something else I wanted to ask you," he said quietly. The seriousness in his tone surprised her.

She sat back, studying his face. "What is it?"

He smiled, his eyes sad and distant. "I'd like to do something for you. I've got plenty of extra money." His gaze went to her feet, then returned to her face so fast her embarrassment didn't even have time to surface. "If you want, I'd like to pay to have your tattoos removed."

She stared at him, unable to believe she'd heard right. She'd never dared dream that was a possibility. It was something she'd never been able to afford. In truth, though, it also wasn't her deepest dream. Her voice choked. "You're amazing. It's an amazing offer. But I don't want to get rid of them. They are a part of my story."

He raised his eyebrows. "Are you sure?" He looked at her steadily. "Is there something else you'd prefer?"

She grinned. "Actually, there is. If you're serious." She gazed into his eyes. "I'd like to turn them into something else—something free and strong, and beautiful. Maybe a river and evergreens."

His lips parted and lifted into a wide smile. "Anything you want. We could even go back there next spring, once the weather gets warmer. Campout. Just the two of us. We could stop by my sister's house on the way. I'd like to introduce you."

"I'd love that." She touched his lips, tracing his smile. He took her face in his hands and leaned closer, looking deeply into her eyes a moment longer before his lips touched hers, a slow, lingering kiss. He smelled like moss and evergreens. Like freedom and new beginnings.

Freedom is not a soul set loose. It is a spirit that's found its home.
—Journal of Emily Adams, age 22
Northern Circle Coven.

Up next in the Northern Circle Coven series
Our Entangled Secrets

Chapter 1

Burlington's flying monkeys.
The originals were crafted out of steel decades ago.
I created mine out of car parts and garden tools
as a gift to my son on his third birthday.
Truly, if I could have made them fly, I would have.
—WPZI interview with artist Chandler Parrish

Chandler set the hand grinder aside and flipped up the visor of her welding helmet. She studied the fist-size heart on the workbench in front of her and smiled, pleased with the results. If she could just find the perfect strands of wire to use for the arteries and veins, then the heart would be ready to install.

She glanced across the workshop to where her latest flying monkey sculpture crouched on a rusty oil drum. It was crafted from scrap-metal like its predecessors. But this one was going to be an updated model with a trapdoor in its chest and a heart—a cross between the Tin Man and the flying monkeys of Oz fame.

"Mama?" Her son's voice came from behind her.

"Yeah?" She turned to see what he wanted.

Peregrine stood in the workshop's doorway, silhouetted against the autumn-orange leaves of a maple that sheltered the entry. Dirt smeared his jeans. His wild blond hair was tangled. Her chest swelled with joy. If she could ask the Gods and Goddesses for anything, it would be for his life to remain as carefree as that of the eight-year-old he was right now.

He looked over his shoulder, then his gaze whipped back to her. "Devlin sent me to get you. Some guy's waiting in the main house."

"Who is it?" Chandler asked, but her mama dragon instinct wondered what was going on in the yard that had required a furtive glance.

He shrugged. "I don't know. The guy saw a shapeshifter turn into a loup-garou. Wish I'd seen it."

Chandler pulled off her welding helmet and thumped it down on the workbench. *Damn it.* Their mystery visitor had to be the journalist. His spotting a shapeshifter illegally transform in public wasn't that recent of news, but his dogged interest in the event—and his intrusion into the coven's ongoing issues in general—was proving to be a major pain. Actually, she was shocked he'd showed up here at the Northern Circle coven's complex. A couple days ago, two coven members had paid him a visit at the fleabag motel where he'd been staying to discover if he truly was a threat to the witching world's anonymity or if he'd only come across as crazy to the average person.

"Devlin thinks the guy's lying," Peregrine added.

"Even if Devlin did believe him, he couldn't tell the journalist what he saw was real, right?"

"I don't think Devlin likes him."

"That's because the journalist is a troublemaker." She walked over to Peregrine and smoothed her hand down his cheek. Devlin was the coven's high priest. At twenty-five, he was younger than her by almost four years, but that made him no less wise. He was Ivy League smart, a powerful witch with polished good looks and kind heart that made him perfect for the Circle's high priest position. She gentled her voice. "Do you know where Brooklyn is?"

Peregrine nodded. "She and Midas are making dinner."

"I need you to go help them until the visitor leaves. Okay?"

Peregrine stuck out his bottom lip in a pout. "Can't I just listen? I wanna hear about the loup-garou. Please?"

"Not this time." She crouched, looked him in the eyes and turned on her mama tone. "You need to stay away from this man. He's dangerous. Understand?"

"He didn't look dangerous to me. He just talked kinda funny."

"No arguing. I want you to hang out with Brooklyn and Midas. Later, I'll tell you all about it."

Peregrine stole another glance over his shoulder. His voice trembled a little. "I—I want to stay with you."

Chandler straightened to her full height. Hands on her hips, she followed his gaze. There was nothing unfamiliar or strange in their front yard or in the parking lot beyond it, except for an old, lime green Volkswagen Beetle in front of the main house, undoubtedly the journalist's ride.

"What do you keep looking at?" she asked firmly.

"Ah—What do redcaps look like?"

In two swift motions, she pulled him all the way inside and slammed the door shut. Heat and the thrum of protective magic blazed up her dragon and monkey tattoo-covered arms and across her shoulders. She studied the yard again through the door's window, hoping to spot a fox or a mangy racoon. Something. Anything.

Peregrine wriggled in beside her, his breath fogging the windowpane. "There was a creepy person-thing next to that guy's car."

She scrubbed her fingers over the soft bristle of her close-cropped hair. *Shit. Shit. Shit.* Not this. Anything but this. Peregrine was the age when most witches' abilities manifested. And—as much as she rarely thought of him—Peregrine's biological father possessed the gift of faery sight, an ability to see through the glamour faeries used to make themselves invisible, fae such as redcaps. The gift was rare nowadays because the gene pool of witches with the ability had shrunk to a handful, after eons of them being murdered or blinded by the fae who preferred to remain concealed. It was an extraordinarily dangerous gift for the few adults who possessed it. But for an eight-year-boy? For her boy?

She wrapped an arm around Peregrine's shoulder, snugging him closer. "Are you a hundred percent sure you saw something?"

"Yeah. Ah—maybe."

Maybe? Her tension eased a fraction. In truth, it could have been nothing more than wishful thinking on Peregrine's part, combined with an imagination as active as hers. Even if he had seen a faery, it could have been a benign and unglamoured garden sprite Brooklyn had invited into the complex to help with her herbs and concoctions.

A movement caught Chandler's eye. Something coyote-size and hunched low to the ground was creeping out from behind the Volkswagen. It slunk along, dragging something—

Chandler shrieked. A body! A child.

She pushed Peregrine behind her, then eased the door open just far enough to get an unobstructed view. She had to have been mistaken. It couldn't be carrying a child.

The creature swiveled to look at her. It dropped the body. Tufts of straw trailed out from where the child was missing an arm.

Chandler let out a relieved breath. She recognized the child and the creature now. "There's nothing to worry about," she said. "It's just Henry with Brooklyn's scarecrow." Well, there wasn't anything to worry about as long as Brooklyn didn't catch Henry, Devlin's golden retriever, making off with her straw man. If she did, then there'd be hell to pay.

Peregrine wiggled past her to look. "I wasn't afraid of nothin'. And that isn't what I saw. What I saw was bigger. A lot bigger." He fanned his arms, indicating something twice as tall and large as the scrap-metal rhinoceros that she'd sold to a client last month, impossibly larger than a redcap.

She gave him a side-eye look. Now he was fibbing, except . . .

A chill traveled up her arms, prickling against the magic in her tattoos. But what if—other than the size—it wasn't a fib? What if he did have the sight like his father?

DON'T MISS THE DARK HEART SERIES

A Hold on Me

Annie Freemont grew up on the road, immersed in the romance of rare things, cultivating an eye for artifacts and a spirit for bargaining. It's a freewheeling life she loves and plans to continue—until her dad's illness forces her return to Moonhill, their ancestral home on the coast of Maine. There she meets Chase, the dangerously seductive young groundskeeper. With his dark good looks and powerful presence, Chase has an air of mystery that Annie is irresistibly drawn to. But she also senses that behind his penetrating eyes are secrets she can't even begin to imagine. Secrets that hold the key to the past, to Annie's own longings—and to all of their futures.

Beyond Your Touch

Annie Freemont knows this isn't the right time to get involved with a man like Chase. After years of distrust, she's finally drawing close to her estranged family, and he's an employee on their estate in Maine. But there's something about the enigmatic Chase that she can't resist. And she's not the only woman. Annie fears that a seductive stranger, who is key to safely freeing her mother, is also obsessed with him. As plans transform into action and the time for a treacherous journey into a strange world draws near, every move Annie makes will test the one bond she's trusted with her secrets, her desires—and her heart.

Reach for You

A world of deception and danger separates Annie Freemont from her mother—and from Chase, the enigmatic half ifrit with whom Annie's fallen in love. But she vows to find her way back to them, before Chase succumbs to the madness that threatens his freedom. The only person who can help is the magical seductress Lotli, a beautiful, manipulative woman…a woman who has disappeared.

Available everywhere books are sold.

CPSIA information can be obtained
at www.ICGtesting.com
Printed in the USA
LVHW041925211019
634862LV00002B/305/P

9 781516 106332